The
Dunbridge
Chronicles

BOOK 4

SAINTS AND SAILORS

Pam Rhodes

LION FICTION

Published by Lion Fiction
an imprint of
Lion Hudson plc
Wilkinson House, Jordan Hill Road
Oxford OX2 8DR, England
www.lionhudson.com/fiction

ISBN 978 1 78264 156 8
e-ISBN 978 1 78264 157 5

First edition 2015

Acknowledgments
Extract p. 72 taken from the song "Holy Ground" by Dave
Bilbrough, copyright © 1997 Thankyou Music. Adm. by Capitol
CMG Publishing worldwide excl. UK & Europe, admin by Integrity
Music, part of the David C Cook family, songs@integritymusic.com.
Extract pp. 141–142 taken from "Make me a channel of your
peace", Prayer of St Francis (80478). Dedicated to Mrs Frances
Tracy. © 1967, OCP, 5536 NE Hassalo, Portland, OR 97213. All
rights reserved. Used with permission.

Agent: Lili Panagi, Panmedia (www.panmediauk.co.uk)

A catalogue record for this book is available from the British Library

Printed and bound in the UK, September 2015, LH26

SAINTS AND SAILORS

For pilgrims everywhere – blessings on you wherever your journey takes you

ACKNOWLEDGMENTS

*T*here are so many people without whose help and encouragement this book would have been impossible to write. Heartfelt thanks to you all!

CHRIS GIDNEY of Christian-cruises.co.uk – I have taken part in several of their Christian cruises now, and have always found it the most wonderful experience. Looking forward to travelling the high seas with them again soon.

CRUISE AND MARITIME and SAGA cruise lines, both of whom have had the vision to encourage Christian cruises on board their ships.

CAPTAIN DAVID WARDEN-OWEN, now retired captain of some of the world's most exclusive cruise ships – the Christian who first had the vision for these cruises.

RHYDIAN ROBERTS – my favourite singing star, a Christian in the challenging world of entertainment who is a truly lovely man. His mum is delightful too.

REVEREND ERNIE REA – formerly Head of Religious Broadcasting for the BBC and therefore my boss on *Songs of Praise* – now an inspiring lecturer.

THE RIGHT REVEREND GEORGE CAREY, former Archbishop of Canterbury – has led the ministerial team on several of the Christian cruises I've taken part in. He and his wife Eileen are not just modest and inspiring, but terrific company.

REVEREND ROSEMARY TAYLOR – friend, story-sharer and chaplain on Christian cruises.

REVEREND ANDREW McLELLAN, former Moderator of The Church of Scotland, and his wife IRENE – both inspirational fellow pilgrims.

DR ANNA ZAHORSKI – my friend, who is always so supportive and full of good ideas.

TONY PARKINS – Cruise Director for Cruise and Maritime. Tony was incredibly helpful, not just with the book's Christian programme on board, but ensuring my description of ship life was as accurate as possible.

TERRY FEARNLEY – retired submariner who provided great ideas and information that helped create the character of Brig Young.

SIMON AUSTIN – on-board entertainer who was very encouraging – and talented!

REVEREND NIGEL BENNETT and his wife DELIA – Nigel shared his story with me during a couple of on-board "Songs of Praise". A truly warm-hearted Christian family, and great travelling companions.

ALISON and BRUCE LANGFORD – fellow pilgrims who have travelled with us on Christian cruises we have taken part in.

LILI PANAGI – my agent and long-time friend.

RICHARD CROW – my husband, toughest proofreader, leader of singing during our events, great dance partner and my favourite shipmate.

WHO'S WHO
IN DUNBRIDGE

From St Stephen's, Dunbridge, Bedfordshire

Iris Fisher – Reverend Neil Fisher's mother.

Harry Holloway – great-uncle to Claire, Neil's wife. Harry is both friend and neighbour to Iris.

Clifford Davies – former show-business keyboard player, now church organist.

Peter Fellowes – churchwarden.

Val Fellowes – Peter's wife.

Brian Lambert – organist; father of Wendy.

Sylvia Lambert – Brian's wife; church choir leader; mother of Wendy, Neil's former girlfriend.

Julia Dawes – member of both the church choir and the Ladies' Guild. Travelling with her mother, **Ida**, who has dementia.

Barbara and John Curtis – stalwarts of St Stephen's, keen on walking and photography.

Raymond Callaghan – big, friendly man, slightly deaf.

From St Jude's, Burntacre, Derbyshire

Reverend Neil Fisher – came to St Jude's as vicar, having finished his curacy in Dunbridge the previous summer. Husband to Claire; son of Iris Fisher.

Claire Fisher – Neil's wife; mum to seven-year-old Sam; great-niece of Harry Holloway.

Carole and Garry Swinton – Carole directs the church choir; Garry is Chairman of the parish council.

Arthur Jones – D-Day veteran, travelling with his son **Pete** and grandson **Callum**.

Deirdre O'Donnell – school teacher at Burntacre School; mum to Brendan; choir member at St Jude's.

Mark Stratton – research scientist; choir member at St Jude's.

Betty, Sheila and Marion – all altos in the choir.

Jill and Rob Grenville – Jill is a soprano in the choir; Rob takes no part in church life.

Ministry team

Bishop Paul Ambrose – Bishop of Bedford, with his wife **Margaret**.

Reverend Ros Martin – vicar from Worcestershire, assistant to Bishop Paul; organizes the Chaplain's Corner.

Reverend Maurice Brown – Methodist minister from Exeter.

Father Peter and Sister Maureen – from a large parish in Birmingham, with a group of Catholic mothers.

Reverend Ernie Rea – lecturer on board, former head of Religious Broadcasting for the BBC.

Pam Rhodes – presenter of BBC Television's *Songs of Praise* series, travelling with husband **Richard**.

Cruise staff and crew members

Captain Stephan Johannson – Scandinavian captain of *The Pilgrim*.

Ramon Moreno – Cruise Director, in charge of the ship's programme.

Jane Thurlow – Assistant Cruise Director.

Brad Osbourn – on-board doctor, travelling with his wife **Joanne**.

Andrew Bragnall – keyboard player in the cocktail bar, on his first professional contract.

Maureen and Bill Bragnall – Andrew's mum and dad.

Sharon – head dancer.

Michael – lead singer.

Other passengers on board

Rhydian Roberts – international singing star.

Bernie Gordon – Rhydian's agent.

Brig Young – former submariner, travelling with his wife **Daisy**.

Nigel, Brian, Margaret and Fiona – all interviewed during the on-board "Songs of Praise" event.

CHAPTER 1

DUNBRIDGE AND
⇒ BURNTACRE ⇐

Forth in Thy name, O Lord, I go.

Charles Wesley

"Will we need wellies?"

"Probably not. I'd take your walking boots, though." Claire answered Neil without looking up from the holdall she was packing.

"Umbrella?" he asked.

"I've got a small one, and you've got a hood on your jacket."

"Should I take one pair of thick socks, or two?"

"One."

"How many dress shirts?"

"You've only *got* one."

"And jumpers?"

"For heaven's sake!" Claire looked at Neil with exasperation. "You go and sort out the paperwork and books you need to take with you, and I'll do the rest."

He grinned. "That worked, then! I hate packing."

"I'd never have guessed," she laughed, aiming an odd sock in his direction as he headed for the door. "And put the kettle on while you're at it."

Ten minutes later, when Neil returned with two mugs of steaming coffee, the holdalls were neatly packed. Claire tidied away the last bits and pieces before sitting down on the bed next to him, lifting her face for his kiss as he handed her the cup.

"I've just had a call from Mum," he said. "She's all ready to go."

Claire chuckled. "Iris has had her case packed for about a week."

"Peter and Val are picking her and Harry up at eleven. But they reckon it should only take a couple of hours for them to get to Tilbury Docks. It's so much further from here – I've no idea how long it'll take us to battle our way down the M1 and around the M25 to get there."

"It'll be nice to see the St Stephen's crowd again," said Claire, taking a sip of coffee. "Even nicer to be on holiday with them. This was a great idea, to get some of your old parish and your new one to meet up. And cruising round Britain sounds brilliant!"

"I'm not sure how much of a holiday it's going to be for me," mused Neil. "I'm thrilled that they asked me to be one of the Christian team on board, of course, but I'd feel better if I had a clearer idea of what it involves."

"That's why you've got all those books on Celtic saints taking up space in our bags," she teased. "I'd be squeezing in a couple of extra pairs of shoes if it weren't for them."

"Well, I wouldn't need so many reference books if I knew for sure that the internet always works reliably on a cruise ship. Do you think it does when you're out in the middle of the ocean?"

"Oh, I should think so…"

"Bishop Paul'll know what he's doing, of course, and it's flattering that he asked me to help with the ministry side of things. After all, I was just a curate in Dunbridge for the three years he was my bishop, and that was only nine months ago. I've still got a lot to learn. I hope I don't let him down."

Claire smiled. "Not many curates find themselves running a busy parish all by themselves when they've hardly been ordained a year. Bishop Paul knows how much you took on when the rector left, and how well you coped. For heaven's sake, by the time you left Dunbridge, your parishioners were asking him to let you stay and take on the parish as their full-time priest. He said himself he'd never known that happen before!"

"Do you ever regret moving to Derbyshire instead of staying there, Claire? After all, we had to take Sam out of his school and leave your Uncle Harry just after his eightieth birthday. It was a big upheaval."

"Sam's OK – he's really settled here. What six-year-old wouldn't love all these trees to climb and space to kick a ball about with a gang of friends? He loves it."

"Quiet, isn't it, without him?"

"Mmm. He loves staying with Mum in Scarborough, though."

"Let's face it, he couldn't wait to get out the door, because she and David always spoil him rotten. He'll have a lovely holiday."

"Do you think he's missing me?"

"Probably not as much as we're missing him, but you know we can ring him."

"I'm looking forward to all the places we're going. I've always wondered what Orkney is like, after years of hearing it mentioned on the weather forecast!"

"And Lindisfarne. A group of us went to Holy Island in my first year at college. I've never forgotten the impact it had on me."

"Dublin, Guernsey and the Normandy coast – so many lovely places."

"And we get to sail round the coast being pampered on a cruise ship…"

"I wonder how the Christianity bit will fit in?" mused Claire, her face thoughtful. "You know, I'm still not completely into this God stuff. I hope it's not going to be all worthy and prim."

Neil laughed. "Because you, Mrs Fisher, are definitely not prim, I'm very glad to say."

Smiling cheekily in return, she continued, "I think the evenings will be good, though, because they put on some big production shows. And then, of course, Rhydian's going to be on board…" Claire's expression became dreamy as she spoke. "I wonder if I'll get a chance to meet him. He's really famous! I love his voice – and he's very attractive…"

Neil looked indignant. "I'm attractive – and I can serenade you, if you like."

"My darling Neil, you have many abilities, but serenading is not one of them."

He laughed. "I remember at theological college when they were trying to teach us various options for singing the responses during the Eucharist. The music lecturer took me to one side and said it would probably be better if I just spoke them. I felt deeply offended."

"The truth hurts," laughed Claire, "and so would your congregation's ears if you put them through that!"

"Anyway, I won't be seeing much of the shows. I've got my evening worship services to prepare, when I say something about the life and spirituality of each saint, and lead worship based on the Celtic tradition. Apparently those gatherings will be held in the ship's chapel, so they'll feel very intimate and hopefully moving. That's the plan anyway. I really want to get everything just right."

"You'll be great," said Claire.

"Oh, and that woman off the telly – you know, Pam Rhodes, who's been on *Songs of Praise* since I was in short trousers – she's coming too."

"Harry'll like that. *Songs of Praise* has been his favourite television programme for years."

"Mum's too."

"Will there be cameras on board, then?"

"No. She'll be organizing our own version of *Songs of Praise* on the ship towards the end of the cruise, but it's not for broadcasting."

"Good job we've got some of our St Jude's choir coming, then," said Claire, "and I think most of the Dunbridge group have sung in St Stephen's choir at one time or another. I'm really looking forward to seeing them again."

"Me too," agreed Neil, glancing at the bedside clock. "Come on, it's nearly midnight. I need my beauty sleep. Early start in the morning!"

She leaned over to rest her head on his shoulder. "It'll be like a second honeymoon, cruising around Britain for nine days."

"I hope I'm not seasick."

She looked up at him. "You've just ruined a romantic moment!"

"Oh," he said, planting small kisses across her cheek until he could whisper in her ear, "don't you worry. There'll be plenty of those. I'll make sure of that…"

Claire turned her face so that her lips met his. "Sounds good to me…"

***

"I haven't slept a wink. I'm worried."

Iris made her announcement the moment she stepped inside Harry's back door. Harry, who was still in his dressing gown, looked at her in surprise.

"It's only eight o'clock. We're not being picked up for three hours."

"I'm ready. I hate being late. And I'm worried."

Reaching for the kettle, Harry sighed. "Let me guess. You're worried about high winds on the high seas?"

She looked at him with disdain. "Of course not. I'm excellent on water. I often went sailing with my father when I was a girl. That was one of the benefits of growing up in Bristol. We had our own boat."

"You did?" asked Harry, plainly impressed.

"A rowing boat called Dumpy."

"Nice!" Harry suppressed a smile as he turned away to fill the kettle. "Well, you can't be worried that you won't have enough clothes to wear. You ended up putting some of your things in *my* case!"

"You don't need to take much. You're a man."

"A mere man I might be – and into my eighties – but I do still like to look smart."

"Yes, but gentlemen don't need to bother as much as ladies to look smart on a cruise ship. We have to dress for dinner, you know. And on formal nights we really do need evening gowns – with shoes to match, of course."

"Oh, of course," smiled Harry, who was really more interested in filling the kettle than Iris's fashion plans. "So, let me guess. Are you worried you haven't got enough handbags?"

"Now you're being sarcastic. I have two for days out, one containing a foldaway shopping bag, plus two evening clutch bags in gold and silver. That should be ample."

"Well, I give up. What's *left* to worry you?"

"The catering. How hygienic can it possibly be if they're having to cook three meals, plus afternoon tea, for around four hundred passengers every day? And that's not to mention feeding all the staff too. *The Pilgrim*'s small fry as far as these cruise ships go nowadays, but then it's really quite old. I've been looking it up. Do you think, in an old ship, the kitchens are up to scratch?"

"Yes, I do."

"But what if someone brings a sickness bug or something on board? What's to stop us all going down with runny tummies?"

"Oh, for goodness' sake, Iris," groaned Harry. "I've not even opened my eyes properly yet, and you're already talking about bodily malfunctions…"

"Rest assured, if that happens, you and I will have a head start. I'm taking our own very comprehensive first aid kit, complete with prescribed medicines. All that's in your bag too."

"There's a doctor on board! And a nurse and a proper surgery. I'm sure they've got infection control well organized. Anyway, we're only going round the coast. The food will probably be as British as you are. You're talking as if you're Doctor Livingstone heading off into the African jungle!"

"You know my stomach is delicate. What happens if the kitchen team all come from the Philippines or somewhere equally exotic? I can't cope with curries. You know that!"

Without answering immediately, Harry placed the full kettle in its holder and switched it on. Then he reached out to take Iris's hand, leading her gently over to the kitchen table, where he pulled out a chair for her before sitting down himself.

"How long is it since you went away on a proper holiday like this? And I don't mean staying with Neil for a week or two, when it's felt like home from home."

She shrugged. "I can't quite recall. The last time must have been when Robert was alive, and we went to the Isle of Wight for a week."

"And Robert died not far off twenty years ago, didn't he? So it must be at least that long since you've done anything even remotely like this."

"I don't see what that's got to do with anything…"

"Robert was with you then. You two may have had your moments over the years, but Neil told me his dad was your rock. And here you are, going off on this great adventure without him by your side. No wonder you're nervous."

"Of course I'm not nervous!"

"Yes, you are – and so am I. It's five years since my Rose passed on, and until then, in all our fifty years of marriage, we did everything together. We never spent a night apart, because I never wanted to go anywhere without her at my side. I've worked all my life and it must have looked as if I could cope with anything – but she was the strong one in our marriage. I was nothing without her."

Iris nodded, her eyes unnaturally shiny as she listened to Harry.

"And I can tell you now, I used to get quite panicky at the thought of being somewhere unfamiliar or different, but it felt all right if we did it together. I think if it had been left to me, we would never have gone on holiday at all. But although I dreaded leaving home, I always enjoyed it in the end. She organized a surprise weekend for us in Dublin once, and for our fortieth anniversary we went to the Scilly Isles, because she'd always wanted to go there. Those two places are the reason I'm booked on this cruise. Rose loved being there then, and I think she'd be pleased I'm going back there again now, taking our memories with me."

Iris smiled with relief and understanding. "I know what you mean. Everyone always said I wore the trousers in our marriage. Even Robert said he was henpecked! On the surface it might have seemed that way – but really, I might have made all the noise, but he was the strong one. You'd have thought, in all these years, I'd have got used to being without him, but I still feel so lost. Not just lonely, but alone, all alone…"

"Even in a crowd…" agreed Harry softly. "And you and I are going to be with hundreds of people for the next week and a half."

"Suppose I can't find my way around the ship? What if I don't remember what deck my cabin's on – or I forget the number or the key?"

"Then, dear lady, we will make sure that our cabins are close together. We will keep each other company and out of harm's way. I'll be there for you, if you promise to be there for me."

Vulnerability was not something often seen in Iris's expression, and Harry was moved to see the uncertainty gradually easing from her face as she considered his words. Finally, she smiled a little as she reached out to touch his hand.

"Of course I'll look after you. You're my friend, my best friend."

"And don't forget, Neil and Claire will be with us too."

"I hope he's packed everything he needs. He can be *so* disorganized. And I've been trying to remember whether he ever did get his badge for swimming when he was in the Cubs. I do know he was never that confident around water – and he's taking us all on a cruise!"

"Well, aren't we lucky that the younger generation in our families – your Neil and my Claire – care enough about us to want us with them on this wonderful trip? They both insisted they wouldn't go unless we came too. So you and I *will* go, and we'll have a bloomin' good time!"

"We will!"

"Now," said Harry, scraping back his chair, "let's get that tea."

Iris looked anxiously at her watch. "Have we got time? I hope Peter and Val aren't late picking us up. You know what that motorway's like! We might get held up in traffic when we leave Dunbridge – and what would happen then? Would the ship go without us?"

Shaking his head with affectionate disbelief, Harry poured a little boiling water in to warm the teapot, then opened the tea caddy.

***

"Please mind my suitcase! It cost a fortune!"

Carole Swinton's piercing instruction cut through the babble of excited chatter from the crowd gathering around the coach. It was parked outside the lychgate of St Jude's Church in Burntacre, a few miles north of Ashbourne in Derbyshire. It was half past eight in the morning and the passengers due to board *The Pilgrim* at Tilbury later that day were putting their bags into the luggage compartment at the side of the coach, before taking their leave of family members with loving hugs and a few tearful goodbyes. The crowd obediently parted as Carole and her husband Garry marched up to the middle of the luggage compartment and pushed other lesser bags unceremoniously to one side as they slid in their elegant leather suitcases.

"We need to sit at the front of the coach," said Carole loudly. "Garry, make sure you tell them to keep our two seats at the very front. I've organized this trip and I'll have to use the mike to give out instructions."

"And that way you and I can be first off too," hissed Garry in her ear. "If there are four hundred other passengers booking onto this cruise today, I've no intention of being anywhere except at the head of the queue."

"Good to see you in your civvies, Vicar," giggled Sheila, one of three ladies who usually formed the entire alto section of the church choir.

"I must say you look very fetching in shorts!" added Sheila's friend, Marion.

Bustling up to join them came Betty, who was almost as wide as she was tall.

"Claire, I am seeing your husband in a completely new light. He's quite a looker without the dog collar."

"Believe me," laughed Claire, "having a job which requires a sort of uniform is a great relief for Neil. He has no fashion sense at all, so it's good he doesn't usually have to think beyond a pair of trousers and a clerical shirt."

"So you've put your foot down while he's on holiday?"

"She certainly has," agreed Neil. "She said shorts are the order of the day. Is she having me on? Do I look ridiculous?"

"Come on, ladies and gents!" called the driver. "Time's ticking on and we've a long journey ahead. Sort yourselves out, please!"

"Hang on!" muttered Jill, who was also in the choir at St Jude's. "Where did I put the passports? Are they in your pocket, Rob? Rob! I'm asking you a question! Did you pick up our passports?"

Her husband turned around to stare irritably at her.

"I've not seen them. You're in charge of paperwork. You're in charge of everything, remember?"

Seeing how flustered and embarrassed Jill was becoming, her fellow soprano, Deirdre, stepped up to lend a hand.

"Could you have put them in your handbag?"

"My handbag!" squealed Jill, looking around her frantically. "Where's my handbag? I didn't leave it on the kitchen table, did I? I bet I did. There was so much to think about before we left this morning, I must have forgotten it. Will the coach be able to wait? Do you think it could take a slight detour to drive my way out of the village?"

"It's not this one, is it?" offered Deirdre, noticing a well-used brown bag on the ground just behind them.

"Oh, that's it! Deirdre, you're an angel. And here are the passports, thank goodness! Come on, Rob. Where's Rob?"

"He's already on the coach, I think," said Deirdre, the Irish lilt in her voice still noticeable in spite of the years she'd spent living in rural Derbyshire. "Look, I can see him sitting towards the back."

"Careful, Dad," came a voice behind them. It was Pete Jones, a popular local builder, carefully guiding ninety-one-year-old Arthur towards the coach steps. Bringing up the rear, carrying a backpack and another travel bag, came Pete's teenage son Callum, earphones in as he chatted away on his mobile phone. Pete's wife had opted to hold the fort at home while three generations of men in the family made this special trip together. The last stop on the cruise was Honfleur on the Normandy coast, near where Arthur had been wounded on D-Day more than seventy years before. This journey would be, without doubt, a very moving pilgrimage for him, not least because his son and grandson would be able to share it with him.

"Hi, Carole," smiled Pete as he reached the top of the steps into the coach. "Would it be okay if Dad and I sat at the front here, to save him having to struggle any further down?"

"Oh, but I've got to sit here!" Carole's voice pitched up a tone in indignant panic. "I have to give instructions over the microphone, so this is my seat – and Garry obviously needs to sit beside me."

"Take my seat, Arthur," said a calm voice on the other side of the aisle. "I'll move back."

Mark Stratton quickly removed himself and his bags, so that Pete could edge into the window seat and manoeuvre Arthur safely into place.

As soon as he stood up Mark saw Deirdre stepping onto the coach. He moved swiftly down the aisle, wondering if there was any chance she might consider sitting beside him. Choosing a seat halfway down on his right, he smiled up at her as she came towards him. She gave him a shy half-smile in return, clearly hesitating about where to sit. In the end, she lowered herself into the window seat directly across from him.

Next, Jill Grenville flapped her way down the coach to where her husband had spread his briefcase and a range of newspapers all over the seat. When it became clear that Rob had no intention of making room for her, she slid awkwardly into the seat in front of him, her cheeks reddening with the knowledge that several people in the coach were watching her reaction with interest.

"Right," announced Neil, as he and Claire eventually climbed on board. "I've done a final check to make sure we've not forgotten anyone or anything. Are we ready to go?"

"One minute, Vicar," interrupted Carole. "I have a few important announcements to make."

"Really?"

"I need to tell everyone about the arrangements for getting their luggage onto the ship when we reach the dock…"

"Tell you what, Carole, why don't you do that a bit nearer to Tilbury? That way we'll be more likely to remember. But first, before we get on the road, shall we ask God to bless us on this journey, and be with us throughout the time we're going to spend together?"

Heads obediently bowed throughout the coach.

"Father, today this group of friends is to become a band of pilgrims – travelling together in the footsteps of the ancient saints who established our faith and inspired our knowledge of you. Be with us every step of the way, guiding our feet and our hearts towards a greater understanding and closeness to you. In the name of your Son, Jesus Christ our Lord, we pray…"

"Amen" echoed throughout the coach.

"Are you done now?" asked the bored voice of the driver.

"Thank you, yes."

"And are you and your missus about to sit down, Vicar?"

"Oh, right, yes we will."

"Good. So can we *finally* get on the road?"

"What are you waiting for?" squealed the excited voice of Betty from the back row, where she had spread out alongside Sheila and Marion. And as the three women launched into a lively chorus of "I Love to Go A-Wandering", while others yelled goodbyes to family and friends who were waiting to see them off, the driver thought dismally to himself that it was a very long way to Essex.

***

The group from Bedfordshire had opted to travel in individual cars to Tilbury. At the same time as Peter Fellowes, the St Stephen's churchwarden, and his wife Val were picking up Harry and Iris, Brian Lambert, the organist, and his wife Sylvia were also setting off from home. As their car was a seven-seater, they had offered to transport one of the choir members, Julia Dawes, along with her elderly mother Ida. Ida had dementia and it had made her withdrawn and frail. Julia, her only child, was devoted to her, bringing her to church on Sundays in the wheelchair. She had often wondered what it was like on a cruise ship – and what had finally decided her to make this journey possible for Mum was that, down the years, Ida had always been drawn to the wisdom and sayings of the ancient saints. Even if Mum missed a great deal about what was going on around her, Julia wanted to do this for her – and without exception, the church group going on the cruise with them thought it was both kind and right that she should make this voyage happen.

As Brian loaded the chair and all their bags into the boot of the car, Julia and Sylvia gently guided Ida into the back seat, surrounded by her favourite, familiar cushions. Ida's face registered nothing – not surprise, not interest, just nothing.

"Are the others likely to be ahead of us?" asked Julia, as Brian pulled away from the kerb.

"Not by much," he replied. "I think Barbara and John were setting off about the same time as us."

At that exact moment, Barbara and John Curtis were picking up Clifford Davies, a rather theatrical but hugely talented organist. Now well into his sixties, he added to his pension by providing the music several times a week for services at the crematorium. Clifford's colourful stories about his time in variety theatre and the early days of television raised a few eyebrows among the more conservative members of St Stephen's, but he rather enjoyed the thought that he occasionally shook things up a bit.

Clifford was a little uncertain about the last passenger due to travel with them from Dunbridge to Tilbury. Raymond Callaghan was a large, untidy man with a sunny smile and great enthusiasm for life, in spite of the fact that he appeared to have no family left around him now, and he was steadily becoming very deaf. Not that he realized it, even when other members of the choir dug him in the ribs in an attempt to at least keep him in time, if not in tune. He simply smiled broadly at them and continued to sing with gusto in his booming voice.

Raymond was waiting at the gate when they arrived, and within seconds he was trying to fold his gangly arms and legs into the back seat alongside Clifford. His smile was infectious and there was an air of excitement in the car as they headed towards the motorway.

"So have you managed to organize cover for yourself at the playgroup, Barbara?" Clifford asked.

"Yes, they've all rallied round. John and I haven't had a holiday for a while, so this break is long overdue, isn't it, love?"

"Well, to be honest," answered John, "it's the itinerary of the cruise that swung it for me. I love history. I can't think of anything better than standing where something important was actually said, done or thought. We're going to such interesting places, the cradle of Christianity and culture in the British Isles. I'm going to make the most of every minute."

"And I'm going to capture it all on my camera, aren't I, love?" smiled Barbara. "Then we can remember those moments over and over again. In fact, we were thinking, when we're all safely back home again, we could organize an evening when we show everyone our holiday snaps. That would go down well, don't you think?"

"Oh, I'd like that," agreed Raymond.

Clifford managed to smother a groan as he turned to watch the world go by through the car window.

CHAPTER 2

⇒ TILBURY ⇐

*Live in mutual harmony with all other
servants of Christ.*

St Cuthbert

John might have been interested in history and events of the past, but there was nothing backward-looking about the way he put his foot down to weave an aggressive route around any motorway traffic that got in his way. Even when Raymond suggested that an urgent "comfort break" was needed, John simply glanced at the clock and told everyone he would stop for eight minutes, no more, at the South Mimms service area, and if they weren't back, he would go without them. Clifford, who'd been pretending to be asleep in the back seat so he didn't have to join in with the excited holiday chatter, looked at John with a new eye. So he did have a bit of backbone after all! What a pleasant surprise.

"My John likes to be early for everything, don't you, love?" trilled Barbara, as the car came to a standstill. "He's got this journey worked out to the minute. It's so reassuring."

While the others rushed off to find the restrooms, Clifford bought himself a paper and a large cup of black coffee before strolling back to the car to wait in the May sunshine for his travelling companions to return. Raymond was last. Clifford watched as the big man puffed out of the automatic doors and looked around uncertainly until he spotted Barbara waving both arms in the air to guide him back in the right direction.

"Right," announced John, as he reset the satnav. "No more stops now until Tilbury. Everyone belted up?"

How I wish they were, thought Clifford before closing his eyes and his mind to everything around him.

***

"May I have your attention, please!" Carole tapped the microphone sharply. "Is this working? Can you hear me at the back?"

"She's got a voice as loud as a foghorn," mumbled Betty to Marion. "What makes her think she ever needs a mike?"

"It's okay, Carole. You're coming through loud and clear!" yelled Sheila, as all three in the back row dissolved into giggles.

"We are approaching Tilbury Docks," announced Carole in the clipped tones of a television newsreader. "The coach is not able to stop for long in the holding area, so you need to identify and collect your luggage as soon as possible, then form an orderly queue behind me and I will lead the way into the terminal building. Please make sure you leave nothing on the coach – and don't leave rubbish by your seat either." She looked pointedly at the back row as she said this. "There is a litter bin just by the door here at the front."

"Huh!" snorted Sheila indignantly, as she stuffed an empty crisp bag into her pocket.

"I am sure," continued Carole, smiling benevolently in the direction of the driver, "that you will want to show your appreciation in the usual way for our wonderful driver, Steve. It's been a pleasure to have such a competent and experienced person at the wheel to bring us safely from Burntacre to our destination here at Tilbury. We look forward to seeing you again, Steve, when you collect us on our return."

"Might not be me," he retorted, "and there's a queue of vehicles waiting to get in here. Can you all hurry up and get out, please?"

Claire squeezed Neil's hand and looked at him with a grin. "Here we go, then."

"Lead the way, Mrs Fisher. I'll bring the bags."

It was as Neil was stepping off the coach that he heard his name being called from a car that was coming to a standstill nearby.

"Neil! Over here!" Barbara had wound down her window and was waving frantically to get his attention. "Oh, and Claire, there you are. It's so wonderful to see you both."

"Burntacre party, stay together, please!" ordered Carole, her eyes narrowing as she viewed the new arrivals. Her instruction came too late. Neil and Claire were already making their way over to shake hands through the window with their old friends from Dunbridge.

"Neil!" snapped Carole, who had no intention of being ignored. "We're ready to make our way inside. Keep up with the group, please!"

Clifford, climbing out from the back seat to greet Claire and Neil, eyed Carole with distaste.

"She who must be obeyed, eh?"

"We have a lot to tell you, Clifford," was Neil's quiet reply.

"And I am looking forward very much to catching up with your news, dear boy," retorted Clifford, his eyes twinkling with mischief.

At just that moment, Peter and Val pulled up behind them, and Carole bristled with indignation as Neil and Claire hurried over to greet the newcomers.

"Leave them, Carole," said Garry. "They may not want to get to the front of the queue before the masses arrive, but we do." And taking his wife by the arm, he led the rest of the St Jude's coach passengers towards the reception area.

Claire got to the car first, pulling open the door to help Harry out of his seat so that she could hug him fondly. Iris clambered out with surprising speed, throwing her arms around Neil as if she hadn't seen him for years.

"You did pass your Cubs' badge for swimming, didn't you?" she whispered in his ear as she embraced him.

"What?" asked Neil, pushing her away from him slightly, so that he could look down at her. "I've no idea. I might have done, because I *can* just about swim the length of the local pool. I'm not confident enough to swim in the sea, though, so I have no intention of jumping in at any time on this cruise. Does that put your mind at rest?"

Plainly relieved, Iris hugged him again. "You know how a mother worries, Neil."

"And I'm glad you do, Mum. Come on. Let me help you with your bags."

Once the cases were safely loaded onto a trolley, Neil and Claire had a chance to say hello properly to Peter and Val. The churchwarden had been a great friend to Neil throughout his three years as a curate at St Stephen's, and they had helped one another through various crises in both the church and their personal lives. The two couples greeted each other warmly, with Neil giving an especially big hug to Val, who had brought such joy to Peter after the ending of his first, unhappy marriage.

"Here come Brian and Sylvia," said Peter, as the last car arrived from Dunbridge. "And do you remember Julia Dawes from the Ladies' Guild, and her mum Ida?"

In fact, Neil remembered Julia and her mother very well, and he was genuinely shocked to see the deterioration in Ida's condition. As Val and Claire helped the elderly lady out of the back of the car and into her wheelchair, Neil moved across to shake Brian's hand. There was still a remnant of reserve between the two men: for a time the Lamberts had hoped that Neil might marry their daughter Wendy, but immediately after Neil had chosen Claire, Wendy had unexpectedly taken herself off to live in Australia – which seemed almost as dramatic as joining the Foreign Legion!

Once all the hellos had been said and the luggage unloaded, Peter and Brian drove their cars to the long-stay car park while the others made their way across to the terminal. Their ears were immediately assaulted by the noise of lively chatter echoing around the huge warehouse-like building, as members of various groups found and greeted each other, and queues formed to register their arrival at the row of desks manned by uniformed members of the ship's crew.

"Neil!" Carole Swinton appeared at his side the moment he and Claire stepped into the building. "You are holding us all up. Bring your cases and your paperwork, and follow me. And please keep up from now on!"

Neil and Claire exchanged a glance that suggested to the Dunbridge group that Carole was one of the more challenging members of his Derbyshire congregation.

"We'll see you all on board," said Claire. "Once we know where our cabin is and we've got ourselves sorted, we'll be heading for whatever sundeck is serving proper cups of tea."

"Lunch too," added Neil. "I'm starving."

Following Carole to the head of one of the registration queues, Neil and Claire presented their paperwork and identification as their cabin was allocated and their luggage taken from them. Then, along with the rest of the St Jude's party, they were ushered through an exit at the other end of the terminal.

Stepping out onto the dockside, there was a general gasp of delight as they got their first view of *The Pilgrim*.

"I didn't expect it to be so big," said Betty.

"I hope I don't get lost on it," added Sheila, eyeing the rows of cabin portholes and balconies with trepidation.

"They said it was old," finished Marion. "It looks new enough to me."

"They paint these ships all the time," said Pete with the authority of someone who was a builder, painter and decorator himself. "They never stop. I reckon we'll see them giving the ship a lick of paint at almost every port."

"So it always looks nice?" asked Jill.

"No." Her husband Rob gave her a patronizing stare. "So it's *safe*, of course. Maintenance is everything on ships like this. They have to follow the rules. Passenger safety's paramount, and that means keeping the ship well maintained."

"Photo?" asked a man who suddenly appeared beside them, camera in hand. "You can see your photo on board near the library after dinner this evening. Are you all together? How about a group shot?"

Carole took charge, ordering that any bags or coats they were carrying should be placed on the floor before arranging everyone into neat lines, so that they looked like a visiting choir rather than a motley group of friends.

"Smile, please!"

"Saints and sailors!" shouted Marion.

"Saints and sailors!" called the rest of the group, as the photographer took the picture that was destined to take pride of place in all their albums once they got back home.

"What are we waiting for?" squealed Betty. "Last one up the gangplank's a landlubber!"

Uniformed members of the crew welcomed them, but insisted that everyone squirt their hands with disinfectant before being allowed up the gangplank to get on board.

"I feel like the queen making her way onto the Royal Yacht *Britannia*," said Sheila with a giggle. "Should I wave?"

Once they'd stepped inside the ship at the top of the ramp, they were each asked to pose for an official snapshot and given an identity card, which they had to keep with them at all times. They then moved on to another table, where a smiling steward gave them their cabin keys.

"We're on Deck C," said Neil. "Are we all together?"

"I think so," said Mark, hoping Deirdre would give some indication of where her cabin was to be. Leaning over as subtly as he could manage, he tried to catch a glimpse of her key number. Ever since he'd booked this trip, he'd been dreaming of magical times when he might escort her back to her cabin after a moonlit evening on deck. He was certainly very relieved when he saw her nod agreement to being on C Deck with everyone else.

"Actually, we're on E Deck, much higher up, near the captain's quarters, I believe," said Carole nonchalantly. "We paid extra for a bit more luxury."

"Ooh!" said Betty. "I fancy a guided tour round your cabin then!"

"So the rest of us are all looking for C Deck, are we?" asked Claire.

"Well," said Pete, smiling in Arthur's direction. "I've got a bit of news. It seems the people from the British Legion have been in touch with the shipping company about Dad being on this trip. You know he wants to see France again. He's not been back since D-Day."

"Oh, that's so moving," sighed Betty. "Brings tears to my eyes…"

"Anyway, apparently the company thinks it's an honour to have a D-Day veteran on board, so when we came to check in, they treated Dad like a VIP. And guess what? They said they've given Dad, Callum and me a big family suite on Deck E – probably quite near to you, Carole."

"How nice," commented Carole through gritted teeth, plainly furious at this invasion of her specially booked space, and the unforgivable upstaging of her status on board.

"Well," said Neil, "apparently it's going to take a while for our bags to be delivered to us. How about we just drop our bits and pieces in the cabins for now, then meet in quarter of an hour or so, wherever they might be serving lunch?"

With general agreement all round, they headed off to the main stairs, where they spent several minutes studying the wall map, trying to work out where they were and locate their cabins.

"C125: this is it," called Claire, who was slightly ahead of Neil as they walked down the long corridor, scanning cabin numbers. Eagerly, she turned the key in the lock and they walked into a surprisingly roomy space that was both homely and cleverly arranged. A door on the right revealed a small shower room with a colourful array of toiletries laid out in front of the mirror. They pulled open the wardrobe doors to find plenty of hanging and drawer space, with a safe secreted on the bottom shelf. There was a desk where Neil could work on his notes, a television complete with DVD player, and a wide window through which they could see the dockside bathed in pale sunlight.

"Oh no!" sighed Neil. "Single beds!"

Claire's face fell as she followed his gaze. "Do you think we could change cabins?"

There was a sudden knock as Betty popped her head round their open door.

"What's your cabin like? Oh, yes, just the same as mine and Sheila's. Marion's looks like this too. They must all be identical on this corridor. Good, isn't it?"

Claire slipped her hand inside Neil's and gave it a squeeze.

"Hmm," was all Neil could manage to reply.

"We've found out that they've got a buffet restaurant three floors up at the back of the boat," squealed Betty, plainly beside herself with excitement. "That's the round end, not the pointy one. We'll see you there when you're ready."

As Betty pulled their door closed behind her, the couple stared down at the two narrow beds on opposite sides of the cabin.

"We'll have to do spoons," said Claire. "It could be fun."

"It'll be one heck of a squeeze. If one of us turns over, the other will end up on the deck – and I bet that's me!"

She turned her face up to his, slipping her arms around his waist. "We'll just have to cling together and be very inventive."

"I love you, Mrs Fisher…"

"And I need some lunch, Vicar. Coming?"

***

"Well, I must say, I'm very pleasantly surprised," announced Iris as she looked around the buffet restaurant. The tables were elegantly set and an army of polite and welcoming staff were on hand.

"Thank God for small mercies…" quipped Harry.

"Look at the waiters serving the food – they're all wearing hygienic gloves."

"Apparently they do that for the first forty-eight hours, to make sure no infection is passed on if a passenger gets on board with a bug of some kind," said Sylvia. "The restaurant manager was explaining to Brian and me while we were in the queue waiting to be served."

"Most efficient," agreed Iris.

"And this coronation chicken is delicious," enthused Harry, until he caught Iris's sideways glance. "Nowhere near as nice as the coronation chicken you cook, my dear Iris, but very good all the same."

"I counted eight different kinds of fish, both fresh and smoked," said Barbara. "Fish is John's favourite, isn't it, love?"

"Need to keep the cholesterol down these days." John patted his stomach, while Barbara looked on fondly.

"I had the roast," said Raymond, who was still managing to smile while shovelling down fork-loads of food at the same time. "And some of that cottage pie. The pasta was good too. And all those different bread rolls! I just tried the three that looked best because I couldn't decide which one to choose."

"I've got my eye on the puds," said Val. "We never usually bother with desserts at home, do we, Peter? But when they're made specially for us and they're just asking to be eaten, what can we do?"

"Well, Mum's always loved puds, so I'm going to pile a spoonful of every single one of them onto her plate," laughed Julia, pushing Ida in her wheelchair to join the group. "I'm sure her eyes lit up when she saw the buffet. You've always had a good appetite, haven't you, Mum?"

Ida's face was impassive as she looked back at her daughter.

Barbara smiled warmly at her. "Lovely food here, Ida, isn't it? We're going to be really spoilt on this trip. Heaven help my waistline!"

Sylvia leaned over to speak quietly to Val, who was sitting next to her. "I know Ida still enjoys her meals. It seems odd when she's withdrawn from so many other things that used to matter to her."

"That's often the case," answered Val. "I've nursed lots of dementia patients over the years, and mealtimes can be the most important part of their day. They may lose connection with people around them, and get frustrated when they can't understand what people are saying to them, let alone make themselves understood, but I suppose there's something so fundamental and comforting about eating. Appetite's often one of the very last things they lose."

"When I booked this cruise," said Clifford, "I promised myself that I would remember my high sugar levels and my low will-power, and make sure that this sylph-like figure – which, of course, you all envy – remains as lithe and lovely as ever!"

"And that treacle pudding and custard is all part of the diet master plan, is it?" laughed Brian.

"There are no calories on board ship, Brian – and I'm telling you that as one church organist to another, so it must be true!"

Laughter was still rippling round their large table when Neil and Claire walked into the restaurant. Instantly there was a flurry of noisy greetings, hugs and chair-moving to make room for the new arrivals. On the other side of the restaurant, closely monitoring the goings-on, one couple was sitting slightly apart from the group of Neil's Derbyshire parishioners.

"That has got to stop," hissed Carole. "Neil is *our* vicar. St Jude's pays his wages. He'd do well to remember that."

"They seem such an unruly bunch." Garry was staring pointedly at the table of people from Dunbridge as he spoke.

"Neil said they've got two organists and a choir mistress in their group."

"Obviously not to the high standard of your musical training, my darling. You've got a *degree*!"

"And I have no intention of letting that uncouth rabble rule the roost where the music is concerned."

Garry reached across the table to cover her hand with his own. "Of course not. Now drink your coffee, then we'll go for a stroll around the deck to get our bearings."

Most of the other St Jude's group members were sitting at the neighbouring table.

"Did any of you have a chance to read this Daily Programme they've left in our cabins?" asked Mark. "There's a bit about a fire drill we've got to take part in this afternoon."

"I've heard that all cruise ships have to organize a fire drill by law before they're allowed to set sail," said Deirdre. Mark's heart lurched to see her smiling at him as she replied.

"What does it involve, did it say?" This was the first time Jill had spoken for a while. She had come to lunch by herself, looking somewhat subdued, after Rob had decided he'd prefer a beer and snack on his own at a bar they'd come across en route to the restaurant.

"We found our life jackets on the top shelf in the wardrobe," said Sheila. "I expect that's where yours are too. Anyway, there's a notice on the back of our door which says where you need to assemble in case of fire. From what I gather, there'll be some sort of bell or announcement at four o'clock this afternoon. Then we all have to put on our life jackets and make our way to wherever we're supposed to be."

"And where's that?" asked Betty. "We must all be going to the same place, as our rooms are so close to each other."

"The Discovery Lounge, I think it said," replied Mark.

"What's the Discovery Lounge?" asked Marion.

"And where is it?" added Betty.

"Well, I discovered it," said young Callum. "I went round the ship while Dad was settling Grandad in. It's a great big lounge with a stage at one end and a bar at the other, with lots of seats and tables in between. It might have been on the floor below this, or was it the next one down? Anyway, I'm pretty sure it was at this end of the ship – but it might have been the other..."

"So is this our cue to do a bit of exploring?" laughed Deirdre. "That way we'll all get lost together."

Getting lost with Deirdre, thought Mark longingly. *What a wonderful thought...*

"Don't forget Carole and Garry," suggested Sheila. "They might want to come too."

"No chance!" grinned Marion, pushing back her chair. "They've already cleared off and left us. I don't think they want to be seen with punters from C Deck!"

"Wait for me!" wailed Betty, struggling to follow them. "I've eaten so much, I can't move that fast. Do you think running late counts as exercise?"

***

A couple of minutes before four, an announcement came over the tannoy, warning everyone that it was compulsory to take part in the fire drill which would happen as soon as the practice alarm sounded. In cabins all over the ship, passengers new to this routine fumbled around locating their bright orange life jackets, then trying to work out how on earth to put them on.

"Do I put the strap round the front and tie it at the back, or round the back and tie it at the front?" puzzled Sheila.

"I can't do this," wailed Betty. "My boobs are too big! A man must have invented these; a man with no idea whatsoever about the needs of ladies with big boobs!"

On the same deck on the opposite side of the ship, Iris opened her cabin door to find Neil, Claire and Harry waiting outside for her, all of them looking stiff and awkward in their jackets, which were stuffed front and back with large rectangular blocks of what was probably polystyrene.

"You look ridiculous," Iris huffed, "and I refuse to look ridiculous with you. If the captain thinks there is any danger at all of this ship capsizing, he should own up now and we'll get off and go home."

"Mum, you must. Everyone has to…"

"I will not. I will, however, escort you as far as the Distress Lounge…"

"… the Discovery Lounge," corrected Neil.

"Whatever it's called," Iris continued, giving her son a hard stare. "And I will *carry* with me this wretched orange monstrosity, but unless this ship is actually sinking, I will *not* put it on."

Like crocodiles of school children, the passengers filed out of their cabins and into the corridors. On the way, they passed business-like members of the crew, all with emergency uniforms and equipment, either striding purposefully in the opposite direction or standing along their way to keep them on the right route.

As Neil and Claire marched on ahead, Iris found her path suddenly blocked by a tall, white-suited officer who stepped out to address her.

"Madam, I see you're having trouble with your life jacket."

Iris flushed. "Well, not exactly. I just think that…"

"It can seem very complicated if you've not come across one of these jackets before," smiled the officer, his blue eyes twinkling and his teeth gleaming unbelievably white. "Please allow me to be of assistance, dear lady."

And with his smile not dropping for a second, he expertly manoeuvred Iris into her jacket, while she allowed herself to be helped as if she were a flustered teenage girl.

"Thank you," she breathed when the procedure was accomplished. "I'm very grateful, Mr…?"

"Stephan," he replied, holding out his hand to shake hers before striding away. "Stephan Johannson. I'm the captain."

Iris still had high colour in her cheeks when she finally reached the packed Discovery Lounge. Neil was surrounded by people from both his parishes who had spotted his familiar face and made a beeline for him.

"Well," chuckled Betty, "this may be the first occasion when Neil's two congregations are all together, but I can't say any of us are looking our loveliest. I know we saw each other across a crowded buffet earlier, but we really are very pleased to be sharing this trip with you."

"And so are we," responded Barbara, who intended to shake Betty's hand in greeting until she realized that was almost impossible when wearing the cumbersome jackets. Instead, she waved both hands in the air and was delighted when just about everyone in the two groups waved too, first at her and then in general to anyone who was waving back. Plainly appalled, Carole and Garry moved a couple of steps away in the hope that no one would think they actually belonged to this large group of grinning, waving, orange-jacketed morons.

"Good afternoon, everyone!"

The voice belonged to an elegant blonde lady in a smart uniform, who was speaking from the mike on stage.

"I am the assistant cruise director, Jane Thurlow, and I would like to welcome you all on board *The Pilgrim*. This fire drill is a necessary precaution which is all part of the high standard of safety procedures we adhere to on this ship. You will see on your safety jacket that, apart from telling you to report here to the Discovery Lounge, there is also a large number written in red. This number refers to the lifeboat to which you are allocated."

Across the lounge, the crowd searched their own jackets and those of their companions to find the number they had to look for. Generally speaking, the passengers who had cabins on the starboard side of the ship were on lifeboats with even numbers, whereas the lifeboats on the port side had odd numbers. What followed was organized chaos, as around the room crew members held up paddles with corresponding numbers to show passengers where they should muster.

"Number 6 over here!" called a young man with glasses, who was waving a paddle in the air.

"Good gracious," said Clifford, who was the first to reach him. "You don't look old enough to be away from home, let alone leading us all to safety should disaster strike."

The young man grinned. "Actually, I'm twenty-one, but I must admit this is my first time being part of the team on one of these drills."

"Not a seasoned sailor, then?" smiled Clifford.

"I'm the pianist in the cocktail bar."

"Well, dear boy, you and I have a lot in common. I've tinkled the ivories in many a cocktail bar in my time."

"You play?"

"A lifetime as a professional, from the West End theatre and the odd television musical, to senior church organist in the home counties – with many good, bad and ugly bookings in between…"

The crowd heading for lifeboat number 6 was gathering around them, so their young leader raised his arm even higher and instructed them all to follow him.

"Form a single file with each of you placing your hand on the shoulder of the person in front of you," he called out, in the hope they could actually hear him. "That way no one gets lost, and everyone remains safe."

Across the huge lounge, rows of chattering passengers clasped hold of each other and disappeared in the direction of their allotted lifeboats. Within a couple of minutes, group number 6 was duly lined up on deck beside an impressive-looking lifeboat, while their bespectacled leader stood in front, trying to look confident.

"So, as seasoned seamen go, you're a good cocktail pianist, are you?" grinned Clifford, continuing their conversation.

"Throw any song title at me, and I'll play it in seconds. Throw a man overboard, and I'd be useless. Thank goodness all the rest of the crew know what they're doing."

"Not been cruising long, then?"

"This is my first contract. I've been here a month now, and I'm still learning the ropes. Everyone in the entertainments team is great, though."

"Well, dear boy, I will look forward to sipping a G&T in the cocktail bar while you entertain us all. I'm Clifford, by the way."

"Andrew – and I play the organ at our church too."

As they waited for the all-clear, Iris's attention was suddenly taken by a familiar voice she heard coming over the tannoy.

"Good afternoon. This is your captain speaking, Captain Stephan Johannson, welcoming you aboard *The Pilgrim* on behalf of all the crew. We are delighted to have your company on this nine-day cruise around the British Isles, and hope that each and every one of you will have a pleasant and inspiring trip. Our itinerary includes many fascinating trips ashore, plus a whole programme of entertainment, activity and interest while you are with us."

"I met him," whispered Iris, tugging at Harry's sleeve. "In the corridor just now – he spoke to me!"

"Really?" chuckled Harry. "You'll be dining at the captain's table before you know it."

"Let me hand you over now," continued Captain Stephan's voice on the tannoy, "to our wonderful cruise director, Ramon Moreno, who can tell you what's in store for your interest and delight this evening."

There was the rustle of the microphone being handed over before the air was filled by a deep, warm voice that lilted with a charming Spanish accent. It certainly got the instant attention of most of the ladies who were listening.

"My friends," Ramon began. "I take the liberty of addressing you in that way because we will all be *very* good friends by the end of our cruise in each other's excellent company. Welcome to *The Pilgrim*. We want you to enjoy every moment of your holiday, and we start by inviting you to the Discovery Lounge this evening, where at nine o'clock, after dinner, The Pilgrim Classical Trio will be playing a popular programme of Chopin, Tchaikovsky and Rachmaninov."

Ramon's voice was warm and inviting like liquid chocolate as he continued. "Those of you who've had time to peruse the Daily Programme which was left in your cabins will also know that there is much more to enjoy around the ship this evening – from a quiz upstairs in the Shackleton Lounge, Film Night in the cinema, and a touch of romance in the cocktail bar, with Andrew playing *Schmoozic* – melodies to smooch to until the wee small hours."

"He makes that sound delightfully decadent," whispered Betty. "Are we allowed to be a little sinful on a Christian cruise?"

"Oh, I do hope so," muttered Sheila.

"What a shame we'll be all by ourselves in the moonlight," sighed Marion. "Where's my Ron when I need him?"

"You left him at home to hold the fort with four teenagers for company. He'll be frothing at the mouth by the time you get home!"

Marion laughed. "At least I'll know he missed me."

"Now…" continued Ramon, "may I remind all those who are taking part in the Christian element of this cruise that there will be an introductory meeting to which you are all invited in the Discovery Lounge at half past five this afternoon. There you can meet the Christian host team, and hear about the services, trips and events that may be of special interest to you."

"Heavens, that reminds me," said Neil to Iris, who was standing beside him. "I'm due to meet Bishop Paul and the rest of the Christian team straight after this, just to make sure that the programme he planned is still what he's got in mind. I must round up Clifford, Brian and Sylvia too. Paul's asked them to sort out any music we need for our services on board. I'd better go!"

"Well, the rest of us are all going up on deck to see the ship sail," said Claire as Neil planted a kiss on her cheek. "If we miss each other, I'll catch up with you at the gathering in the lounge."

***

By the time people started arriving in the Discovery Lounge for the meeting at five thirty, the organizing team had rubber-stamped the final arrangements, and agreed on how to divide up the range of contributions needed to provide ministry, lectures, Bible study and chaplaincy throughout the cruise. As Bishop Paul stepped up to the mike to get the meeting underway, he was delighted to see that there was standing room only in the packed lounge.

"Good evening," he began. "I am Paul Ambrose, Bishop of Bedford, and I am heading the Christian team who will be leading worship and praise during our time on *The Pilgrim*. We embark together on a journey which is indeed a pilgrimage, following in the footsteps of the ancient Celtic saints like Aidan, Cuthbert, Bede, Columba and Patrick. They shaped our faith, informed our belief and inspired our country to know the truth of Christ's gospel. Each day as we go ashore, there will be a chance to choose from several different trips. You will have the chance not just to hear about the history of the location and appreciate its beauty, but also to learn of the spirituality and teaching of those great saints, who stretch down the years to inspire and guide us today.

"First, I would like you to meet the people who form our main ministerial team during this pilgrimage, starting with the chaplains. As a team, we will not only be leading prayer and worship each morning before we set off on our travels, but also Bible study every evening. Each of us will also be available for quiet prayer and individual counselling, if you would like that."

One by one, as Bishop Paul called out their names, the ministers took their place at the side of the stage.

"May I introduce my good friend Reverend Ros Martin, who is now the rector of a large parish in Worcestershire. Next on the team, there's the Reverend Neil Fisher, who's brought with him quite a few members of his church in Derbyshire.

They are joined by Methodist minister Maurice Brown from Exeter, who's here with his party. We're also delighted to have Father Peter and Sister Maureen from Birmingham, with a group of Catholic mothers. We are also pleased to know that on board there are several other members of the clergy from all denominations, some travelling individually, others with their own groups from churches up and down the country. We are looking forward to meeting you all as we worship together. We are one body, one church here. Getting to know each other and building the fellowship between us will be one of the greatest pleasures for us all as we travel together.

"Next, I would like to introduce you to a Presbyterian minister who was working right in the centre of Belfast during its most troubled times. He became involved with broadcasting for the BBC in Northern Ireland, before moving over to the mainland, where he was responsible for all the BBC's religious programming on both radio and television. Ladies and gentlemen, please welcome the Reverend Ernie Rea."

Ernie stepped up to take the mike offered to him by the bishop. He was a tall, slightly built man with a kindly face and a Northern Ireland accent.

"I am very pleased to be a member of the worship team on board *The Pilgrim*, taking part in our daily services, and travelling with you to visit places where the great saints lived, worked and wrote in years gone by. And as we visit some of these important sites, I will also be presenting a series of lectures which will explain some of the history and background to the lives of these men, hopefully giving you context to the wisdom and insight they've left as a legacy for us."

As Ernie left the stage to a round of applause, Bishop Paul spoke again.

"Now I'd like to introduce you to a lady who has been the familiar face of BBC Television's *Songs of Praise* programme for almost thirty years – Pam Rhodes!"

Necks craned among the audience as they tried to see whether Pam looked older, fatter or just different from the way she seemed on their television screens. In fact, she looked reassuringly familiar as, smiling, she came up to take the mike.

"Hello, everyone! Like all of you, I am looking forward to sharing services and Bible study while we're on the ship, as well as visiting places that have the power to inspire and move us."

"Rose used to love her," Harry whispered to Iris.

"She's got a lisp," commented Iris. "I always thought it was my television, but she's still got it."

"That's one of the things Rose always said she liked best about her."

"Towards the end of our time on board together," continued Pam, "I will be presenting our own 'Songs of Praise'. No cameras, just us, but we'll be following the same pattern that's made the television programme popular for more than fifty years, not just in the UK, but in many other countries around the world. We'll be singing together some of the most loved and moving hymns, both traditional classics as well as modern favourites – but in between our singing, I hope to talk to some of you about the challenges you've been through, and how your faith has supported you.

"So my first request is to say that if any of you feel you have gone through an experience that you would like to share during our 'Songs of Praise', perhaps you could let me know, and I can arrange to talk it through with you. Everyone has a story to tell – everyone has been challenged in their faith – and it would be very encouraging for us all to hear some of those stories. During our 'Songs of Praise', I'll only have time to include four testimonies, so I'll choose the four that together offer the greatest variety of experiences for us all to hear. In finding those people, I'm really looking forward to talking to any of you who would like to contribute to our Christian fellowship in this way, so feel free to chat to me at any time.

"Apart from that, I know how much many of you enjoy singing, so I'd like to suggest that we form a very informal gospel choir. We'll need a few rehearsals, because the choir will be performing at our very last worship time together, up on deck as we sail away from Honfleur on our final evening. Bearing in mind how we've come together from all sorts of different backgrounds, I think we should call it the 'Good Heavens!' choir. What do you think?"

A general chuckle of approval rippled around the room.

"How many of you already sing in a choir?"

About forty hands went up across the room.

"And how many of you sing along with the hymns on *Songs of Praise*?"

Just about every person in the lounge put their hand up then.

"Well, if you're interested in being part of our 'Good Heavens!' choir – and I assure you I'm looking for enthusiasm rather than skill – perhaps you could join me over in this corner when we've finished here, so that I can tell you more. And before I go on, I'd like to introduce you to the musical team who will be so essential to our worship. First of all, please take a bow, Clifford Davies! We are so lucky to have Clifford with us, because he brings with him a lifetime of experience, not just as a church organist, but from his professional career in West End theatre television too. Clifford will be the musical maestro behind the arrangements for the gospel choir."

Clifford duly greeted the crowd as Pam continued.

"For our more formal singing together, we are very privileged to have with us a husband and wife team who excel in all aspects of church music, both traditional and modern. Please welcome Brian Lambert, who plays any kind of keyboard he can lay his talented fingers on, and his wife Sylvia, who brings with her years of experience as a musical director for church choirs."

In the front row, Carole Swinton, sitting among the group from St Jude's, visibly bristled.

"Well, if those two think they're going to lord it over those of us who are *highly* qualified in church music, they have another think coming."

"You must have a word with Neil immediately," snapped Garry. "This is a Bedfordshire stitch-up. Burntacre will not be brushed aside in such a high-handed manner. It's outrageous!"

As Pam stepped down from the stage, Bishop Paul went on to announce that there would be leaflets by the door as they left, detailing places and times for the various services, Bible studies and choir rehearsals throughout the coming days.

"On your seats you will already have found the book we have prepared as a companion throughout our pilgrimage. We've called it *In the Footsteps of the Saints*, and in it we have collected a selection of prayers in the Celtic tradition. Some of them were written a thousand or more years ago by Christians who saw God in his creation around them, and who dedicated their lives to his service. Others are prayers written by modern-day Christians who feel the same connection with God in everything around them. So this will be a handbook to keep with you as we worship on board, as well as when we go out on trips. You'll also find it contains the words of about forty of our best-loved hymns, and I hope we get a chance to sing them all before we arrive back in Tilbury."

There was a flurry of page turning and chatter as people took a closer look at the book.

"Right!" Bishop Paul finished. "Tomorrow morning we arrive in Berwick, where some of us will be taking coaches over to Lindisfarne, the legendary Holy Island of St Aidan and St Cuthbert. So I would like to finish this evening by asking God to bless us as we set out on this pilgrimage together. Let us pray: *Be with us, Lord, as we set out together on this pilgrimage of discovery and faith. Guide us as we follow in the footsteps of the ancient saints. May we learn from their wisdom, be strengthened by their courage, and recognize your hand in everything, everywhere. We ask for your blessing, now and always. Amen.*"

Chapter 3

❧ Berwick-upon-Tweed ❧

*See in each herb and small animal, every bird
and beast, and in each man and woman, the eternal
Word of God.*

St Ninian

"*T*he trouble is, they're too cosseted on these great
big ships nowadays."

A bald-headed, rather rotund man had
taken the seat next to Mark on the open deck, where passengers
could have their breakfast with a view of the border town
of Berwick laid out before them. Mark's unknown table
companion stopped speaking only long enough to pop a piece
of sausage and ketchup into his mouth.

"I was in *boats*. Oh, sorry, if you've not been in the navy,
you wouldn't know what I mean by that. I mean submarines,
of course. I was a submariner for twenty years. Once a
submariner, always a submariner…"

A piece of fried bread topped with black pudding was the
next morsel to disappear.

"You see, nowadays these ships are more like floating
towns. They hardly notice the weather. It isn't a matter of
life or death to them, as it was to us. I was on A boats in the
Singapore Squadron – in Borneo, of course…"

"For heaven's sake, Brig, let the poor man eat his breakfast in peace!"

A small, round woman with neatly curled hair and a flowery shopping bag joined them at the table. "I do apologize. I hope my husband's not bothering you."

"Oh, don't worry, please," said Mark, hoping his reply would come across as more sincere than he actually felt. The man had taken the chair next to him five minutes previously, laying his plate – loaded with a very full English – on the table with a flourish. Since then, he'd not stopped talking (or eating) for more than a couple of seconds.

In fact, Mark had chosen this table because it was near the door, so he'd be able to see when Deirdre came in to join the line for the buffet. To his delight, he'd finally managed to catch her eye, and she'd waved across at him. He hoped she'd notice there was a spare seat beside him. He'd imagined a long chat about the ship and the people and the weather and the trip today…

No chance of that once "Brig" had plonked himself down and put paid to his well-laid plans!

"Submariner Young, reporting for duty, sir," grinned the old seaman, "and this is my wife Daisy, who's never understood the pull of the sea and what it means to a seadog like me. Once a sailor, always a sailor! It gets you right here."

Mark watched in alarm as Brig emphasized his point by thumping his heart with the hand that still held his breakfast fork.

"You're dripping egg on your shirt sleeve," snapped Daisy. "Just finish your breakfast. It's gone half past eight, and we're supposed to muster for the coach to Lindisfarne in fifteen minutes. Get a move on!"

"Hello, Mark."

Mark looked up in surprise to see Deirdre walking towards their table.

"Deirdre, good morning! Did you sleep well?"

"No one ever sleeps well on their first night at sea," stated Brig with an air of authority.

Deirdre smiled back at Mark. "Actually, I slept like a baby. I think it's the gentle rocking motion as we sail. I don't even remember putting the light out."

"Are you all set for Lindisfarne today?"

"Oh, are you going there too?" asked Brig. "Well, would you believe it? We've opted for that trip as well. We could all travel together."

"Really?" asked Deirdre, while Mark's heart sank.

"Brig, leave them alone!" interrupted Daisy. "They don't want a silly old fella like you hanging around."

Her husband doggedly ignored her, holding out his hand to Deirdre. "Brig Young, at your service, ma'am. And you two are…?"

"Deirdre O'Donnell…"

"… and Mark Stratton."

"And where are you folks from?"

"Burntacre in Derbyshire. Brig, did you say?" answered Deirdre.

"The lads called me that on the boats. The name sort of stuck."

"Don't encourage him," said Daisy. "It's a daft name for a daft old man who lives in the past. His real name's Frank."

Brig glared at Daisy, then turned his best smile in Deirdre's direction. "I've never heard of Burntacre. Small place, is it?"

"Quite small. I like it, though," replied Deirdre.

"You want to live in a big city, like us. Pompey, that's where we're from. That's *Portsmouth* to landlubbers. Never could bear the thought of living too far from the sea. I don't think I'd ever sleep at all if I couldn't hear waves breaking night and day."

"We live eight miles from the coast," interjected Daisy. "All we ever hear is the occasional seagull. And we're going to be late if you don't come right now! You've got to take your medication before we leave."

Brig nodded his head thoughtfully. "That's what happens

when you've been a fighting man. Some wounds never really heal. They blight your life and need constant treatment."

"He's developed Type 2 diabetes caused by too much beer and not enough exercise," explained Daisy. "Right, well, I'm off. Please yourself whether you catch that coach."

As she marched away, Brig smiled apologetically at Deirdre and Mark, and wiped his mouth with the serviette he'd had tucked in the collar of his open-necked shirt. He pushed back his chair and gave them a jaunty salute before trotting off after Daisy.

Watching him go, Mark caught Deirdre's eye and they both burst out laughing.

"Well, I'd better go too," said Deirdre at last.

"Yes, we don't want to be late. I'll see you at the coach, then."

"I hope so," she smiled, hesitating for just a second before turning to walk away.

She hopes so! Mark's mind was racing as he swallowed his last mouthful of toast, gulped down his coffee, then hurried back to his cabin to collect his things – and dab on an extra splash of aftershave.

***

"Ladies and gentlemen, may I have your attention please!"

Facing the crowd who had gathered in the Discovery Lounge waiting to leave for the day's outings, Assistant Cruise Director Jane looked as neat as a pin in her smart navy suit, her blonde hair scooped back into a business-like bun at the nape of her neck.

"Welcome to Berwick-upon-Tweed, the border town that has changed hands between the Scots and the English at least thirteen times. It stands on the English side of the border at present, but I'm told the Scots feel the match is still on!

"Now, we have several different trips heading out from the jetty this morning, so please make sure you collect the right boarding card for the coach you're supposed to be on. If you're booked onto the *Wild Life* boat trip to see the seals and puffins on the Farne Islands, please wait until you're called, which will be in about fifteen minutes. The *Historical Highlights* tour will visit Bamburgh Castle and a museum dedicated to the courage of Grace Darling, who was a Victorian lighthouse keeper's daughter who saved the lives of many sailors when their ship was wrecked on the rocks just off Bamburgh. If you're on that trip, your coaches are due in about ten minutes. Please listen out for more details.

"But if you have tickets for the full-day trip to the Holy Island of Lindisfarne, there are two coaches waiting now. Would you kindly make your way to the exit, which this morning is on D Deck near the main reception area."

"That's us!" Iris was immediately on her feet. "Come on, Harry. We don't want to be last. We need to get good seats on the coach."

"Don't worry, Mum," soothed Neil. "I've already had a word to make sure you two can sit near the front. You should be able to get in and out of the coach quite easily then."

"Oh, you haven't told them I'm a doddery old woman, have you? That would be unforgivably embarrassing."

"Heavens, Iris! The very idea." Harry's eyes were twinkling as he spoke. "You do, however, keep company with an extremely doddery old man who needs you to stop talking and take me down to D Deck immediately."

Even though they hurried down to the exit point from the ship, others had beaten them to it, notably Carole and Garry Swinton, who were chatting and laughing loudly with the uniformed officer who was waiting to show the passengers off *The Pilgrim*.

"How does she do that?" grumbled Sheila, as she and her two friends joined the end of the queue. "That linen suit Carole's wearing hasn't got a crease in it. Does she iron it full of starch, do you think?"

"Her housekeeper probably does," added Marion at Sheila's side. "Garry earns a fortune, so Carole told me."

"What exactly does he do?" asked Betty.

"Financial advisor; something like that."

"Well, I don't like to speak ill of anyone," said Marion, "but I really can't warm to him."

Sheila nodded in agreement. "Always seems a bit superior to me – just because he's Chairman of the parish council…"

"They're both a bit full of themselves, don't you think?" hissed Betty. "Calling herself *choir* director when there's only a handful of us and you could hardly describe us as singers."

"True," conceded Betty. "She does have an uphill struggle knocking us into shape. Credit where credit's due, though. She's got a nice voice."

"Pity she hasn't got a nice personality to go with it," mumbled Marion.

Down on the jetty, Mark headed towards the coaches for Lindisfarne, looking out for Deirdre as he went. There was no sign of her. Thinking she might already be on board, he was halfway up the steps of the first coach when he felt a tug on his sleeve. Turning, he looked down into the worried face of Jill Grenville.

"Sorry to ask, Mark, but you haven't seen Rob, have you?"

"Can't say I have."

"He seems to have done a disappearing act. Odd, really. He knows how much I'm looking forward to this trip."

"Perhaps he's already up in the coach waiting for you."

"Do you think so?" Her expression brightened. "You're right. He might be sitting over the other side where I can't see him."

"Come on," offered Mark, "let me take that bag for you."

But there was no sign of Rob on the bus.

"He'll be here soon," suggested Mark, worried that Jill was close to tears. "Why don't you choose a seat for the two of you now? The bus is filling up fast."

Reluctantly, Jill squeezed into the seat across from Mark's own, looking anxiously through the window as passengers made their way to the coaches. She recognized Brian, Sylvia and Clifford, because they'd all been introduced at the meeting the previous evening as the music team from Dunbridge. They were chatting as they climbed into the coach.

When Mark glanced towards Jill a few minutes later, he was alarmed to see her absent-mindedly scratching the back of her hand until her skin looked red and raw. Still Rob didn't come, not even after the time it took for Pete and Callum to help Arthur up the steps, followed by Julia skilfully manoeuvring her mother into a nearby seat. Jill's scratching became more and more frantic.

"Oh, there he is. Rob!" She banged noisily on the window to get his attention.

He heard her. He stopped for several seconds to stare right at her, then turned away to join the queue for the other coach.

"Rob!" she shouted, thumping the window even louder. "Over here. Rob!"

But her husband was plainly ignoring her, sharing a joke with a fellow passenger as he climbed into the bus opposite. Her shoulders slumped, her whole body shivering as she fell silent. Unsure what to say, Mark slid across to sit beside her, gently taking her blood-streaked hand in his own.

"Perhaps he didn't see me through this thick glass…"

Mark said nothing.

"I'll find him when we stop. These buses *are* going to the same place, aren't they?"

"I think so, yes."

"We'll be able to meet up at the other end. That's what we'll do…" Every now and then, she twitched with anxiety. "Why didn't he try and find me, though? He knows how much I was looking forward to this."

Beneath their hands, Mark could feel her knee trembling.

At that moment, Deirdre stepped onto their coach. Seeing Mark sitting so close to Jill, their hands clasped together and obviously deep in conversation, she kept moving to take a seat further back.

It was as Neil was about to step on board that Bishop Paul caught up with him.

"I'm on the other coach, Neil, so we can all meet up at Lindisfarne? Are you still OK to lead the prayers at our service?"

"I'm looking forward to it. Holy Island's very special to me. I came for a week's retreat when I was at theological college. If it weren't for the soul-searching I did then, I doubt I'd be standing here as an Anglican minister now."

Paul smiled. "Then there'll be a real sense of home-coming for you today. You know we only have five hours there at most before the tide covers the causeway and the island's cut off again. Can you tell everyone on your coach that our service will start by the priory ruins at one? We need to make sure everyone's ready to leave by half past two before the road disappears."

Neil boarded the coach and realized at once that it was almost full. Claire grinned up at him from her position next to Iris, who'd decided the seats were impossibly narrow for any normal-sized person, and that she needed to sit beside someone who was so slightly built that they took up practically no room at all – Claire! On the other side of the aisle, Harry was having an animated conversation with Arthur, who was surprisingly sprightly for a ninety-one-year-old.

Making his way down the coach, Neil passed Jill and Mark, and finally opted for the centre aisle seat right in the back row, where he was surprised to see a man sitting completely out of sight, tight against the window.

"Sorry," said Neil. "You might be wanting a bit of peace and quiet without me thumping down beside you. I'll move…"

"No."

Neil was shocked by the bleakness in the man's eyes. He looked as if he was in his early forties, dressed casually in a sweatshirt and jeans, but there was a desolation about him which was almost tangible. Neil responded with nothing more than a friendly smile, sensing that the man really didn't want company, so it came as a surprise when he spoke again.

"I've been to Lindisfarne before."

Neil nodded. "It's an island you want to come back to."

"I made a decision there."

Neil was silent.

"I need to make a decision again."

At that moment, the microphone squeaked into life as a fair-haired woman, looking delightfully bohemian in a flowing skirt and long knitted jacket, introduced herself.

"Hello, I'm Lydia, your guide for our visit today to the Holy Island of Lindisfarne. Unspoiled and steeped in history, it lies just off the north-east coast of England, about twenty minutes' drive south of Berwick. It has stood for centuries at the mercy of the elements, with the tides cutting the island off from the mainland twice every day as the causeway is submerged by the North Sea.

"People seek out our island for a variety of reasons. We welcome bird-watchers, walkers, fishing parties, artists, writers, photographers and film-makers, historians and natural historians, scientists, theologians, wildfowlers, yachters, golfers – and, of course, pilgrims in their thousands, some of them traditionally Christian, others seeking God's truth in their own way, just as the ancient saints did more than a thousand years ago. What they all find here is peace. In the midst of God's creation at its most raw, people are drawn here to find the peace of God."

"Is she a hippie?" Iris leaned towards Claire, whispering under her breath.

Claire smiled. "Perhaps a little alternative – but then so am I. You always told me you half expected me to put flowers in this spiky haircut of mine!"

"I am a member of the small community who live and worship on this holy island," continued Lydia. "I will tell you more about why it's always been so special as we get nearer, but this is a place you should travel to with purpose and prayer. So still your minds and open your hearts as I share these words with you:

> In the roar of the wind and the sway of the waves,
> We see your power.

In the cry of the birds,
We hear your voice.
In the calm of dusk,
We feel your peace.
Lord, with the depths around us,
We find rest and solace in you."

Neil sensed rather than heard the sob that came from the man alongside him. He'd turned his head away, so Neil felt he couldn't intrude. Instead, he bowed his head and said a heartfelt prayer for himself, his ministry, for those he loved – and for the man beside him who was so obviously hurting.

***

A silence fell over the passengers as the coach turned onto the causeway that stretched out ahead of them for more than a mile across to Holy Island.

"Imagine how this island must have looked to St Aidan when he first saw it, just as you are seeing it now, nearly fifteen hundred years ago." Lydia's commentary was quietly dramatic, catching the hushed mood around her.

"In 635, St Aidan and a group of twelve Irish monks were summoned from their community founded by St Columba on the Scottish island of Iona. They were invited by one of the first Christian leaders in England, Aethelfrith, who established himself at nearby Bamburgh Castle as King of Northumbria. He was determined that his new subjects, who were mostly pagan, should have the opportunity to hear the good news of Christ.

"So Aidan was sent to establish a monastery here on the island. In those early days, there would have been little more here than a church, a cluster of small circular dwelling huts, workshops and probably one larger building for communal gatherings. The monks led a disciplined life of prayer and poverty. They studied learned texts, and by the end of the eighth century they'd produced the beautifully illustrated Lindisfarne Gospels, all in Latin.

"Mission was a great part of their work too, and once they'd mastered the English language, Aidan and some of the brothers who crossed from the island to the mainland, where they walked the lanes, talking to everyone they met. Gradually they began to sow the seeds of Christianity in the communities around them; seeds of faith that eventually flourished to bring the knowledge of Christ to every corner of the British Isles."

Allowing a few minutes for her listeners to soak up both the information and the spectacular vista around them, Lydia didn't start talking again until the shore of the island came into clearer view.

"St Aidan founded the monastery in AD 635, but St Cuthbert, who followed Aidan as Prior of Lindisfarne, went on to become one of the most celebrated of this country's holy men. When Cuthbert died in 651, he was buried on the island until, eleven years later, the monks removed his body from its tomb in order to place it in a specially created pilgrim shrine. It was then that they became aware of the great miracle of Cuthbert: that his body had remained undecayed, a sign of great purity and holiness.

"At the end of the eighth century, the isolated island with its rich monastery became easy prey for Viking raiders. Eventually in 875 the monks left, cherishing their saint's remains as they fled, carrying him with them across the north of England. Their wanderings lasted for more than two centuries, until finally they were able to lay Cuthbert to rest at a bend in the river, where Durham Cathedral and his shrine remain today.

"It was only after that time that the Durham monks felt able to return to re-establish a priory on Lindisfarne, and the dramatic ruins of the richly decorated priory church they built at the start of the twelfth century, with its famous rainbow arch, still stand on the island today.

"A small community lived quietly on Holy Island until

1537, when Henry VIII caused devastation across the country by dissolving the monasteries, Lindisfarne amongst them. It's said that stones from the demolished priory church were used to build Lindisfarne Castle, which can still be seen from miles away, standing as it does on an ancient volcanic mound. It has passed through many hands and renovations since, but it's still an evocative and fascinating place for you to visit today."

At this point, the coach pulled up alongside several others in the car park by the village.

"Right!" announced Lydia, her voice now snapping with authority. "Please pick up a map of the island as you leave the coach, and then you are free to wander at will until quarter past two, when everyone must, I repeat *must*, be back on the coach, so that we can cross the causeway back to the mainland before it's submerged in water. Did everybody hear that loud and clear?"

A chorus of agreement echoed around the coach. Neil stood up to make his way down to the front and took the mike Lydia handed him.

"Can I remind everyone that we are holding our own service of worship beside the priory ruins at one o'clock sharp? Everyone is welcome to join us. They describe this as *a thin place*, where the veil between heaven and earth seems to fade almost to nothing. So discover for yourself what a special island this is – and God bless you."

The passengers tumbled untidily out of their coaches, poring over maps to try to get their bearings.

"This place is right up my street," announced John Curtis, as he and his wife Barbara emerged from their coach. "Spectacular landscape steeped in history."

"John loves history, don't you, love?" beamed Barbara, as she slung her rucksack over her very new waterproof jacket. "And we both love walking. That's right, isn't it, John?"

"Certainly is, dear. And you have your camera at the ready to record every little detail."

John looked down at the map, up to the horizon, then down at the map again before glancing left and right. "That way, I think!"

And with their unnaturally pristine walking boots squeaking slightly, the two of them set off at a determined pace.

"Rob!" called Jill, hurrying towards her husband the moment she spotted him. "I'm really sorry we missed each other. Were you OK being alone on that other coach?"

He barely looked at her as he replied, "Actually, the company was better than I've had for days."

"Oh dear, I'm so sorry I got things mixed up – but now we're here, what would you like to do first? Do you fancy walking up to take a look at the castle? Apparently there's a shuttle…"

"No. You go off and do your happy-clappy-churchy thing, and I'll sort myself out."

"Well, we're not meeting for our service until one," replied a flustered Jill. "We could do a bit of sight-seeing before that."

"The only sight I want to see is a nice pint in that pub over there. A newspaper would be good too, but I suppose it's too much to ask that they'd have a daily newspaper in a God-forsaken place like this."

"The one thing this place is *not* is God-forsaken," interrupted Marion, who had been standing near enough to hear the whole exchange. "Come on, Jill, he's not worth your worry. Just let him get on with whatever he wants to do. Come and join us. We're going to have a cup of coffee, then head for that castle."

Jill hesitated, looking pleadingly at her husband, but he was already striding away. Her expression was bleak as Marion led her over to where Betty and Sheila were standing. They both reached out to put their arms around her.

Mark had followed Jill off the coach, and he was appalled at Rob's reaction to his wife's obvious distress. He had a strong urge to march after him and punch him square on the nose.

"I feel like giving him a kick on the shin," said Deirdre,

suddenly appearing at his side and staring after Rob as he marched away.

"Hardly a good Christian response from either of us, then," grinned Mark.

"Ah, well…" agreed Deirdre, her eyes dancing with mischief. "What do you think? Coffee – or a walk to the castle?"

Without thinking, Mark offered his arm, and immediately she linked hers in his.

"The castle, I think."

Their eyes met in complete understanding. Then, as one, they walked out of the car park and veered off to the left, so deep in conversation that their heads were almost touching.

***

It was getting on for eleven o'clock by the time Iris, Harry, Claire and Neil had wandered around the village and made a trip to the café. Claire soon realized Neil was getting restless.

"Go on, hop it!" she smiled, putting her arms around his waist to draw him close. "I know how special this island is for you. You need some time on your own here. I'll look after the others."

He bent his head to kiss her. "Thank you for being so understanding. I'll see you at the priory ruins at one, OK?"

He knew exactly where he wanted to go: down to the shoreline, then back past the causeway where, all those years ago, in the rolling sand dunes that lined the shore, he had stumbled across a corner hidden from man but known to God – because it was there his despair and confusion had been met by God himself.

That moment had come just as he was reaching the end of his first year of theological training; a time when his confidence in his faith, in his understanding of God and in himself should have been steadily growing in depth and certainty. He could see that was happening for other candidates studying with him. His best friend had an easy way with people, combined with a talent for the theatrical. He always seemed able to connect easily with others, whether it was leading worship in a packed church, or being alongside a grieving wife as the life of her dearly loved husband ebbed away. Neil doubted that he would ever be capable of the right abilities, and that made him question whether he really understood what God wanted of him. Perhaps it wasn't ministry? After all, shouldn't there be Christians in every walk of life? Maybe he would make more impact on the faith and understanding of others if he were a teacher, a doctor or an accountant like his father?

He had been so near to quitting. He had come to this remote place, this holy island where the shadow between heaven and earth was smudged and fluid. He needed time to question everything he felt and thought he knew. After all, for years he'd been absolutely certain that he could hear the "still, small voice of God". He'd recognized its truth, reassuring, guiding and infinitely loving. He had no doubt of God's plan for his life. He was sure he could hear his voice above the clatter of the everyday, pushing him towards ministry, focusing him on what he understood to be God's purpose.

But, looking back, he knew that he had neither heard nor understood anything – not until he sat amid these windswept dunes, opening his mind and himself in utter surrender to God's holy will. It had seemed as if the ancient saints were drawing him there, whispering to his soul in the swirl of the wind, the rustle of the grass, the whistle of the pipits and the heave of the waves. He remembered lying flat as if his body was rooted in the ground, his arms stretched out towards the arch of heaven, exposed, vulnerable, inadequately human. A line of Scripture was rolling around in his head, and he remembered hearing a voice, *his* voice, saying the words over and over again: "You have searched me, Lord, and you know me." *If you know me, Lord,* he remembered praying in thoughts rather than words, *if I am a creation of yours, let me know your purpose for me. Grant me the skills and wisdom to fulfil your will. Let me be all I can be, what you intended when you breathed life into me…*

Later, he was unclear about what had happened – what he heard, what he saw, what was actually real. He remembered how the roaring in his brain seemed to subside, as silence descended around him like a warm dark blanket. No stirring wind, no rush of waves against the shore – just dark warmth, like loving arms that enclosed him. If there were words, he couldn't recall them, and yet he had complete understanding of what he heard; a deep reassurance in his heart of God's presence and purpose. He *would* become a minister, a channel of God's love to all. *Thy will be done, O Lord; thy will be done.*

His mind racing with the emotion of his memories, Neil made his way now through the dunes. They changed with every breath of wind and yet seemed comfortingly familiar. This was it. Just here, in a basin of calm from the weather – this was where it had happened. This was where his absolute belief in God, his sense of mission and his truest love were decided forever. Exhilarated, walking faster as he neared the spot, he climbed until the long grasses cleared a little so that, at last, he could re-live that moment of facing his nemesis.

And that was when he saw him. Hunched in a corner of the dip, his head in his hands, was the man who had sat alongside Neil on the coach. It was difficult to tell which of the two of them was more shocked and irritated by the intrusion, but finally it was Neil who spoke, thinking that if there was anywhere on earth where he had a responsibility to put care for others above his own wants, it was here in the place where the glory of God had been revealed to him.

"I'll go, if you like," said Neil. "Unless you could do with the company of someone who's a good listener."

The man stared at him through reddened eyes. "You're a minister?"

"Yes, in the Church of England."

"I'm an Anglican. At least I was a long time ago."

"Sometimes we drift away from religion, but that doesn't necessarily mean we lose our faith…"

"Are you asking if I believe in God? Yes, with all my heart.

65

Do I think God has any business with me? No, I don't. I don't deserve it."

"What makes you think that?"

"Because if I were half decent as a man, a husband, a father…" His voice trembled, pausing for a while before he could carry on. "If I'd been half decent as a father, my son wouldn't be dead because of me."

Neil moved over to sit beside him on the sand, watching as the man tore off a long blade of grass, shredding it savagely between his fingers as he continued.

"He died nine weeks and four days ago. Chris, our son. He was just eighteen."

Seconds passed.

"He overdosed. Heroin. It was cut with something else, backstreet stuff, contaminated. It killed him."

His head dropped as he struggled to go on.

"I could have helped him. I could have done something, the right thing. He came to me begging for help. As usual, I knew best. I gave him a lecture; told him he was a failure, a disgrace. Said I was ashamed to call him a son of mine. I turned my back and walked away – and he died. My son died in agony, in squalor, all on his own. Our boy, who was brought into the world with so much love and joy, died in pain and fear. I did that."

"Were the two of you close?"

The man grimaced. "It's hard to have a relationship with a father who's always working. Well, of course I work. Dads do. A family needs money, and I'm the provider. I didn't *want* to be away. I had to be. That's how things are."

"Who else is in the family apart from you and Chris?"

"My wife, Joanne – and Livvy. Chris is two years older than her." His voice broke again. "I mean, he *was*. They were always together, those two. She adored her big brother. Followed him round like a shadow when they were kids."

"And Joanne? How's she doing with all this?"

"Devastated. Grieving."

Another silence while he looked down at the mangled piece of grass in his hand.

"Do you know what Chris threw at me the week before he died? He said he hadn't asked to be born…"

Furiously, he slung away the grass he was holding.

"What do you say to that? What can a father say when his son tells him he didn't ask to be born? He was blaming me, as if everything going wrong in his life was my fault – and my first failure as a father was to give him life. He wished he hadn't been born."

"So how did you react?"

"I left. I told him he was an ungrateful, selfish, immature little boy, then I left. Six days later, they found him in an alley – and he was right. That *was* my fault…"

He wiped his fingers roughly over his face, taking a long, deep breath before raising his head to look out towards the sea.

"Years ago, I came here to make a decision. Now I wonder if I got it right. I'd fallen in love with Joanne, but our lives were so different. I didn't know if I could make her happy. I couldn't imagine living without her, but was I right for *her*? I couldn't think straight when we were together, because the passion between us was so strong. It was almost frightening that we wanted each other so much. So I came here to think things through. I sat on this shore for hours, thinking about her and me, and whether it was possible for two such different people to make a life together. There's something about this place, isn't there? Almost as if there's old wisdom in the air. Is it the saints? God?

"Whatever it was, I left here absolutely certain that Joanne and I could make a go of it. We didn't have mobiles then, but as soon as I got back on the mainland, I called her from a phone box by the side of the road. I asked her to marry me – and she said yes."

"And now you're back to make another decision?"

"I think I should leave her. That's what I have to decide.

I think she'd be better off without me. I made the wrong decision then, and it's time for me to put it right."

Abruptly, he got to his feet. "I need to walk. See you back on the coach."

And without a backward glance, he strode away towards the seashore.

***

Betty elbowed Sheila in the ribs as they sat on a bench munching ice-cream cones.

"Don't they look good together?"

Sheila followed her gaze to see Mark and Deirdre walking hand in hand down the road towards them.

"About time too. He's been gazing doe-eyed at her for months."

"He's quite shy, I think. Probably doesn't need to talk to people much in his line of work. It's something to do with cancer – a research scientist, I think he said. Anyway, he's a bit of a boffin. Nice man, though." Giving her cornet another lick, Betty looked at him thoughtfully. "How old do you reckon he is?"

"Mid-forties?" suggested Sheila.

"Hmm, probably. Good looking, if you like the tall, lean sort."

"Pity his hair's going. He must have been quite a looker before the bald patch."

"Well," said Betty, leaning closer to Sheila. "You know what they say about men who are bald…"

"What?"

"That they're very virile – you know, manly…"

"Oh, I don't think so," protested Sheila. "My John's bald and I can't think of one manly thing about him. Oh, yes I can: *two* things. He's got smelly feet and he won't let me have control of the TV remote *ever*!"

"Mark's been married, hasn't he?"

"His wife went off with a fella where she worked, so I

heard. It must have been years ago, though. I don't remember ever seeing him with anyone."

"And Deirdre's not got a husband, has she?" asked Betty. "How old's that boy of hers now?"

"Well, he used to be in the choir, didn't he? That was years ago, before I was a member. I guess he must have been about thirteen then."

"I'd say he's in his early twenties now," said Betty. "Maybe twenty-three, twenty-four? He turned out really well – went to university to study law. He's a solicitor down south somewhere, so I heard."

"She must be very proud of him, bringing him up on her own like that."

"Is his dad around?"

"Never heard him mentioned."

"Ooh…" said Betty, a knowing look on her face.

The two women fell silent, licking their cornets as they watched Deirdre and Mark walk by.

They were joined on the bench by Marion and Jill, who had been browsing in the shops in the village, ending up at the Lindisfarne Centre.

"Jill's treated herself to something really beautiful. Show them, Jill."

With the excitement of a small child, Jill dug into her handbag to produce a small, velvety bag in midnight blue. Untying the ribbon, she drew out a soft mound of tissue paper, which she unfolded with care. Inside its layers was an exquisite silver Celtic cross.

"It's lovely!" enthused Sheila.

"Rob will be so angry. He doesn't like me wasting money…"

"You're here on a Christian pilgrimage," countered Betty. "This is Holy Island, steeped in the Christian faith. What a special place to buy a cross. It will really mean something to you for the rest of your life."

"He'll still be mad. After all, he's the one who works to earn that money."

"And you don't work because you've been bringing up the family, *his* family."

"Yes, but he never liked the idea of his wife working."

"What were you doing when you met him, Jill?" asked Sheila.

"I was teaching maths at one of the senior schools in Derby."

"And you carried on till you had children?"

"I stopped three months before Martin was born. Rob didn't want me to work after that."

"So before you became a mum, you'd held down a very responsible and highly qualified job. Didn't you miss that when you were at home with the children?"

"Well, Rob thought the kids needed their mum at home, and I agreed with him…"

"Did you? All the time? What about when the boys were both at school themselves? You could have worked the same term times as theirs. You could have gone back to a job that suited your training and ability."

"He wouldn't have liked that. And I wouldn't have wanted to upset him."

"Jill, listen to yourself! If your husband had been saying you should stay at home out of love for you, fair enough. But we've seen the way he belittles and bullies you. He's done it for years. And somewhere inside you, there must still be a confident, capable woman who studied and worked and excelled at maths. I don't believe you never missed it."

"Yes!" Suddenly Jill's voice was strong and certain. "Yes, I did. Rob works for a big insurance company and it's a job he loves. I watch him going off to work each morning, knowing he can't wait to get his teeth into the challenges of a new day. I listen to him talking on the phone, and see how animated and on the ball he is when he's speaking to his team – and how different that is from the dismissive, patronizing way he talks to me. He says I bore him.

"Well, to be honest, I bore myself. I've got nothing to

talk about apart from the daily grind of housework: washing up, making beds, vacuuming, tidying, shopping, ironing, preparing dinner. I'm not saying I don't enjoy being a home-maker, because I do, but there's more to me than that, and I know it. Yes, I do feel resentful that Rob has always had a fulfilling job but won't allow me to have the same, not even now the kids have left home. There! I never dared say that out loud before, and now I have."

A cheer went up from the friends around her.

"And do you know what makes it worse?" she went on, really getting into her stride. "He doesn't come home. Most evenings he says he's working late at the office, but he's never back until after nine, and his breath stinks of booze. He wants his dinner, his favourite television show and bed – and it doesn't make an ounce of difference if I'm sharing that bed with him, because he hasn't been remotely interested in me for years."

"Why's he come on this holiday?" asked Betty. "I've never seen him at church, so I wouldn't think the fact that it's a Christian cruise would hold much appeal for him."

"I won some money on my Premium Bonds, the ones I've had for years. It was £2,000 that came out of the blue. I said I wanted to spend it by coming on this trip, and he was terrified he would miss out on his share of my winnings if he didn't come. He didn't really care where the ship was going, but he fancied the idea of cruising. He just took the whole thing over. It's taken the joy out of it for me, really."

"Well," said Marion, putting her arm around Jill's shoulders, "it's good that you're finally talking about it. And we're here to support you in any way we can."

"Oh, there's nothing I can do about it," said Jill, her expression suddenly anxious. "I'm married. He's my husband. Our marriage is just what it is."

"Unhappy," replied Marion gently. "For you, at least. Look at what you do to yourself because you're constantly fearful of his reaction." She looked down at the back of Jill's hand, which was red raw with angry scratches.

"Come on," said Sheila, picking up her bag. "You've got quite enough to think about for now. Just know we're here if you need us."

"I do need you." Jill's eyes were filling with tears. "I realize that now. And I don't know how to thank you."

"You can start by putting on that lovely Celtic cross, because we're all about to worship together at the ruins of the old priory. It's an ancient place, and God's people have prayed there for centuries. And my prayer for you is a new beginning, the courage to recognize all the wonderful talents you've been blessed with, and the strength to be everything God knows you are."

"Amen to that," agreed Betty. "And have we got time to call in at the Ladies before the service begins?"

***

"Holy ground, I'm standing on holy ground,
And the Lord my God is here with me."

The lines were sung prayerfully, as they stood in a circle, equal in worship, in communion with God and each other.

"We are indeed on holy ground," began Bishop Paul as the singing faded. "We stand in the footprints of St Aidan and St Cuthbert in this holy place, surrounded by the beauty, magnificence, wildness and wholeness of creation. Down the centuries, holy men have looked in wonder at the world around them, and given thanks to God. Let's hear how David felt when he did exactly that three thousand years ago."

It was the Methodist minister, Maurice Brown, who stepped forward to speak.

"This is the start of David's Psalm 24. 'The earth is the LORD's, and everything in it, the world, and all who live in it; for he founded it on the seas and established it on the waters. Who may ascend the mountain of the LORD? Who may stand in his holy place? The one who has clean hands and a pure heart, who does not trust in an idol or swear by a false god. They will receive blessing from the LORD and vindication from God their Saviour. Such is the generation of those who seek him, who seek your face, God of Jacob.'"

"Thank you, Maurice," said Bishop Paul. "The Celtic saints who lived here understood that everything on earth is the Lord's. Their lives weren't divided into their relationship with God on one side and everyday life on the other. Their whole existence was prayer. Whatever they did, thought, shared, felt or experienced was one long, heartfelt prayer of thankfulness. God was beside them and within them, just as they knew he was in every speck of life around them.

"But they were wise enough to realize that by choosing to live on a remote island, they could not run away from the temptations and challenges of the world beyond. St Cuthbert said, 'If I could live in a tiny dwelling on a rock in the ocean, surrounded by swelling waves, cut off from the knowledge and sight of all, I would still not be free from the cares of this fleeting world nor from the fear that somehow the love of money would come and snatch me away.'"

Bishop Paul paused for a moment, looking around the circle of worshippers.

"Cuthbert knew that money was only one of the factors of life, both for him then and for us now, which can claim our thoughts, cause us worry and lead us down the wrong path. He knew that wherever we are, whatever we're doing, our problems go with us. And so each one of us stands here now as ourselves, a complicated mix of what we've been through, what our hopes are, what we regret and what we feel we can't achieve. And God is here: the God known and loved by those ancient saints then, the God who knows and loves us now. We stand before him, just as we are…"

From the other side of the circle, Sylvia Lambert quietly began to sing the familiar words of a much-loved hymn. Others joined in, some with their eyes closed in prayer as they sang from memory, others finding the words in their *Pilgrim Companion* books.

Just as I am – without one plea
But that Thy blood was shed for me,
And that Thou bidst me come to Thee,
O Lamb of God, I come!

Just as I am – though toss'd about
With many a conflict, many a doubt,
Fightings and fears within, without,
O Lamb of God, I come!

Just as I am – poor, wretched, blind;
Sight, riches, healing of the mind,
Yea, all I need, in Thee to find,
O Lamb of God, I come!

Just as I am – Thou wilt receive,
Wilt welcome, pardon, cleanse, relieve;
Because Thy promise I believe,
O Lamb of God, I come!

"In 1835, when Charlotte Elliott wrote those words," continued Bishop Paul, "they came from the heart. She had been bed-bound with illness for years, deeply depressed, feeling useless and of little worth to others. On this particular occasion, she was especially frustrated when the rest of the family were busily preparing a bazaar to raise funds for a school her minister brother was setting up in Brighton. Left alone, convinced she had nothing to offer, she penned those words, asking God to accept her just as she was, in spite of everything she simply couldn't be.

"There is something in that plea which resonates with each one of us. We are all a blessed mix of qualities, abilities, opportunities and limitations – but God knows that, because he created us. He accepts us as we are, but his wish for us is that we become all he knows we can be. And the story of Charlotte and her hymn shows how small accomplishments or kindness can resonate far and wide. Those words she wrote when she was feeling particularly worthless have brought comfort and encouragement to Christians around the world, and raised a great deal more money than anything else for her brother's school!

"When St Aidan and St Cuthbert carved a life for themselves on this remote island, they established the Christian faith not only for this corner of England, but for the whole of the British Isles and beyond. And you may never know how something you do today could become a legacy of inspiration for others tomorrow. Do all you can do. Be all you can be – for your fellow man and for God.

"Now, Neil is going to lead us in prayer, using some of the many inspirational words written by David Adam, who was the vicar here on Lindisfarne for thirteen years."

Heads bowed around the circle as Neil began to speak.

"Within each piece of creation,
within each person,
hidden God you wait
to surprise us with your glory.
Within each moment of time,
within each day and hour,
hidden God you approach us,
calling our name to make us your own.
Within each human heart,
within our innermost being,
hidden God you touch us,
awaken us and reveal your love.
Everything, everyone is within you,
all space, all time and every person:
hidden God help us to open
our eyes and our hearts to your presence."

In the silence that followed, no one moved as the moment, the place and the Spirit of God filled them. And then, as someone quietly started singing again, many in their own way felt comfort come, pain fade and hearts open.

"Holy ground, I'm standing on holy ground,
And the Lord my God is here with me."

***

"We've been invited to a cocktail party in the captain's suite," said Claire, looking down at the embossed invitation that had been slipped under their cabin door. She continued reading before she spoke again.

"It looks as if the idea is that the Christian team on the cruise, and their partners, should have a chance to meet the ship's crew, along with a few other guests."

"How nice." Neil inspected the invitation himself, suddenly looking up in horror. "Heavens! Have you noticed? This is for half past six. That's only thirty minutes away. Can we be ready by then?"

"With my natural charm and good looks," grinned Claire, "just a lick of lipstick, and I'll be ready to go. You, however, may need considerably longer."

"You're right," he laughed back. "You do look fetching in your walking boots and anorak. But even with my limited knowledge of ladies' fashion, I know that's not exactly the smart cocktail look."

She slid her arms around his neck and kissed him. "I'll be ready. Just make sure you are."

Across the corridor, Iris was knocking urgently on Harry's door. When he finally opened it, she waved an envelope under his nose.

"Look! That nice captain is obviously a very mannered gentleman. He must have made enquiries as to who I was when we met, and he's invited me for cocktails in his cabin this evening."

Harry smiled as he read the card before turning towards his dressing table to pick up an identical invitation.

"Then, dear lady, you must allow me to escort you, because I feel very fortunate to have been invited too."

76

If this burst Iris's bubble of excitement, she recovered quickly.

"Well, you need to get a move on, Harry. Your grey trousers and navy jacket will do. You can call for me at twenty-five past six."

She was almost out in the corridor before popping her head around his door again.

"You'll need your blue tie – the plain one, not the one with swirls on. And your black shoes. Definitely not brown, even if you do keep saying how comfy they are. *Black* shoes!"

And with that she was gone.

Thirty minutes later, when Harry, in very shiny black shoes, walked into Captain Johannson's suite with Iris on his arm, she looked splendid in a plum velvet dress embroidered with tiny sparkling beads around the neckline. Neil and Claire led the way, immediately catching the attention of Bishop Paul and his wife Margaret, who were chatting to Ros Martin, who'd abandoned her dog collar for a sparkling top. Not far off, the Methodist minister Maurice and his wife were deep in conversation with the Roman Catholic priest, Father Peter. Bishop Paul stepped forward to introduce Neil to Captain Johannson, and Neil made further introductions to Claire and Harry.

"And this is my mother, Iris," Neil said, watching her cheeks blush a pretty shade of pink when the captain made the slightest bow in greeting as he took her hand.

"We have already met, I think," he said with a smile. "I must say, madam, that your dress this evening is so much nicer than the bright orange jacket you were wearing when we last spoke!"

Iris positively glowed, much to the amusement of both Neil and Harry, who stifled a laugh as they saw her grip remain on the good-looking captain's hand much longer than he probably expected.

"Captain Johannson!"

Neil immediately recognized the voice cutting across their conversation, heralding the arrival of Carole.

"How kind of you to invite us! I am Carole Swinton, Director of Music at St Jude's Church in Burntacre, and this is my husband Garry, Chairman of the Parish Council."

Releasing his hand from Iris's grasp, the captain greeted the newcomers politely. Neil and his group watched as Carole gushed and Garry launched into some detailed explanation with the bemused captain, who found himself gently but definitely led away into their private conversation.

"Hors d'oeuvres?" An immaculately tailored waiter offered a plate of colourful bite-size treats. Iris's varnished fingernails hovered for several seconds before she made her choice.

"These nibbles are nice, Daisy," said Brig, who, as an old naval man, had also been invited to the gathering. "Shall I pick up one or two for you?"

"I'd like to choose my own, thank you."

"Did you ever go to sea?" Brig asked, turning to Arthur, who hadn't let the fact he was in his wheelchair stop him wearing an impressive array of medals.

"I was in the artillery," replied Arthur. "Only saw the sea once, and that was on D-Day."

"You were never really *on* boats, then?"

Arthur wasn't given a chance to respond before Brig continued. "We went to hell and back. These people who never left home, how can they possibly understand what we went through? They can't. They don't know about the brotherhood that exists between a man and his comrades. I'm Brig Young, by the way. Whatever my wife calls me, Brig was my name with the boys – and when you've been through what *we* went through, it's what *they* think of you that matters most. Brothers in arms, we were – in Borneo, of course. As a military man yourself, you'll know what that meant…"

"Not really," said Arthur. "I don't know anything about boats. I've been fishing once in a while…"

"Submarines. I was in subs…"

"Oh, not a life I'd have liked," said Arthur.

"No, you have to be a real man for a job like that. Very

tough to get in, you know! Many try; only a handful of the best are picked…"

Arthur didn't comment, quickly realizing that this was a monologue for which no response was required.

"Twenty years I was in the service. The sea's been my life. We had it hard, though." Brig's arm waved expansively around the captain's suite. "No luxury like this. None of this modern technology. We relied on teamwork, instinct and courage. No namby-pamby could ever become a submariner. He wouldn't have lasted an hour with the work we had to do!"

"Brig!" barked Daisy.

"Sorry," she said apologetically to Arthur and Pete as she led him away, still talking as he left.

"Ladies and gentlemen," announced Captain Johannson, "welcome aboard *The Pilgrim*. We are delighted to be hosting this special Christian cruise around the British Isles, and it is good to meet those of you who are contributing to the ministry and music that I know means a great deal to many of our passengers. I would now like to hand over to our cruise director, Ramon Moreno, who will ensure that everyone here is introduced to the members of the entertainments team who'll be working with you."

"The cruise director? That's the one with the voice that sounds like expensive chocolate, isn't it?" whispered Sylvia, touching the arm of Val Fellowes, who was standing beside her.

"I bet he's gorgeous with a voice like that," replied Val.

For a moment, the two women were uncertain where his voice was coming from as they listened to him greet the assembled crowd. Moving to one side so that they could see better, Sylvia and Val were soon staring at each other with open mouths.

"He's tiny!" hissed Val. "Not even five foot, I reckon…"

"That voice," retorted Sylvia, "in that body! Well I never."

Ramon was indeed small in stature, but it took no time at all for him to convince the visitors that, as cruise director, he was extremely entertaining. He was funny and charming, and it was soon clear that most of the ladies in the room were hanging onto his every word.

"You will already have seen The Pilgrim Band," he explained in his delightful Spanish accent: "all top professionals who provide the music for the wide variety of evening entertainment we offer on board. Of course, most of them are busy entertaining our guests at this time in the evening. However, should you require their help during any of your events, they are at your disposal. On a daily basis, though, our extremely talented cocktail pianist, Andrew, who is himself a church organist, has volunteered to be on hand to help in any way, especially if you need to find or print out any particular hymns, music or words. I believe you have two organists of your own amongst your group?"

"Yes," replied Neil, indicating Brian and Clifford, who were standing together. "Brian Lambert's the musical director for our worship together, and Clifford Davies will be taking charge of the music for the gospel choir we're hoping to form."

"Have you had a good response to that?" asked Ramon.

"About seventy people came up after our welcome meeting," said Clifford. "Our first rehearsal is tomorrow night, when we're all back from our visit to Orkney. We'll have a better idea then whether the choir's going to work."

"Well," said Ramon smoothly, "I have an announcement to make. The international recording star Rhydian joined the ship just before we set sail this evening. We are very fortunate to have an artiste of the calibre of Rhydian performing on our ship. He is, of course, a devout Christian, and he is very much looking forward to sharing the whole experience of this trip for the few days he's with us."

"How long is he staying?" asked Carole, her eyes shining with interest.

"He'll be rehearsing on board tomorrow when we're docked at Kirkwall in Orkney, then he'll be performing for us all in the Discovery Lounge the following evening on Saturday.

He will be leaving the ship the next morning when we reach Dublin."

Neil looked round as excitement rippled through the crowd. For the first time, he noticed that Pam Rhodes and her husband Richard were standing on one side of the room. She gave him a friendly wave when she noticed he was looking in her direction.

Neil gave a small gasp of surprise. Standing behind Pam, almost as if he was trying to disappear into the corner, was the man he'd been speaking to that afternoon on the beach at Lindisfarne. Now he was smartly dressed in the uniform of a senior member of the crew. Who was he, then?

"Now, my friends," continued Ramon, looking towards his assistant cruise director, "my assistant, Jane Thurlow, is the person to ask if you need any help at all. In the meantime, dinner is now being served in the restaurant. Would you like to make your way down to take your seats?"

"Hello, Andrew," said Clifford as he passed the young cocktail pianist. "It sounds as if we may well be working together."

"Well, I'm probably not up to your standard, with all your years in the business, but I'm happy to help if you need me."

"Are you going down to dinner?"

"I'm not usually allowed to dine in the passengers' restaurant, but this week's different, as my parents are on board. This is my mum and dad, Maureen and Bill."

"We chose to book this cruise so we can see Andrew in action," explained Maureen, her eyes gleaming with pride as she shook hands with Clifford. "This contract on *The Pilgrim* is his first professional booking. Well, to be honest, it's the first time he's been away from home. We've missed him dreadfully and worry about him being far away with such a lot of responsibility…"

"Mum…" interrupted Andrew, who was plainly embarrassed.

"Well, son," added his dad, "we've coughed up for all those

music lessons since you were five years old. We're just here to see if our investment has paid off!"

"Dad…"

But Bill was in no mood to stop. "He's a brilliant pianist, you know – can play anything either from music or memory. And he knows all the *real* songs: the good stuff like Cole Porter and Irving Berlin. No wonder they've snapped him up. They recognize talent when they see it."

"I'm sure they do," smiled Clifford. "I'm looking forward to paying a visit to the cocktail bar later this evening."

"Well then, please join us," enthused Maureen. "We'll be there."

Andrew's mum and dad left the captain's cabin, and Clifford chuckled to see their son throw his hands up in mock despair before following his parents down the corridor.

As the room started to clear, Captain Johannson caught sight of the officer standing in the corner, and called him over to be introduced to Neil's group, who were still chatting together.

"Ladies and gentlemen, before you leave, may I introduce you to Brad Osbourn, our ship's doctor?"

Neil sensed Brad looking at him, desperately willing him not to react. Then, after a general greeting to the whole group, Brad excused himself and quickly walked away.

CHAPTER 4

KIRKWALL, ORKNEY

Bless, O Lord,
The earth beneath our feet,
The path whereon we tread,
The people whom we meet.

Based on an old Hebridean prayer

"A word in your ear, Neil." Bishop Paul spoke as the two men left together after leading the early morning worship.

"I've been cornered on several occasions by a rather formidable lady from your Burntacre congregation…"

"Don't tell me. Carole Swinton."

"Her husband has a very direct personality too."

Neil sighed. "Those two certainly are a force to be reckoned with in a small parish like ours."

"Well, they're making their presence felt on board too. She plainly wants to take charge of the music, but the team we've put in place are really experienced, and they're more than capable of providing everything we need here."

"I must say, she does have a nice voice."

"So do a lot of people."

"And she certainly makes a good job of knocking our motley crew of singers into some semblance of a choir."

"Hmm," grunted the bishop. "Well, we need to think of something to smooth her ruffled feathers before she drives us all to distraction. I don't suppose it's worth reminding her that St Cuthbert famously said, 'Do not ever think yourselves better than the rest of your companions who share the same faith'?"

Neil grinned. "Probably not. I can't see her thinking that is relevant to her in any way."

"Well," said Bishop Paul, smiling back at him, "I chose you for this trip because I know you're a man of great resource and ability…"

"Passing the buck, eh?"

"Definitely. I shall leave the matter in your capable hands."

"Thanks," groaned Neil, as the two men set off, each in the direction of his own cabin.

***

"I heard him this morning."

"Who?" asked Marion, as she and her two friends followed some distance behind Neil.

"Where was he?" Sheila was deeply engrossed in her conversation with Betty.

"Who?" repeated Marion.

"I don't know where he was," replied Betty. "I asked our steward and he said he was probably up on the top deck where the tennis court is."

Marion tried again. "Who are you talking about?"

"Well, I can see why he'd take himself as far away as possible, especially when he's obviously doing exercises."

"*Who?*" shouted Marion so loudly that Betty and Sheila looked at her in astonishment.

"Rhydian, of course."

"He was singing this morning."

"What a superb voice."

"It could fill the whole ship."

"Never heard anything like it," finished Betty with a flourish.

"Has anyone actually seen him yet?" asked Marion.

"I really don't know," replied Sheila. "But I'm hoping he might be at breakfast. Even a superstar has to eat."

"Well, I'm no superstar," retorted Betty, "but I am starving. Are you coming?"

The three ladies were sitting down with their plates loaded from the buffet when Jill came over and asked to join them.

"Of course," said Sheila. "We didn't see you last night. What happened when you got back to your cabin? Have you smoothed things over with Rob?"

"He hasn't said a thing to me since the coaches arrived on Lindisfarne yesterday morning and we had words."

"You mean when he stomped off to the pub rather than look around the island with you?" said Sheila.

"Is he coming on the trip this morning?" asked Betty.

"Honestly, I've no idea. We've both got tickets, but he just kept his head under the covers and totally ignored me when I told him the time and offered to bring him back a cup of tea."

"He can get his own, then," said Betty.

"So how are you feeling now?" asked Marion. "Is his silence upsetting you?"

"Do you know, I think I actually prefer it to his constant snide remarks. He's done nothing but criticize me for years."

"You stood up to him yesterday," said Sheila. "He wasn't expecting that."

"Well, *you* all stood up to him. I just went along with it…"

"But you didn't back down," said Betty. "You haven't gone running back to him, apologizing and accepting blame for everything he throws at you."

"It's a terrible atmosphere, though," said Jill forlornly, "being in a small cabin on top of each other without a word passing between us. I'd been looking forward to this cruise so much. I thought it might rekindle our relationship, even be a bit romantic – but there's no chance. He's as rude and awful to me here as he is at home. It's not just that he doesn't like me any more. He acts as if he really despises me. Honestly, I can't think what I've done to make him feel that way. I do everything I possibly can for him, not just because he demands it, but because he's my husband and I want him to be happy."

"It sounds as if there's no pleasing him," said Sheila. "As my old nan used to say, it's being so miserable makes him happy."

"You were in the main restaurant for dinner last night, weren't you?" asked Marion. "I thought I saw the two of you on a table across from ours."

"Well, we walked down together and even sat next to each other, but he turned his back on me so he could talk to the man beside him, and I was left to chat to the lady next to me. Heaven knows what they must have thought of us."

"Look, Jill, one thing I've noticed ever since I've known you, and that's quite a few years now," said Sheila, "is that you say sorry in practically every sentence. You apologize for everything to everyone, even when there's absolutely nothing you should be apologizing for."

"I don't, do I?" Jill frowned as she answered. "I'm sorry…"

Everyone burst out laughing, including Jill, who suddenly realized what she'd said.

"The thing is," Sheila went on, "you've got so used to Rob telling you you're useless at everything, you've started to believe it. But you know, you're an extremely capable woman. Look at how well you've brought up your kids, and your house is immaculate. Even the garden looks as if it's been pruned with manicure scissors, and I know that's all down to you."

"You are woman! You are invincible," grinned Betty.

"You're a wife," said Sheila more gently, "and you've had all the confidence knocked out of you by a husband who feels big by making you look small."

"So you've got to stop apologizing for being the wonderful woman you are," added Marion, "and let that husband of yours see you're made of stern stuff."

"Oh, I'm really not. I'm boring. Rob thinks so, and he's right. I feel boring. I bore myself."

Sheila was looking at Jill thoughtfully. "You know, tomorrow afternoon we've all booked ourselves in for a pamper session at the beauty salon downstairs. We're going to have our hair done, a manicure and make-up ready for the formal evening tomorrow. Do you fancy coming with us?"

"How much will it cost?" asked Jill, her face worried.

"Actually, it'll cost you nothing," said Sheila, "because the three of us are going to treat you."

"I'm sorry. I couldn't possibly accept that…"

"Christians have a duty to give," said Marion, taking Jill's scratched hand in her own, "but it's also our Christian duty to learn to accept gracefully. Let us do this for you. Do it for yourself because you deserve it. Do it for Rob, so he can see what an attractive and wonderful woman he's married."

There was a conflicting mix of doubt and temptation in Jill's expression.

"Go on," challenged Betty. "We dare you. Dare to be different."

"You'll have fun, if nothing else."

Jill chuckled, and once she'd started, laughter bubbled up from deep inside her until they were all laughing out loud.

"Yes," she announced. "I'm going to give it a go – and if Rob doesn't like it, tough."

***

Neil, Iris and Harry joined the rest of the Dunbridge group assembled in the Discovery Lounge ready for their half-day trip on Orkney.

"May I have your attention, please?"

Jane Thurlow's announcement brought a lull in the chatter, as the passengers waited to hear which coaches they should be on and what time they'd be leaving.

"Welcome to Kirkwall in Orkney. This port has been

welcoming cruise ships to its shores for many years now, earning a reputation as one of the most popular cruise ship destinations in the United Kingdom. And that's not surprising when you see the variety of interest this group of islands has to offer visitors.

"Many of you are aware that Orkney is famous as a habitat for birds and wildlife, with several conservation areas across 750,000 acres of wildlife reserves. Those with tickets for the six-hour *Orkneys Wildlife* excursion should make their way down to the quayside now, where your coaches are waiting.

"If you're booked on the *Ancient Orkneys* trip this morning, you'll be visiting a World Heritage site dating back to 3000 BC, which includes Skara Brae, Maeshowe Chambered Cairn, the Standing Stones of Stenness and Orkney's own Stonehenge, the Ring of Brodgar. Your coaches should be ready to leave in approximately ten minutes.

"*Going North* is our third excursion this morning, visiting the most northerly cathedral, royal residences and distillery in Britain. I'll be calling you for your coaches within quarter of an hour.

"Also waiting on the dockside at the moment is the coach for one of Orkney's most famous relics from the Second World War, the Italian Chapel. Can passengers booked on that trip kindly make their way down to the transport now?"

"What did she say?" asked Raymond, his smile as beaming as ever. "Is that us?"

"It certainly is," said Peter Fellowes, who was sitting next to him. "Ready for the off?"

"Neil," snapped Iris, "I will allow you to escort me, but only if you promise not to dawdle. Harry, try to keep up!"

"Tell you what, Uncle Harry," whispered Claire, linking her arm through his. "Let Iris do all the rushing around. You and I will take our time so you can just slip into the seat she's saved for you."

Clifford, who was working his way towards the exit along with Brian and Sylvia, heard a voice behind him.

"Good morning, Clifford. Did you enjoy Andrew's playing last night?"

Clifford swung around to see the eager faces of Maureen and Bill Bragnall directly behind him in the queue. Andrew was with them, but he was distracted by the extremely attractive young lady beside him, along with a tall, handsome young man whom Clifford instantly recognized as the talented lead singer in the ship's company of performers.

"We were so proud to see Andrew being applauded like that," enthused Maureen. "And he looks really elegant and mature in his dinner suit. My little boy is all grown up."

"He certainly did very well," agreed Clifford, smiling towards Andrew, who was now aware of their conversation. "You've got a wonderful feel for the music, Andrew. You're a talented musician."

Andrew couldn't keep the delight from his face.

"This is Sharon," he said, drawing his companions into the group. "She's head girl of the show dancers. And here's our lead singer, Michael."

Clifford shook hands with both of them, smiling warmly as he congratulated them on the company's performance the previous evening.

"It's good to see you all taking some time ashore," he added, "especially to visit the Italian Chapel. I remember coming here years ago. It was very moving."

"It's nice to get off the ship sometimes," said Sharon. "Andy, Mike and I have made a pact that we'll try and go on trips at least a couple of times a week. It's easy not to bother, especially when we've all been working late the night before. But if we don't, we could end up cruising round the world and seeing nothing but the sea."

"They don't have to pay, you know," beamed Maureen. "Because they're staff members, they go along as escorts on the coaches, counting passengers on and off and handing out the bottles of water and mints when they come back on board. It's a very responsible job."

"And we'd better go," said Sharon, sensing Andrew's embarrassment at his mother's comments. Hurriedly saying their goodbyes, the three of them headed for the exit.

"Legs up to here," quipped Bill, watching appreciatively as Sharon walked away. "A talented couple, Andrew and Sharon – one providing the music and the other one dancing to bring it alive. The perfect pair."

"Mr Davies," said a commanding voice to one side of their group. Clifford turned to see Carole Swinton looking directly at him. "I wish to arrange a time when you and I can have a little chat."

"Certainly, dear lady," said Clifford smoothly. "Perhaps during afternoon tea this afternoon, before the gospel choir rehearsal? I do hope you plan to come along to that."

"I wouldn't miss it for the world." Carole's reply sounded as if every word was loaded with meaning.

"Morning, all!" The jaunty greeting came from John Curtis, who had stopped beside them to give Barbara a chance to make last-minute adjustments to her camera. "This Italian Chapel's a must for us. A living legacy from the Second World War."

"We've been looking forward to seeing it since we first read the itinerary for this cruise, haven't we, dear?" trilled Barbara, looking adoringly at her husband. "And I'll capture every moment on my camera. I've been meaning to say to you all, by the way, that if you want copies of my photos once we're back home again, I'll be pleased to organize it."

"She'll be the group's official photographer before we know it," chuckled John. "You should be very proud of what you're doing, love."

"Oh, it's nothing really," giggled Barbara, glowing at the compliment. "I'm only an amateur."

As they all filed out towards the coach, Julia and Ida were just settling into the front seat, next to Arthur and his family. Handing over their tickets, the rest of the group clambered into seats further down the bus.

"Ahoy there, shipmates!" called Brig as he and Daisy arrived last.

"There are two seats up the back," directed Daisy. "Keep moving!"

Deirdre and Mark were already sitting close together in the middle of the bus, their hands lightly touching.

"I can't believe it," he said so that only she could hear. "After all this time, longing to get to know you better, it's taken a trip like this for us to get our act together at last. This feels so special, Deirdre. It's a dream come true."

"For me too."

"Please tell me if it gets too much – if I'm crowding you and you want a bit of space…"

"I've had nothing but my own space for far too long," she smiled back at him. "It never occurred to me that anyone would find me interesting enough to want to get closer."

He gazed directly at her. "I do. I hope you'll let me be closer still."

"You may not like what you find."

"What do you mean?"

She shrugged her shoulders. "It's early days, isn't it? Let's just take it as it comes."

"Of course," he agreed, weaving his fingers around hers. "But I need you to know my heart's in this. I think I've been a little in love with you from the first moment I saw you."

A faint flush coloured Deirdre's cheeks before she spoke again. "I've always wondered what brought you to St Jude's in the first place."

"Work. I head a research team that moved to new premises in Derby. I was tired of living in a city. I wanted a house in the country…"

"… with roses round the door?"

He shared her smile. "Exactly. That's just what I found when I discovered Sunnyside Cottage. It felt like home the moment I walked through the gate."

"Have you always been a churchgoer?"

"Not really. That was work too. I travelled a lot and often didn't make it back at the weekends. I made all sorts of excuses not to go, probably because I never found a church where I felt really at home. My faith's never been in question, though."

"Aren't scientists supposed to find faith and science totally incompatible?"

"Quite the opposite for me. Every time I look at life in minute detail through a microscope, I'm even more amazed at the intricacy of creation. I don't believe perfection can be random. It's not just my heart and soul – my logical brain tells me there must be a creative power behind it all. Being a scientist has made me even more of a believer."

"So once you'd settled in Burntacre, you decided to pop into St Jude's?"

"Yes. It was late September, and it turned out to be harvest festival. The church was all decked out with sheaves of corn, flowers and vegetables, and there were lots of children there. The whole building felt full of life and laughter. One of the hymns was 'We Plough the Fields and Scatter', and I hadn't sung that for years. There was a shaft of sunshine streaming through the stained-glass window, and I just felt swept up in the fellowship of it all. I wanted to belong. I needed to put down spiritual roots again and be part of a Christian community. So I went along the next week and the next, and before I knew it, I was on the readers' rota and joining the tenors in what passes as the choir."

"We couldn't believe our luck when a proper tenor joined us," grinned Deirdre.

"You noticed me, then?"

"I certainly did."

"You didn't say much."

"Well, I wouldn't. That's not me at all."

"I did try and talk to you a few times. Do you remember?"

"I remember very well, but I'm not good at small talk with people I don't know."

"Is that shyness?"

"Perhaps, a bit. I always find myself trying to fade into the background in mixed company."

"Why? Is there anything in particular that worries you?"

Deirdre looked as if she was about to reply, then changed her mind.

"I'm sorry. I don't mean to pry," he said, giving her hand a reassuring squeeze.

"You're not. It's a reasonable question."

"I guess," he said slowly, "you've been badly hurt in the past…"

"You could say that."

"Tell me to mind my own business, but does that have anything to do with Brendan's father?"

"I've heard nothing from him since before Brendan was born. Twenty-four years ago."

"Were you married?"

She looked him squarely in the eye. "No. I'm an unmarried mother. Does that shock you?"

"It only shocks me that you'd think for one minute I'd judge you in any way at all. It's Brendan's father who disappeared. You, on the other hand, have been a wonderful mother – everyone says so. And as a teacher, your whole life is devoted to children. I'm not the only one who admires you."

For a moment he thought she was going to cry, but instead she simply looked down at their clasped hands.

"Thank you," she whispered, and the two of them fell silent, words no longer needed when their interlocked fingers seemed to say it all.

As the coach started to pull away from the dockside, the microphone crackled into life.

"Good morning, everybody, and welcome to Orkney!" The smiling guide's weathered complexion and practical jacket and jeans indicated someone well used to an outdoor life. "My name's Morag, and I'm pleased to be your guide as we travel from Kirkwall across the Orkney mainland, over to the small island of Lamb Holm. There we're going to visit a remarkable chapel, quite unlike anything you'll find anywhere else in the world.

"To get to the start of its story, we need to go back to the dark days of World War Two. Here, to the east of Scapa Flow, there were four channels leading into an anchorage for naval ships. There were sunken ships conveniently blocking these channels, so it was thought an attack by sea from that direction was impossible. Not so. On 13th October 1939, a brilliantly planned and executed attack by the Germans took everyone completely by surprise. During an exceptionally high tide the commander of U-boat U47, Lieutenant Gunther Prien, found a gap in the defences of Holm Sound. He managed not only to penetrate the Flow, but also to get U47 safely back out again, having sunk the battleship *Royal Oak* killing eight hundred and thirty-three men."

"That German captain had a lucky break," called out Brig from the back of the bus. "Their U-boats weren't a patch on our subs, and their men weren't ever as well trained. Who won the war, then? It wasn't them, was it!"

"Brig!" commanded Daisy, plainly embarrassed. "People can't hear what she's saying."

In fact, it seemed that Morag hadn't heard the interruption, because she simply carried on with her commentary.

"That episode taught the navy a hard lesson, so a major plan was put in place to lay massive barriers of stone and concrete on the sea bed from island to island. It was going to take several years to build them, bearing in mind that about one and a half miles of barrier needed to be constructed in water up to sixty feet deep.

"It soon became clear that the work was moving too slowly and that more labour was needed. So, in early 1942, Italian prisoners of war were shipped up to this windswept northern isle to work on the huge building project.

"These prisoners came from a land of sunshine and song. They were devout Roman Catholics who missed their churches but cherished their faith. What we are going to see was their solution to that dilemma: their very own chapel. It was made from nothing more than scrap bits and pieces, but it still stands today as a beacon of resilience and inspiration to every generation that's followed them."

By this time, the passengers realized they were travelling across a narrow road with sea on both sides.

"The barriers were immediately named after the man who commanded they should be built – and so, ladies and gentlemen, we are now driving across the first of the Churchill Barriers. Once we reach Lamb Holm, we will be turning off towards the place where prisoner-of-war Camp 60 once stood. Several hundred Italian soldiers, captured during the North African campaign, were sent here. At the start, they were greeted by about thirteen cheerless huts, but the Italians soon got busy improving things. They built concrete paths and planted flowers. They even made a statue of St George in the camp square as a symbol of their triumph over defeat and loneliness during their years of captivity on Lamb Holm."

The coach parked and the passengers followed Morag up a path towards the low red and white building. There she waited beside a large, beautifully carved figure of Christ on the cross. Once everyone had gathered around her, she began to speak.

"Whatever other work the prisoners did to improve their rather bleak living conditions here at Camp 60, what they missed most of all was their church. It wasn't until late in 1943 that the camp padre persuaded the new, very supportive, camp commandant, Major Buckland, that two Nissen huts should be made available to create a chapel. And what you see here are those two huts, laid end to end and joined together. But it's not until you step inside that you realize what a masterpiece this chapel is."

They all made their way through the chapel entrance, and what they saw quite simply took their breath away. They no longer stood in a Nissen hut, but in an ornate, beautifully decorated church, with brickwork walls and carved stone vaulted ceilings leading up to a chancel, complete with a beautiful painting of Madonna and Child looking down benevolently from behind the altar. It was only on closer inspection that they realized that all the depth, perspective, shade and contour were created purely with the skill of a paintbrush on basic flat plasterboard.

"Wow!" breathed Claire. "This is amazing."

"All you see," continued Morag, "was planned and created by a great artist, Domenico Chiocchetti. He was just one of the prisoners, and yet you can see that his artistry was superlative. He led a small band of workers who had the right skills to make his plan a reality – a blacksmith, a cement worker and a couple of electricians. A year later, on 9th September 1944, the prisoners were released from Orkney to return home, but they left behind this exquisite chapel, which has been looked after with love and pride by Orcadians ever since."

"Would you mind," asked Father Peter who, like everyone else in the group, was plainly touched by what he saw, "if I said a prayer of thanksgiving while we're here?"

There was a general murmur of agreement as heads bowed in quiet reverence.

"Heavenly Father, as we stand here together now, we hold in prayer the hardship, the endeavours, the fellowship and the skill of those who created this wonderful chapel. We thank you for Domenico Chiocchetti and all who worked with him in faith and love, inspired by their need to worship and praise you. How could they have known that their creation would draw others to worship here too, just as we are now? We feel united in spirit with those prisoners of war more than seventy years ago, and with all who have stood here in prayer ever since.

"Lord, we are humbled by the beauty and resilience of the human spirit, just as we are moved by the beauty and resilience of this glorious part of the world through which we are pilgrims together.

"We pray in the name of the Father, the Son and the Holy Spirit. Amen."

***

The passengers were allowed about an hour to look around before it was time to get back on the coach. Val and Peter eventually found a low wall where they could bask in the breezy sunshine while they took the weight off their feet. It wasn't long before they were spotted, first by Brian, Sylvia and Clifford, and then by Neil and Claire, who all came over to join them. After a few minutes, their conversation slowed to a halt as they watched Carole and Garry striding across the path some way ahead of them.

"She's asked to speak to me," said Clifford.

"I can imagine what that's about," replied Neil. "The bishop collared me this morning."

"I hear," added Brian, "she has a degree in music."

"Well, that doesn't mean much," scoffed Clifford. "I haven't got a degree. Have you?"

Brian shook his head with a chuckle of laughter. "My mum taught me. For years she was the organist at the church I grew up in. She still is – in her eighties! That's my only qualification."

"Me too," agreed Clifford. "I learned to play the piano in the pub where my dad was part of the resident band three nights a week. Couldn't read a note of music until I was seventeen and realized I'd never get a job playing for variety and musicals unless I could read along with the others. I taught myself in a week, got a job at the Plaza in Stockport, and that was the start of forty years of never being out of work unless I wanted to be."

"Well, I was trained to lead church choirs by the Royal School of Church Music," said Sylvia. "It wasn't a full-time course, just evenings and occasional weekends, but it was very good. Do you think that counts?"

"Definitely," replied Neil. "And whatever qualifications you all have or haven't got, you've been invited to lead the music on this trip because you've got years of experience and you're excellent at the job."

"It's not always just about the score and the notes, though," said Clifford. "It's about being sensitive to the occasion and knowing what music's most appropriate."

Brian burst out laughing. "I can't believe you said that, Clifford Davies – the man who belted out a rendition of 'There Was I Waiting at the Church' during that ceremony when the groom didn't turn up."

"It lightened the atmosphere. If we hadn't laughed, we'd have all been in tears."

"But you're right, Cliff," said Sylvia. "It does take experience to understand the role of music in creating atmosphere for worship. Sometimes a big choral piece works best. Sometimes what's needed is something quiet and prayerful during the Eucharist, or joyous and full of praise when we feel like raising our hands in the air, even if we don't actually dare."

"Well, Mrs Swinton and I have arranged to meet later for afternoon tea," Clifford eventually continued. "I wonder if any of you might care to join us? I mean, what on earth am I going to say? I could do with a bit of moral support here."

Neil laughed. "Knowing Carole, you won't be required to do much of the talking. It'll take her no time at all to discover that you're more than a match for her, but she's a woman who relishes a challenge. She'll love you."

"You're going to abandon me to that woman's clutches, aren't you, the whole rotten lot of you!"

The rest of them looked at each other, nodding in gleeful agreement.

"You're the man for the job, Cliff," said Brian. "We're relying on you. And having worked with you for more years than I care to remember, all I can say is, heaven help that poor lady! Please be gentle with her."

***

Once they were all back on board *The Pilgrim*, Neil left Claire to take Iris and Harry back to their cabins before lunch, and set off down several decks until he found the destination he was seeking. When he knocked, the door was opened by a uniformed nurse.

"I wonder if Dr Osbourn is available for a few minutes?"

"It's OK." Bradley appeared from the consulting room. "This is a social rather than a medical call. In fact," he added to the nurse, "it must be almost time for your break. Why don't you slip off early today?"

Delighted at the thought, the nurse picked up her bag, shutting the door behind her.

"I thought you'd come," Bradley said when the two men were alone.

"As long as I'm not intruding."

"I need to apologize to you about the other day. You must have thought I was a mad man…"

"I thought you were a man in turmoil, and no apology is needed."

"Thank you for your discretion the other night in the captain's suite."

"I must admit I thought our paths might cross again, but I didn't expect to see you in uniform."

"So now you understand what's been tearing me apart. When Chris came to see me the day before he died, it wasn't just a cry for help to his dad. He came because I'm a doctor."

"So what *did* he want?"

"Heroin."

"Why would he think you'd give him that?"

"He said the market price for heroin was going through the roof. The only stuff he could afford was rubbish, mixed with all sorts of other substances. He knew it was toxic and he shouldn't touch it, but he needed his fix. He said if I loved him, I'd get some good, clean stuff for him."

Neil whistled softly under his breath.

"There was no question of me doing anything like that. I'd be struck off and lose my licence to practise. I told him that."

"Was there anything you felt you could do?"

"I tried saying I could get him onto a substitute like methadone, but he wasn't interested. Addicts need to be in the right frame of mind to start that treatment, usually when they're desperate enough to know they really want to change. The doctor has to be certain the patient is at the point where they're honestly committed to getting off drugs – and I knew he was nowhere near that stage. Besides, I couldn't prescribe methadone without doing a proper examination – blood, urine tests, there's quite a list – and he wasn't going to wait for any of that. He wanted heroin, and he wanted it now. He got angry and abusive, with a lot of colourful language in the names he called me."

"But as a doctor, you had no choice but to respond as you did."

"Chris wasn't asking a doctor. He was asking his dad. He needed heroin. He knew that if I'd really wanted to, I could have helped him get the proper stuff and clean needles – but I chose not to. I shouted at him. I told him I was ashamed of him, that he was a mess and a failure, a disappointment and embarrassment to his mother. And then he said… he said…"

He stopped, covering his face with his hands for several seconds until he was able to go on.

"He said if he was found dead in an alley somewhere, it would be my fault."

Brad's words hung in the air as he struggled to continue.

"I could tell he was just about to stamp out of the room – and then, suddenly, the fight seemed to go out of him. I've never seen such anguish in anyone's eyes as I saw in Chris's at that moment. He started crying like a little boy, calling out to me, 'Dad, I need help. I need your help. Please, Dad, please…'"

Brad's face contorted with pain as he relived the memory.

"And I turned my back on him. I told him I couldn't help and it wasn't fair of him to ask. I walked away. Then, seconds later, I thought better of it and turned back, but he'd gone."

Brad looked up at Neil, his expression wretched and bleak.

"The next time I saw him was three days later. He was on a slab in the mortuary. I did that, Neil. I killed my son. Can you blame his mother for hating me?"

***

"Earl Grey, Mr Davies?" Carole Swinton's manicured hand was poised over the bone china teapot.

"I'm a builder's tea man myself," replied Cliff, turning to wave to a hovering waiter. "That's what years of being in the theatre does for you. We mostly had neither the time nor the money to eat properly, so tea was our staple diet, the stronger the better."

Not a muscle on Carole's face moved, but her disapproval of the man sharing the table with her and her husband was absolutely plain.

"And gin and tonic," added Clifford, relishing every moment of her disdain. "I always found I played better with a good slug of gin inside me. I just had to watch it didn't make me play faster. The chorus line girls always gave me a hard time when I did that."

"Mr Davies." Carole's steely tone cut the conversation dead. "Garry and I are very concerned about the standard of music provided for worship on this Christian cruise. Apparently, you are the one responsible. That being so, we intend to list our concerns and demand that you take action to remedy them with immediate effect."

If Carole expected an instant reaction, she didn't get one. It was almost as if Clifford hadn't heard her. Instead, he deliberately picked up his pot of English breakfast tea, pouring the golden liquid into his cup before dropping in two sugar lumps. After what seemed like an age of stirring, he replaced the spoon, lifted his cup and saucer, and sat back comfortably in his seat to look directly at her.

"I'm all ears, dear lady."

"I have a first-class honours degree in Music and Performance from Manchester University."

"And you've performed professionally?"

"She was in the chorus at Glyndebourne," interrupted Garry. "She'd have been in for more than just a month if I hadn't swept her off her feet and got her to marry me."

"How long have you been married?"

"Coming up for twenty years," said Garry, ignoring the blackening of Carole's expression as he placed his hand possessively on her knee. "She's still got a beautiful voice, though. You should hear her singing around the house. And she's knocking that awful choir at St Jude's into shape. She's a real pro, aren't you, darling?"

"Do you teach?"

"I have done," said Carole, shifting herself away from Garry. "I'm very selective about the pupils I take on."

"And what instruments do you play?"

"Piano, of course."

"To what standard?"

Her expression hardened. "A high standard."

"Do you play the organ?"

"I prefer not to. At St Jude's we have a man to do that. I am the choir director."

"And how big is the choir?"

"Numbers are growing as its reputation increases. I only took it over a year ago, and since then it's been a challenge which has needed all my qualifications and experience."

"And your concerns about the music on this cruise are what?"

"Well," she began, warming to her cause, "it's a takeover bid by the Bedfordshire musical mafia! It's all been stitched up by your cosy little group who – correct me if I'm wrong – haven't got a musical qualification between you. We need to represent the very best of the Anglican musical tradition: choral anthems, four-part harmonies, and traditional hymns with presence and gravitas. At our services to date, your ill-prepared team have come up with far too many modern choruses which may be known today, but will certainly be forgotten tomorrow. And what makes you think the passengers on this cruise, who, let's face it, are mostly aged fifty and upwards, are likely to have any interest at all in all this happy-clappy rubbish? Heaven knows what the bishop thinks of it! Oh, but then he chose *you* to provide the music, so perhaps he knows no better. He wouldn't understand the need to provide a mature, considered, traditional music setting which adds depth and meaning to our worship. That is its purpose – and that is your failing!"

Once again, Clifford took a sip of tea before replacing his cup to reply.

"So," he started at last, "you were a student of music more than two decades ago, and apart from a few performances soon after leaving university, you've rarely performed professionally since. You mostly sing at home for your husband's pleasure. You play the piano but not the organ, which is the usual instrument in most churches, and by your own admission the St Jude's choir is still not performing up to standard, even though you have been its musical director for a year.

"I suggest that as you have such an aversion to the widely acclaimed pieces written by current Christian songwriters, you have only limited knowledge of the rich variety of excellent music that is used in worship these days. I agree with you of course, dear lady, that a first-class honours degree in music is a significant achievement, but so is the combined treasure of decades of experience in churches of all denominations and styles which our current team is able to offer."

"And your experience stems from downing gin whilst you played for chorus girls in end-of-the-pier summer season shows, does it, Mr Davies?"

"Absolutely," Clifford agreed with a smile. "Although I did manage to fit in a few other productions too…"

"I demand," continued Carole, her face getting redder as

she rallied to her cause, "indeed, I *insist* that you and the St Stephen's road-show loosen your grip on the provision of music on this cruise, and allow me to bring a bit of decorum for those of us who are mature enough in our musical appreciation to recognize what is suitable and what is simply show business!"

"Well, I'll be blowed!"

They all looked up at the sudden interruption. A man got up from a table a short distance away and was now approaching them. He was probably in his late fifties, looking cool and elegant in light, tailored trousers teamed with a smart beige jacket.

"Cliff Davies! Fancy meeting you here."

"Bernie!" exclaimed Clifford, genuinely delighted to see the newcomer. "You look wonderful. You haven't aged a bit. Whatever you're on, I want some. How many years has it been?"

Bernie pulled up a chair to sit alongside Clifford. "That last Royal Variety Show with Shirley, I should think…"

"And how is Ms Bassey?" grinned Clifford. "As entertaining as ever, I hope."

"She never changes. That's what I like most about her. And you, Clifford? Is this cruise a well-earned rest for you?"

Bernie took in the astonished faces of Carole and Garry.

"Oh, I'm sorry. Forgive the intrusion. I'm Bernie Gordon, and I can't tell you how delighted I am to run into this marvellous man so unexpectedly. He's just the best, but then you obviously know that. I was never comfortable allowing my artistes to get involved in any big production or live television show unless I knew *he* was the musical director. They all wanted to work with him – Lulu, Sir Cliff… How long did you do that series with Cilla?"

"Oh, a few years," smiled Clifford.

"She called him her lucky charm," Bernie explained to Carole and Garry. "If Clifford wasn't available, she would simply turn down the booking."

For once in her life, Carole seemed genuinely lost for words.

"So what brings you on this trip?" asked Clifford.

"Rhydian's one of mine. He's a real rising star, you know; in demand around the world. I wouldn't normally have considered letting him do something as small fry as this, but he insisted. He's a Christian, you see. That means a lot to him. When he heard about the invitation to join this cruise, he jumped at it. I've just come along to make sure things run smoothly and to keep an eye on him. Oh, here he is now."

Carole's jaw dropped as she watched the famous operatic star making his way across from the table he'd been sharing with Bernie. A shock of pale hair rose from a face with chiselled features and strikingly blue eyes. His broad shoulders, muscular frame and confident stride gave him an air of strength and presence.

"Rhyd, come and meet a great friend of mine, the best keyboard player in the business: Clifford Davies."

"I'm honoured to meet you, Cliff. I've heard Bernie mention you often," said Rhydian, shaking his hand. "Is there any chance you might be accompanying me during my set?"

"Not on this occasion," replied Clifford. "I assume your musical backing will be provided by the on-board musicians."

"Well," huffed Bernie, "if they're not up to scratch, I'll be calling on you."

"I'm sure that won't be necessary. They seem very competent."

"I don't want mere competence, though," replied Rhydian in his lilting Welsh accent. "I want art and passion. I take my singing very seriously. I haven't met the band yet, but if they struggle at all with my material, it would be good to know I could call on you."

"Tell you what, let's talk about it over dinner tonight," suggested Bernie. "Please join our table this evening, Cliff. We've a lot to catch up on."

Clifford laughed. "And a lot that's probably better forgotten! Of course I'd love to join you."

"Shall we say half seven in the à la carte restaurant?" smiled Bernie.

"That will be perfect," agreed Clifford, standing to scoop up his newspaper and key from the table. "I'll walk out with you, Bernie. We're pulling together a gospel choir from the passengers on board, and our first rehearsal is in fifteen minutes. I do hope you'll join us, Carole. You too, Garry. We could do with some good chorus singers."

And with a gracious wave in their direction, he joined Bernie and Rhydian as they wove their way between the tea tables towards the door. It wasn't until they were safely around the corner and well out of sight that the three of them collapsed in laughter.

"That woman's face was a picture," chuckled Bernie. "She looked as if she was sucking a lemon when we first arrived, and by the end her jaw was practically on the table."

"I can see what a formidable team you two must have been during all those years you worked together," grinned Rhydian.

"Well, there may have been a bit of poetic licence in what I said just then," said Bernie, "but Clifford really is the best keyboard player I've ever known."

"All in the dim and distant past now," smiled Clifford ruefully. "They were great days, though. Variety theatre was such fun then. Of course, I started in the business while you were still in short trousers, Bernie…"

"But Cliff, you taught me a lot. It was no good me calling myself a producer until I'd done my apprenticeship and learned the business inside out. We had some tough times, didn't we? I'm not sure I'd have stuck with it without your encouragement. You certainly set me on the right road."

"And then television claimed you, and that was that. And now you're an agent…"

"It's a much easier life, believe me, especially when I have superb artistes like Rhydian here to look after."

"Well, I'm grateful to you both for playing along with my little plan. I enjoyed having my rather humble professional career rocketed to dizzy heights."

"Dinner tonight then?"

"Half seven it is!"

And with one last conspiratorial grin at each other, they parted company.

***

"I'm not asleep, Claire. Just resting my eyes…"

Harry had heard his great-niece tiptoe into his cabin to peer down on him as he lay stretched out on his bed, the Daily Programme sheet still clasped to his chest where it had fallen as he'd started to doze off.

"You OK?" Concern was written all over Claire's face. "You're not finding all these visits too much?"

Harry turned his head to smile at her. "Not at all. My mind and heart are loving every minute of it. It's just my old bones that are struggling to keep up."

"You probably need to find ways to pace yourself – perhaps give some of the visits and meetings a miss, so you have enough energy for the occasions that are really special to you?"

"Easier said than done, especially when there's so much I'd like to see. At my age, if I don't do it now, the moment will be gone forever."

"Well, you did say you'd like to come to the gospel choir rehearsal, and Neil's just knocking for Iris now."

"Oh yes, I'd like to try that." Harry's answer was a sigh of weariness.

"I reckon there'll be a lot of sorting out and talking things through in this first rehearsal," said Claire carefully. "Probably not too important, really, and I could bring you back any words or music you need, so we could run through it ourselves if you feel like coming to the next one."

"Would you?" Harry rested back against his pillow with relief. "I'll just have a little snooze before dinner. And I really want to see that show in the theatre tonight…"

"'Hooray for Hollywood'," grinned Claire. "Right up your street. You'll know all the words."

When Harry didn't answer, she realized he was already sinking into slumber. Gently taking the Daily Programme sheet from his hands, she tucked the cover around him, kissed him softly on the forehead, and quietly closed the cabin door behind her.

***

They're all here, thought Clifford, spotting familiar faces amongst the crowd of seventy or more people who had crammed into the Shackleton Lounge to sign up for the gospel choir.

It was a relief to see Brian and Sylvia Lambert from Dunbridge – they would both give a good musical lead. Peter and Val Fellowes were chatting to them, along with Raymond, whose smile was beaming as his voice boomed with excitement. John and Barbara Curtis were sitting at a table so she could line up her camera to capture the moment. Sitting alongside in her wheelchair was Ida, with a cup of coffee thoughtfully placed near to hand by Julia before she went over to chat to some of the new friends she'd made from Neil's Derbyshire parish.

Neil and Claire were there with them, along with Iris, who was still trying to make up her mind whether to join in or simply watch. The "girls", Betty, Sheila and Marion, had been joined by Jill, although there was no sign of her husband Rob. No surprise there, as he'd never previously shown any interest in singing. Deirdre and Mark, on the other hand, were enthusiastic members of the St Jude's choir, and Neil had to stifle a smile when he saw their hands were discreetly clasped as they stood at the edge of the group.

"Welcome to our first rehearsal for the Pilgrim Gospel Choir!"

Pam Rhodes had taken her place at the front, keen to get the rehearsal underway. "It's great to see so many of you here. Now, we are rehearsing for a contribution I'd like us to make to the 'Praise Away' worship gathering that's planned for the last day of our cruise. In other words, next Wednesday evening, as we sail out of the ancient harbour at Honfleur in France, on the final leg of our journey back to Tilbury, we'll be holding a praise and worship service up on deck, to which all passengers are invited. I would like our choir to provide the grand finale, a selection of familiar gospel songs to which we'll choreograph simple movements. Our aim is to encourage the audience to be moved, entertained and inspired by our singing, as well as joining in themselves if they feel like it.

"First," Pam continued, "let me introduce you to our team, who've volunteered to help us with our performance. Our musical director is Clifford Davies, whom I think most of you know from the worship we've already shared together. Cliff has written the arrangement for the music, and will be accompanying us on the piano. His role is to help us get the singing just right, and he promises to be gentle with us! However, I'm delighted to say that he has enlisted help in the form of Andrew Bragnall. Those of you who've been up in the cocktail bar in the evenings after dinner will know what a talented musician he is."

A murmur of recognition led to a smattering of applause for Andrew, who was sitting at a very sophisticated electronic keyboard.

"Oh, he's good," said Betty, nudging Sheila, who was standing next to her. "He was playing when we were all singing that Frank Sinatra number the other night."

"Andrew can make that keyboard of his sound like a full orchestra," smiled Pam, "so the music to accompany our gospel choir will be wonderful. Now we just have to get to work on the words and the music."

"What are we singing?" asked a demanding voice from the back of the crowd. Cliff recognized Carole immediately and realized that, following their tea together, curiosity had obviously got the better of her. Her high principles about the standard of music and singing on board seemed to matter less than making sure she didn't miss out on anything now she knew that Clifford was a man of stature in the entertainment business!

"Carole, I'm glad you're here," replied Cliff smoothly. "I wonder if you would be kind enough to hand round these song words to everyone? While that's being organized, can I ask you to put your hands up if you've sung as part of a choir before?"

About thirty hands shot up around the room.

"Very encouraging, but please don't worry if you've not done anything like this," continued Cliff. "I'd like you to divide yourselves into four groups: sopranos over here on the left, then the altos. Tenors over this side, with the basses on the far right."

Good-natured chaos followed as those who knew which category of voice they were worked out exactly where they should stand, while those who had no idea about their voices simply joined people they knew.

"Hello!"

As the tenors and altos shuffled into place beside each other, Julia turned to find a face she recognized smiling down at her. She knew Paul as the dance host, always on hand after dinner to partner any lady who fancied a waltz, quickstep or cha cha cha around the dance floor before the main entertainment of the evening.

The previous night she had taken Ida down to hear the band, and had been a little alarmed when Paul asked her to dance. She refused, saying she didn't feel she could leave Ida, but as she watched, she'd almost wished she'd had the courage to accept his invitation. She hadn't danced for ages, not since those ballet and tap lessons she'd had as a child years before. She loved watching *Strictly Come Dancing*, though, and always thought she'd enjoy taking up that kind of exercise again. She told herself the reason she'd never got around to it was that she had a busy career running her own accountancy business. That claimed most of her energy and attention. The rest was taken up by Ida, her widowed mother, who for some time had been slowly descending into dementia. This weighed heavily on Julia, as the only child in the family. Plus, of course, she didn't have a partner of her own. She assumed most dancers went in couples. Being a wallflower didn't appeal to her at all.

"Oh, hello," she smiled back at Paul. "Can you sing as well as dance, then?"

Paul shrugged with a grin. "No, I'd never call myself a singer, but when Pam said at the meeting the other day that they were looking for enthusiasm rather than skill, I thought I'd come along to see if they really meant it. If not, I reckon they'll be asking me to leave very soon."

Julia laughed. "Me too. I just thought it would be nice for Mum to come along to hear all these old gospel songs. I remember she loved singing them when I was growing up."

"Well, she's certainly got a good view from her wheelchair. She'll be conducting before we know it."

"Oh, I'd love to see that! She doesn't really engage with much around her these days."

"My dad had dementia for several years, too. It's tough. You lose sight of the person you've loved all your life…"

Julia looked at him for a moment, touched by his empathy and understanding of what life was like now for her and Mum.

"Your attention, please!" called Clifford. "These songs should be pretty familiar to most of you. Does anyone *not* know them already?"

No hands went up, so he continued. "The music is very easy to follow – but putting it simply, we will start with two choruses of 'When the Saints Go Marching In', then once through 'This Little Light of Mine' and 'Down by the Riverside'. Then the tempo slows a little as we sing 'Soon and Very Soon' followed by 'Kum Ba Ya, My Lord'. We pick the rhythm up again for 'Go Tell It on the Mountain', with two choruses of 'He's Got the Whole World in His Hands' as the big finish. So let's give it a go – in unison, just to make sure we've got the notes right. All together on my count! Huh-one, huh-two, huh-three: 'Oh, when the saints…'!"

111

SAINTS AND SAILORS

An hour later, the Pilgrim Gospel Choir was making a very acceptable sound indeed. With Clifford conducting and Andrew providing a strong musical accompaniment, the choir had got to the stage where Pam was able to suggest some quite easy moves, which most people seemed to be managing very well. Raymond's arms and legs seemed to move more expansively and in a different direction to the rest of the crowd, but somehow it didn't matter. Their faces were alive with pleasure and concentration as they tried to fit words and movements together, mostly with great success.

Suddenly Paul touched Julia's arm and indicated in the direction of Ida. Julia caught her breath. Ida's face was usually expressionless – but not now. Her mouth was moving. Not forming any recognizable words, but as if she was trying to join in with the familiar old songs.

Julia's eyes filled with tears at the unexpected sight. "I don't believe it. Just look at her."

"I noticed her last night. I could have sworn she was trying to sing along with the dance music then," said Paul quietly.

"Really? Was she? I haven't seen her do anything like that for a couple of years."

Pam's voice interrupted them as she picked up the microphone.

"That's really coming along. Thank you so much for your hard work. Please could you all pick up a sheet detailing the rehearsal times and the arrangements for the performance on the way out?"

"And don't forget to learn those words," instructed Clifford. "Next time, you'll be doing it without the sheet in front of you."

"Does anyone want to come up on deck with me now as the ship leaves the Orkneys?" shouted Brig over the chatter of the crowd. "I'm willing to give a commentary from a seafaring point of view, if that interests anyone?"

"No one's interested!" snapped Daisy. "And we've only got half an hour before our sitting for dinner."

"Save me a seat then," said Brig, as he realized that several people, including Neil, Peter Fellowes and Brian, were lining up to join him. "Follow me, shipmates! These waters around the far north of the British Isles are notoriously difficult, even for the most seasoned sailor. Let's see just how good this captain of ours is."

CHAPTER 5

⇒ TOBERMORY ⇐
THE ISLE OF MULL

Iona of my heart, Iona of my love,
Instead of monks' voices shall be the lowing of cattle;
But ere the world come to an end,
Iona shall be as it was.

St Columba

"Rough night!" commented Brian, as he and Sylvia joined Peter and Val for breakfast.

"It certainly was," grimaced Val. "I've rather enjoyed being rocked to sleep since we joined the ship, but last night I wondered if we were going to end up on the floor a couple of times."

"Well, Brig said it'd be rough," said Peter, "and he was right. He said all the waters round the top of the British Isles are treacherous, because of the strong currents and high winds. It's just as well I didn't end up going to sea. I always wanted to when I was a lad. You know, join the navy and see the world! That sounded quite appealing when I was a spotty eighteen-year-old."

"Why didn't you join up in the end?" asked Sylvia.

"My mum said no," grinned Peter, "and whatever she said

went. You know, I was in my fifties when she died, and I never did get anywhere when I tried to argue with her."

"And you ended up as an estate agent."

"That's right, in the middle of Bedfordshire, which is just about as far away from the sea as you can get!"

"Brig came across as really knowledgeable last night, didn't he?" said Brian. "His career in the Royal Navy certainly sounded colourful."

"It's his wife who puzzles me," mused Sylvia. "They seem so ill-matched. She's always putting him down and criticizing every word he says."

"He is a bit like a long-playing record though, don't you think? Has anyone heard him talk about anything *except* his life at sea?"

When it was clear that no one had, they all had a fit of the giggles. They were still laughing when Neil, Claire, Iris and Harry sat down at the table next to them.

"How are you, Harry?" asked Val. "I thought you looked a bit tired yesterday."

"Oh, I'm fine," replied Harry with a smile. "Just getting my sea legs, and that's not so easy when you've got gammy knees and arthritic ankles."

"And I bet you're not taking all your medicine," accused Iris. "He's terrible. He always thinks he knows better than the doctor. If he doesn't like the colour of a tablet, he won't bother to take it."

"I hope that's not true, Uncle Harry," said Claire.

"Of course it's not true. I don't give a fig what colour the tablets are. I don't like any of them."

"But if you need them...?"

"Look, love, I just don't fancy the idea of all those chemicals inside me. I've never smoked, hardly ever drunk, so why should I start filling myself with drugs and chemicals now? I'm old. Parts of me are wearing out. I'm going to die some time – and I don't mind. I know where I'm going. I'll be with my Maker and with my true love, my Rose. In fact, I'm rather looking forward to it."

"Harry!" The blood seemed to have drained from Iris's face. "That's a dreadful thing to say."

"No, it's not. Is it, Neil? I'm only telling the truth, my truth. I don't dread the thought of no longer living, though of course I'm sad to think of leaving you all behind. No tears, though; not for me. When the time comes, dance at my funeral. Celebrate my life. Wherever I am, that's exactly what I'll be doing."

This conversation was interrupted by Bishop Paul, who was making his way towards their table, along with his wife Margaret and their friend, Ros Martin.

"Morning, Neil," he said. "Are you all prepared for our service on Iona this afternoon? Did I tell you they've given us a slot at the Michael Chapel at one o'clock?"

"Yes. Ros and I are going to lead it together," replied Neil.

"It'll be very special," said Ros. "We'll be worshipping in a sacred place where Columba himself lived, prayed and is buried. In many ways, it's the cradle of Christianity in Britain."

"Amen to that," agreed Neil. "And you're organizing some music, aren't you, Brian?"

"Yes, I've prepared an unaccompanied piece for some of the more confident singers. A cappella singing should fit the occasion and the surroundings very well, except…"

"Except?" There was a note of concern in Neil's voice.

"Except I've asked Carole Swinton to be in the group."

"Goodness, how did she react to that? Does that mean war or peace?"

"Honestly, I'm not sure," replied Brian. "She didn't come to our rehearsal, because she was down in the spa having a stress-relief massage, so Garry told me."

Neil shook his head. "That doesn't sound like a good sign."

"But she assures me she sight-reads perfectly and that she'll fit in without any trouble."

No one looked convinced.

"Well," said Neil at last, "this isn't about individual

performance. It's about our communal worship. Carole can be charming – Garry too. I'm sure it'll all be fine. By the way, we've got two coachloads going to Iona today. Apparently it takes a couple of hours to get from Tobermory right down the Isle of Mull to Fionnphort. Hopefully we'll all arrive in time to get on the same ferry to Iona, but just in case, if Claire and I look after everyone on Coach A, could you take care of the group on Coach B, Ros?"

"Of course," she smiled. "Hope our mobiles work, then, so we can keep in touch."

"Those coaches will be going without us if we don't get a move on," said Peter, glancing at his watch. "We're due to collect our tickets in fifteen minutes."

Just at that moment, Daisy Young walked past their table with a couple of other ladies.

"Morning, Daisy," said Neil. "Your Brig was great last night as we were sailing out of Orkney. Very impressive. Where is he, by the way?"

Daisy stopped, her face expressionless except for tightly pursed lips. "He's had his head down the toilet all night. Seasick. He's always been a rotten sailor. I don't know why he wants to come on these cruises, really."

The crowd stared at her in shock as that revelation sank in. Then, suddenly, her mouth twitched and she began to laugh – and once she started, her cheeks grew redder and her eyes filled with tears as she threw her head back with laughter. It was infectious, and by the time everyone was making their way out of the restaurant, they couldn't help but laugh along with her, even though they weren't quite sure they should…

***

Rob was under the covers when Jill crept back into their cabin. Being as quiet as she could in the bathroom, she emerged to slip on her anorak and walking boots, then slung her rucksack over her shoulder.

"I'm off now," she whispered, in case he was just pretending to be asleep.

"Bye, then." His voice was muffled beneath the duvet.

"You're quite sure you don't want to come? Only, Arthur's decided not to do the trip after all, so there's a spare seat."

"He's over ninety." Rob pulled back the covers so that he could stare at her. "It was a pretty stupid idea to think of letting him do such a long coach trip in the first place. Two hours of driving just to get to the ferry? That son of his must need his head tested."

"Actually, Arthur would love to see Iona, but the journey's got nothing to do with it," answered Jill, trying to ignore his patronizing tone. "It's because he loves Scotch whisky, and he's just realized we're moored right next to the Tobermory Distillery. Something about a fifteen-year-old single malt that's more than 46 per cent proof?"

Rob whistled under his breath. "That could kill him."

"I think he'd die happy. Anyway, he's off for a tasting, and Pete and Callum say they'll *have* to go too, just to make sure he gets back to the ship in one piece."

"Right…!"

"So if you fancy coming to Iona, it'll be a wonderful drive. Iona's full of history…"

"You're old. You'll enjoy that."

Tears stung Jill's eyes as she replied. "I'm the same age as you."

"The difference is, you're old before your time," retorted Rob. "You're set in your ways, stuffy and predictable."

"Rob, that's cruel and unfair."

"Oh, Jill, admit it! We've got nothing left to talk about. We don't enjoy each other's company. All we've got in common is the kids, and they don't need us any more. And you're right, we are the same age, but you seem to be happy with that. I just see the months and years slipping away from me. I'll only live once, Jill. With you I feel as if I'm treading water, getting nowhere – with someone who's lost the will to do anything except dress and act like a pensioner. If I didn't have my job to get me out of the house and away from you, I'd go completely mad."

Gulping with indignation and hurt, Jill turned to head for the door. Then she looked back and said, "Well, you're the one who can't be bothered to get out of bed and see where we're moored right now. I'm the one who's going off to spend the day visiting a lovely island with people who value me. The only company you're likely to keep is any bartender willing to pour you a drink or six. Who's the boring one, Rob?"

And with that she slammed the door, only to collapse against the corridor wall as hot tears coursed their way down her cheeks.

***

As the coach wove its way out of the pretty town of Tobermory, Mark and Deirdre sat together looking out at the red, pink, yellow and blue houses clustered around the small harbour, which was sheltered on three sides by a steep wooded bank. At first, Deirdre tried to concentrate on what their guide was telling them about the three hundred miles of rugged coastline that encircled Mull, and the island's native grey seals, red deer and white-tailed sea eagles with their wingspan the size of a barn door. It wasn't long, though, before the words blurred as she gazed out in wonder at the wild beauty and vibrant colours of the landscape.

I need to cherish these wonderful memories, she thought, feeling the warmth of Mark's hand encircling hers. *Tomorrow everything will be different. By tomorrow, this lovely man will know the truth about me – and he won't want to know me then.*

"Look out to your left," said their guide, who was adept at weaving local history and folklore into his description of the geology and wildlife of the island. "On a clear day like this, it's often possible to catch a glimpse of the massive shape of Britain's highest mountain, Ben Nevis. Over there on the mainland. Can you see it?"

"No," said Sheila, taking off her sunglasses to peer through the window. "Can you?"

"I'm not keen on Scottish mountains," said Betty in the seat alongside, her head turned away from the window.

Sheila turned abruptly to check out her friend's unexpected lack of enthusiasm. "That's cryptic. Why not?"

Betty shrugged. "Oh, I tried skiing in Scotland once. A woman at work asked me to fill in when her friend had to back out of a week's holiday in Aviemore. I was so thrilled to be asked, although I did wonder why me? She was Miss Popular: tall, slim, always wore trendy clothes – quite the opposite of dumpy, frumpy me. I was the office comic, really. Very early on I worked out that everyone likes someone who makes them laugh, so that's what I tried to do."

"How did you get on with skiing?"

"Well, she'd been going on winter holidays for years, so once she'd dumped me in the beginners' class, she was off up the mountain and I didn't see her all day."

"Good idea to learn the basics, though," said Sheila.

"Yes, I thought that too. I might even have enjoyed it if I hadn't been the only person in the class who was over ten years old."

"Oh, I see…"

"I stuck it out for the first day, and I really thought I was beginning to get the hang of it. You know, though, how the weather in Scotland can change so quickly? The next morning, I was going up in the chairlift in freezing fog, with my fringe hanging down in icicles in front of my eyes. I just wondered what on earth I was doing there. It was supposed to be fun."

"And was it, once you got going?" asked Sheila.

"Well, I got up to the slope for the class, and I was struggling to get my skis on when a little show-off – she couldn't have been more than about five – shimmied up and skidded to a halt right next to me. She asked if I'd been in her class the day before. I was ridiculously pleased to think I'd made a friend, even a small one, so I said I was and that it was nice to know she remembered me – and she said she didn't really, but her mum told her there was a big girl at the back who kept falling down."

"Oh, Betty…" said Sheila, hands across her mouth as she struggled to stifle a giggle.

"So that was it. I decided that if God had wanted us to walk on snow, he'd have made skis easier to put on. I was back on that chairlift like a shot, and spent the rest of the week on a bike cycling round the loch near our hotel. It was great, really beautiful down at ground level. I enjoyed it. But the Scots can keep their mountains."

Sheila laughed out loud as she hugged her friend. "Of course you enjoyed it. You always make the best of everything. That's what I love about you. And I hope you spoke your mind to that heartless madam who abandoned you in the kids' class."

A slow smile spread across Betty's face. "She twisted her ankle…"

"No!"

"For the rest of our holiday, she was stuck in bed with her foot propped up on pillows. I was very sympathetic, of course."

"Well, you would be…"

"… while I had a great week out in the fresh air all day, then lots of Scotch broth and hot toddies in the evening. Après-ski without the bother of skiing. I loved it."

The two friends collapsed into giggles together.

"They sound as if they're having fun," smiled Claire. She and Neil were sitting just behind Betty and Sheila. "It's been good introducing people from our new congregation to the crowd from Dunbridge. I think it's working well. Don't you?"

Neil looked up from the book of Celtic prayers he'd been thumbing through in preparation for the service at Iona.

"Yes. I reckon some genuine friendships are being forged this week. Of course, the exceptions are Carole and Garry. They seem to think the St Stephen's crowd are their arch-rivals, for some unfathomable reason."

"I didn't realize how much I've missed all our friends down

in Dunbridge. I don't mean Uncle Harry and Iris, because we're always in touch with them – but people like Peter and Val. They're obviously still in love, after all the difficulties his ex-wife put him through. And Clifford! He always makes me laugh because he's so outrageous, but you can't possibly take offence. And there's Julia and Ida, although I didn't know them so well. And Raymond's a dear. He never changes, does he? Always smiling…"

"Well, it's easy to envy his attitude to life," agreed Neil, smiling too. "He breezes through life loving everyone and everything."

"Especially singing…" grimaced Claire. "What key is that he sings in?"

"A very loud one," chuckled Neil.

"And then there's Brian and Sylvia."

"Yes, they're great."

"Is it awkward for you? It's not so long ago they had you lined up as their son-in-law…"

"Until you came and claimed me from Wendy's clutches," grinned Neil, squeezing her hand.

"Seriously, though," Claire persisted, "how do they feel about that now?"

Neil shrugged. "If Brian and Sylvia hold any grudge, they certainly don't show it. I've noticed they're inclined to mention Wendy quite a bit, just to make sure I know how wonderfully well she's doing and how much she isn't missing me."

"Isn't it odd to think of her out in Australia with Ben, of all people? I mean, Ben was my boyfriend years ago when he was in Dunbridge – and he's Sam's dad, so he'll always be in our lives to some extent. But when he belted back to Australia leaving me to bring Sam up on my own, I honestly thought I'd never see him again. It was shocking enough that he came back last year expecting I'd welcome him with open arms, but when he finally got the message that I wasn't interested, I never thought he'd end up with Wendy. After all, she was still throwing her hat in your direction. And she always gave the impression she was so cultured and highbrow. It's hard to imagine her taking off for a new life in the middle of nowhere with a humble garage mechanic. It was all so dramatic; a bit like joining the Foreign Legion!"

Chuckling at the thought, Neil nodded in agreement.

"Are they a couple now, do you think?" asked Claire.

"Brian and Sylvia have never said and I haven't asked. I know Wendy's teaching at a school in his town, and from what her dad said, I think she's already head of the music department there. Presumably she's enjoying it, or she'd have been on the first plane back again."

"Do you have any regrets about making the choice you did?" There was a vulnerability in Claire's expression as she asked the question.

Holding her gaze, Neil leaned forward to kiss her with a tenderness that left her in no doubt of the answer.

"I love you," he whispered, "till death do us part. That means always. I will always love you, my darling Claire, always and forever."

With a sigh of contentment, Claire rested her head on his shoulder. "That's OK, then."

Two seats ahead of them, Jill turned her face to the window. She blew her nose and dabbed her eyes with a now-sodden tissue. Sitting beside her, Marion's voice was full of compassion as she spoke.

"Look, love, marriages have their ups and downs, especially when you've been married for years. I can't count the number of times I've been on the point of leaving Ron. Once, I even got as far as going to live with my sister for a whole month."

"But you came back." Jill's voice was barely audible. "You must have felt there was something in your marriage worth coming back for."

"Actually, my sister threw me out and said I was a pain to live with. She said I expected other people to do too much for me, and told me I was moody and didn't pull my weight. It was a bit of an eye-opener, really. Of course, I had a huge list of things that irritated me about Ron, but it had never occurred to me that perhaps he had to put up with quite a bit from me too."

"Did you bore him? Did he think you looked and behaved like a pensioner? Did he make it perfectly clear that he had no interest in you whatsoever, and that his life would be considerably better if you just cleared off and left him to it?"

"No, I think it was me who said all those things about him."

"But how can either of you step back from the point where you feel like that? Rob's said it all now. It's out there. I've heard it loud and clear. He doesn't love me any more. How can I stay when I know that's how he feels? Why would I want to?"

"Do you love him?"

"I thought I did, but then I thought he loved me too. What's the point of even trying to love someone who really doesn't want you? I've got to have some pride."

"Definitely. So give him something to notice – you. Prove to him and yourself how much you're worth – and then you can decide if you think he's worthy of you!"

"Hmm," grunted Jill, plainly not convinced.

Marion squeezed her hand reassuringly. "Trust me. Wait till this evening after you've been top-to-toed at the beauty salon. Then see how you feel."

Jill's face was filled with uncertainty, but she finally answered with a hint of a smile. "All right, fairy godmother, do your stuff! Of course, I'll be back in rags by midnight, but tomorrow's another day!"

"That's the spirit," grinned Marion, and the two women relaxed back into their seats to gaze out at the magnificent countryside beyond the coach window.

Just over an hour later, they drew up in front of the ferry terminal at Fionnphort, stopping alongside the other coach carrying passengers from *The Pilgrim*. Across the water they could see the outline of the Isle of Iona looking enticing and mysterious, just as pilgrims had seen it for centuries.

"Those ancient pilgrims didn't have a nice warm ferry boat to take them over to the island, though," smiled the

Reverend Ernie Rea, who was guiding the party during their visit. The passengers had gathered around him to gaze out towards the island as they watched the ferry make its steady way towards them.

"You see before you a sacred island," continued Ernie, "a place of inspiration, peace and healing where, more than one thousand four hundred years ago, the Celtic saint Columba founded a small monastic community which has inspired generations of Christians ever since.

"But it's not only faithful pilgrims who have been drawn here over the years. For centuries this was the seat of the great Stone of Scone on which kings of Scotland were crowned. Even after the stone had been moved over to Scone on the mainland, the kings of Scotland came back to Iona to be buried. Duncan and Macbeth weren't just fictional characters dreamed up by William Shakespeare. They were real Scottish kings whose bodies lie together somewhere on Iona.

"When we approach the landing point on the island, take a look towards your left, because there you'll see Martyrs' Bay, where the bodies of the kings were brought to their final resting place. From there, the Street of the Dead led through the ancient town of Sodora to the churchyard and the Chapel of St Oran, the oldest surviving and most hallowed place on Iona, where many Scottish and Irish kings are laid to rest.

"And somewhere on this island lies the body of St Columba, the monk whose teaching helped to establish the Christian faith in Scotland and eventually across the whole of the British Isles. When Columba and his fellow monks arrived here from Ireland on the day of Pentecost in 563, this island was wild and rugged, battered by strong winds and restless tides. Their lives were a daily struggle with the elements, illness and hardship. In the rawness of creation around them, they saw both the power and the love of God, and this oneness with God was reflected in their prayers and worship.

"Today, members of the Iona Community are committed to seeking new ways to live out the gospel in our modern world. The community was established in the late 1930s by the Reverend George MacLeod, who worked with a team of volunteers from some of the poorest areas of Glasgow to renovate the ancient monastic buildings of Iona Abbey. The community there today echoes the lifestyle of St Columba himself, bringing together work and worship, prayer and politics, the sacred and the secular."

At this point, Ernie broke off as the ferry arrived, and the passengers clambered on board. Some of them stood in awed silence as the boat made its way across to the island. Others captured the moment on their cameras, or texted the image to their friends back home. But as the group finally disembarked and gathered around Ernie again beside the ferry landing point on the Isle of Iona, there was a palpable air of excitement among them.

"You're welcome to wander around the island with me," said Ernie, "so I can explain the history of this place and the relevance of the buildings here. Or you may prefer to explore Iona quietly by yourself, as so many pilgrims have before you. Walk in their footsteps. Experience something of what Columba and his founding monks felt here on this blessed island. Whatever you decide, please bear in mind that at one o'clock we'll be holding our own act of worship in the Michael Chapel, at the back of the main abbey building. We look forward to you joining us then. But however you choose to fill your time, make sure you're back at the ferry here by two. Is that clear?"

There was a general murmur of agreement as the crowd started to disperse.

"I'm heading for the Ladies, then a café and a cupcake," announced Betty.

"I thought you were on a diet?" asked Sheila.

"My weight's perfect," retorted Betty. "Unfortunately, I'm about a foot shorter than I should be. Besides, I'll be keeping my diet in mind when I tuck into that cupcake. I'll ditch the sprinkles." And with that she marched off in the direction of the main street.

"Did she say cupcakes?" asked Raymond, his smile as broad as ever as he puffed up to join the group.

"I thought she said chocolate cupcakes," grinned Sheila, and with that she and Raymond turned to race after Betty, as Marion and Jill hurried along behind, hoping to catch up.

"Carole!" called Neil, as he spotted her walking with Garry towards the abbey. "I'm so pleased you're joining our choir for the service in the Michael Chapel today. I just wanted to check you've got everything you need."

"Why should I need anything?" Carole replied, turning to stare stonily at him. "I'm a professional. I can read music. I can sing anything asked of me."

"Of course," mumbled Neil hastily.

"Brian asked me specially. It's plain he needed a singer with expertise – a commodity in very short supply on this trip, I must say."

"Well, it's good of you to offer your services, and I'm sure it will be an enjoyable experience for us all."

"The setting will be very special," Carole agreed. "As for the standard of the singing in general – well, my guess is *that* will leave a lot to be desired."

"We're starting the service at one. I believe the choir are planning to gather a little earlier than that."

"I'm never late, as you know, Vicar. Now, if you'll excuse us, we have a lot we'd like to see before that service begins."

Feeling like a schoolboy dismissed by his headteacher, Neil turned away and counted silently to three before he walked over to where Claire had found a seat with Harry.

"Rose always wanted to come here."

Claire squeezed Harry's hand as he spoke.

"She had one of St Columba's prayers on a plaque in the kitchen. She often said how much she'd like to visit, but it always seemed too long a journey. I wish now I'd made it happen for her. She'd have enjoyed that coach journey this morning. In fact, she'd have loved this whole cruise."

Neil nodded agreement as he sank down on the seat beside them.

"I miss her." The old man's eyes seemed to be focused on a long-ago memory as he spoke. "There aren't many moments in my day when I'm not imagining what she'd be saying, if she were here."

"And what would she be saying now?"

There was a smile on Harry's face as he considered Neil's question. "I think she'd be most pleased at the company I'm keeping. You now married to Claire – she'd have approved of that! And Iris too. Rose would want to know a strong woman's keeping an eye on me, because she'd never have trusted me to look after myself. She's wrong, of course. I muddle along at home just fine – not that Iris would ever admit it. Actually, Iris needs me to look after her just as much as I do her, but I'd never dare tell her that. We're friends, good friends. I do appreciate her friendship, Neil, even if she does drive me to distraction at times."

"Oh," grinned Neil, "say no more. As a fellow sufferer with years of experience, I understand exactly how frustrating my mother can be."

Bang on cue, Iris's voice broke into their conversation. "No dawdling, Harry! We've not been round the abbey yet, and I've no intention of running out of time to see St Oran's Chapel. After all, it's the oldest building on the island, so it must be the most interesting."

"Rose used to nag me too," hissed Harry so that only Neil could hear. "Perhaps that's why I feel so at home in Iris's company."

"You're not flagging, are you?" challenged Iris. "We've only just had that coffee. Surely you're not giving up before we've properly started?"

"Wouldn't dream of it, my dear," smiled Harry, offering her his arm. "St Oran's first, I think, and then a stroll through the cloisters at the abbey in time for the Michael Chapel at one."

***

It was in the cloisters that Mark and Deirdre found a quiet corner seat after a brisk walk during which they'd covered as much of the island and its buildings as they could. Their conversation hadn't faltered at all, as if they had years' worth of feelings and experiences to share with one another – until now, when the quietness of the place, and the atmosphere of centuries of worship seeped into the ancient walls around them, made conversation unnecessary.

After several minutes, when Mark stretched out to cover Deirdre's hand with his, he was surprised to see her draw her hand back onto her lap.

"Mark, there's something I need to tell you."

The sudden bleakness of her expression shocked him, and he deliberately reached over to take her hand again. "There's nothing you can't tell me."

"You may change your mind after this."

"I don't believe anything could ever change my feelings for you."

"Don't say that until you know. This is something I've carried around with me for years, and never wanted to share with anyone – until you, now."

He squeezed her hand gently. "You're safe with me, Deirdre. I'm not going anywhere."

There was a silence while Deirdre was plainly gathering her thoughts. When she finally began to speak, her voice was low and her eyes never lifted from their clasped hands to look at his face.

"The only reason I booked this cruise was because of tomorrow. We're spending one day in Dublin. Just one day, that's all I need. I don't have to stay. I don't even have to go, if I lose my nerve. One day, I can cope with."

"Cope with what?"

"Dublin was my home. I grew up there. I haven't been back for twenty-four years."

"The year Brendan was born?"

"Six months before. I couldn't stay, so I left. I caught the ferry from the same harbour we'll be docking in tomorrow morning. I had no choice. There were no abortions in Ireland, so London was my only option. I had an address on a scrap of paper in my pocket. I remember wrapping my hand round it as I stood on the dockside watching the ferry come towards the terminal. I wanted to pull that paper out and throw it into the waves so the nightmare would stop. It felt as if everyone was looking at me, as if they knew what I was: a stupid, easy, immoral slut who'd brought disgrace to my family. That's what Da said I was, and he was right. I deserved it all, guilty as charged."

"Your family turned on you?"

"Da disowned me. The rest of the family had no choice. Oh, my mum didn't really want me to go. I'd always been her favourite. But I'll never forget the disappointment and shame I saw in her eyes that morning. After all she'd done for me, all that love and encouragement, her hope that I'd be the first in the family to go to university and make something of myself – after all that, I'd fallen for the oldest trick in the book. A man told me he loved me and I believed him. And I proved how much I loved him by giving him everything he wanted – because I wanted it too. I wanted him even more two months later when I was a girl in trouble and he'd disappeared off the face of the earth."

"Who was he?"

"The drummer in a band that came to my da's social club. His name was Brian. He kept catching my eye, and bought me a Coke at half time. Da never saw. He was on the committee and too busy with the raffle tickets to notice." She hesitated, breathing deeply to pull herself together before she went on.

"Brian asked me to come backstage after their set finished, and I said I couldn't possibly do that. He was trendy and good-looking. I was just a silly little girl who'd never got further than holding hands with the boy next door because I thought if I let him kiss me, I'd get pregnant. That was the extent of my sex education."

Mark moved closer, stroking her hand as she spoke.

"I was all dressed up that night. I'd just started work and splashed out on a pair of knee-high boots that made me feel fashionable and sophisticated. I'd got a new skirt and a top that was lower than anything I'd ever worn before. I knew I looked good. And I wanted him. I'd never seen such a beautiful man in my whole life, and I wanted to prove I was a modern girl, in charge of my own decisions. I knew he liked the way I looked. His tongue was practically hanging out. But then I was a girl used to playing hard to get – so hard that no one ever got anywhere with me – and I wasn't planning to change that just for a grubby backstage fumble with a man who didn't even want to know my name. By the end of the show, with a drink or two inside me, I had enough Dutch courage to think I could flirt and tease and show him how in control I was, then walk away with my head held high, knowing he was gagging for more."

Mark watched as tears filled her eyes and spilled down her cheeks.

"But in the end, it wasn't him who was gagging for it. It was me. Oh, he knew all the tricks. He'd probably had dozens of girls, stupid little groupies queuing up for him, just like me. When he kissed me, I couldn't care less what it might lead to as long as he didn't stop. I threw myself at him and he loved it, but it was me who loved it more. I couldn't get enough of him, even when he started putting his hands inside my new top. I knew it was wrong. I knew I should stop him, but it was the most wonderful feeling I'd ever known. I thought I heard him say he loved me – but by that time, it didn't matter. It wasn't only him ripping my clothes off; I was doing the same to him – or at least, as many clothes as we needed to lose to do what we both wanted…"

Releasing her hand from Mark's grasp to wipe her tear-stained cheek, it was some time before she felt able to go on.

"I remember afterwards trying to put my clothes back on, feeling so happy and warm – but he didn't even look at me.

He got dressed, picked up his bag and walked round the front to pack up his drum kit. I just watched from the side. He was laughing and joking with the rest of the band as they loaded up their van and drove off. He never spoke to me again."

"And he never knew he'd left you pregnant?"

"No. I didn't know myself until I'd missed a couple of periods and finally plucked up courage to talk to my sister Clodagh. She was already married."

"How did she react? Did she help you?"

"She was furious with me. She couldn't believe I'd been so gullible and stupid. She said I had to tell Mum and Da and take the consequences."

"Was it Clodagh who suggested an abortion?"

"She knew that wasn't possible for a good Catholic girl in Ireland, certainly not in those days. She said having a baby would ruin my life, and I had to do something. I was so confused I hardly took in what she was saying, but I knew abortion wasn't an option for me there."

"So you had to face your parents?"

"I told Mum first. I thought she might understand and just put her arms round me and make everything all right, like she always did when I had a problem."

"And did she?"

"It was the look in her eyes that floored me. Disgust, disbelief, disappointment – it was all there. She said nothing. She didn't need to. She just took my hand and dragged me down the stairs to the back room where Da was reading the paper before tea. 'Tell him,' she said. 'Tell him what you did!'"

Deirdre shuddered at the memory, and Mark put his arm around her shoulders to draw her close.

"So I told him. I told him about Brian and the night at the club, and I watched as his face turned black with anger. He was staring at me with such coldness that I had to look away. And then he turned to Mum. 'Get this immoral slut out of my house.' That's what he said. 'She has no place here. She's no daughter of mine.' And then he got up from his chair and walked out of the room without a backward glance. My mum ran after him, and they were arguing upstairs for a while, but in the end she came down with a small suitcase packed with a few of my things. She stuffed a couple of banknotes into my hand and pushed me towards the door. I screamed. I remember screaming and begging her to let me talk to Da, to give me time to sort things out – but she never said another word. She just pushed me through the house, threw me out into the street and slammed the door behind me."

"Where did you go?"

"To Clodagh's. Her husband Terry was there, and his reaction was much the same as Da's, so I knew I couldn't stay there. It was Terry who said I'd have to leave Dublin straight away; that to stay would bring shame to the whole family. He went to bring his van to the front door so he could take me to the ferry port, and while he was gone, Clodagh gave me the note with the address of the abortion clinic on it. To this day, I have no idea how she knew about it.

"There was another address on the paper too, of her old school friend Catherine who had married an Englishman and lived in north London. She said she'd ring and let her know I was coming, and ask her to let me stay for a while so that things could be organized. And then the horn on Terry's van was blaring, and she took me outside and waved goodbye.

"I knew what a difficult position I'd put her in. If Da knew Clodagh was helping me, he'd never forgive her. She'd be an outcast too. She did what she could, but I knew I was on my own. So there I was, standing on the dockside watching the ferry coming in, knowing I was leaving Ireland forever."

"And you've not been back?"

"No. I've never got over that feeling of shame and disgrace; never been able to get that vision of Da's face or the hurt in Mum's eyes out of my head."

"But surely you've been in touch since?"

"No, not with my parents. I do speak to Clodagh every now and then. I even saw her a couple of times when she came to

London to see Catherine and her family, but my name's not been mentioned in my parents' house since the night I left."

"But do they know what happened to you? Has Clodagh told them?"

"They've never asked, and she's never felt able to say. She thinks that Mum's wanted to find out about me, but nothing's ever actually been said. And Mum and Da are getting on now. They're in their mid-sixties. Da's retired. He worked as a drayman for a local brewery. After all these years, they've probably forgotten all about me."

"I doubt that very much."

"You may be right. Or perhaps it's me who can't forget, and they don't want to remember."

"What happened when you got to London? Did you go to the abortion clinic?"

"No. I couldn't. I was carrying a new person inside me, a part of me and of my parents. That baby might have started life in the worst possible way, but he deserved a chance to be all he could be. I knew I could never live with the knowledge that I'd disposed of that life for my own convenience, as if it meant nothing."

"But you had nothing. No family, no money. How on earth could you bring up a child?"

"Well, Catherine was wonderful and so was John, her husband. They'd got a young baby of their own, so they were appalled at the thought of me ending my pregnancy. And Catherine was a nurse at the Royal Free Hospital in Hampstead. She was being offered a lot of extra shifts, which would mean good money for them while John was setting up his own business as a plumber. So in the end, they asked if I'd like to stay with them for free as a nanny for Caitlin, their daughter. That way I'd have somewhere to live while I was pregnant, and then I could carry on taking care of both babies when my own came."

"And six months later, Brendan was born."

"I gave him my da's name. And the moment I held

Brendan in my arms, I knew that being a mother made my life complete. I didn't need anything or anyone apart from him."

"Did you stay with Catherine's family for long?"

"For five years, in the end. They encouraged me to study, and I managed to qualify as an infant teacher while I was with them. That way I could always work school terms and still be there for Brendan during the holidays. I applied for several jobs – but there was one that felt right the moment I walked in the door: Burntacre School. I'd never even visited Derbyshire before the day of my interview."

"And you've never married?" There was gentle concern in Mark's voice as he asked.

"To this day, I've not been with another man."

"No! I can't believe that. Surely you've had offers from perfectly nice men who could have been a good partner for you as well as a father for Brendan?"

"Perhaps there was the occasional man who looked in my direction, but I never looked back. It was Brendan and me against the world. That's how it felt. He was all I needed."

"And now? Do you still feel that way?"

She looked directly at him then, her eyes filled with emotion. "Now there's you. I've watched you for so long, and wondered if I could ever let my defences down enough to trust any man again. I didn't even know if you'd be interested in me, but I hoped – and I thought about you more than you could ever know. And Brendan's left home now and has his own life…"

"… so it's time for you to start yours?"

"I'd like to – with your help."

"Darling Deirdre, I told you before that I was falling in love with you. Well, I do love you, and nothing you've told me today has done anything except make me love you more. You're a brave and capable woman and a devoted mum. I know you'd make a wonderful wife too – *my* wife, I hope, if you'll have me."

"But this is all happening so fast. How can you be sure?"

"We've known each other for years, and it's obvious that for most of that time we've been longing for each other without ever plucking up the courage to say how we really feel. But that's behind us now. We're together and I've got no doubts about my feelings. Have you?"

She shook her head with a small smile. He kissed her then and she melted into his arms, returning his passion with the longing of a lifetime. Suddenly she drew back, her eyes gleaming.

"You've kissed me. I won't get pregnant, will I?"

"Perhaps," he grinned, "but not today. And certainly not from a kiss in such hallowed surroundings!"

She leaned forward so that their foreheads were touching.

"One day, though," he continued, "one day very soon, I'd like to stand in our church in Burntacre and make you my wife. I want to ask for God's blessing, to bring you comfort and a sense of forgiveness after all the pain and guilt that's been your burden for so long. I want to fill your life with my love until death do us part."

"Amen to that," she whispered. "I do. I will. I'd love to…"

Another kiss followed, before she spoke again. "First, though, I have to get through tomorrow."

"We'll do it together, if you'd like me to come."

"I'd like you to be nearby, but I think I have to knock on my da's door on my own. Just me – the girl he threw out, returning as a woman with a successful career in *spite* of him, and an album full of photographs of the wonderful grandson he's never known."

"Do you plan just to turn up unannounced?"

"Clodagh's going to meet me on the dockside."

"Then I'll look forward to meeting her. And whatever happens, you'll never be alone again. *We're* a family now. Let's hope that family can include your mum and dad after tomorrow."

"I pray for that."

"Me too."

And she laid her head on his shoulder as he drew her close again.

***

"Are you coming to the chapel? It's nearly one o'clock." Val Fellowes was calling out to the group of formidable ladies who were on the cruise to celebrate the anniversary of their local Catholic mothers organization.

"We are," replied Sister Maureen, who was travelling with them. "Just not quite sure which way to go."

"Follow us. It's round the back of the abbey building, I think."

"Don't forget Father Peter," warned one of the ladies. "He's gone to find Teresa. He thinks she's still in the gift shop."

"We'll wait for him, then," decided Sister Maureen, clucking like a mother hen at the trials of keeping tabs on the only man travelling with them. "He'll get lost if we don't."

Val and Peter joined the others from Dunbridge as passengers from *The Pilgrim* made their way towards the Michael Chapel, chatting and laughing as they walked. The atmosphere changed instantly, though, once they'd squeezed through the door of the ancient building to join the crowd filling the little church. The building was long and thin, lined with dark wooden pews down both sides leading up to a simple altar. A Celtic cross was framed against a Gothic window looking out over the grassland that tumbled down to the shore, then across the sea to the mainland.

"We're here! Don't start yet," puffed Sister Maureen as she and Father Peter arrived leading a gaggle of apologetic Catholic mothers. Obligingly the crowd squashed together even more to make space for the late-comers.

"Welcome, everyone," began Neil. "We are gathered to worship in the Michael Chapel here on Iona, in the place where St Columba and his monks also worshipped way back in the sixth century. Theirs was a tough life. You can imagine how bleak it must have been at times, on this tiny island battered by the elements. The community had to work together in order to survive, and to accomplish their aim of spreading the gospel of Christ. They all had to play their individual part for the common good.

"And so St Columba's message has become an inspiration for all the thousands of faithful who have worshipped here since – his belief that what's important is not just the universal community that exists between Christians, but the individual responsibility that rests on each and every one of us, to surrender our lives to God's will and purpose. Jesus asked a simple question, not just to the disciples in his time, but to all of us who have the choice to be his disciples now. 'Will you come and follow me?' Will you? Could this be the moment in your life when God's purpose for you becomes clear? Are you willing to put the needs of others before your own? Are you prepared to live out your faith in Christ, not just in church on Sunday, but every second of every day? Will you share all you have, do all you can, be all you should be?

"One wonderful example of a Christian man whose every thought and action was to live out his faith and encourage others to do the same was John Wesley, who, along with his brother Charles, established the Methodist Church. They started life as Anglican ministers, but they both went through a remarkable conversion experience which inspired them with the knowledge that each of us is able to have our own individual relationship with God. It's because of that relationship we are all called to make our own commitment to the care of others.

"Let's hear Reverend Ros remind us now of the words written by John Wesley as a prayer of covenant between himself and God."

Ros then got up to read the words:

"I am no longer my own, but thine.
Put me to what thou wilt, rank me with whom thou wilt.
Put me to doing, put me to suffering.
Let me be employed for thee or laid aside for thee,
exalted for thee or brought low for thee.

Let me be full, let me be empty.
Let me have all things, let me have nothing.
I freely and heartily yield all things to thy pleasure and
disposal.
And now, O glorious and blessed God,
Father, Son and Holy Spirit,
thou art mine, and I am thine.
So be it.
And the covenant which I have made on earth,
let it be ratified in heaven.

Amen."

Ros finished the reading and looked at the small group of
people who were standing to her right to one side of the altar.
"Our first hymn is number 15 in our *Pilgrim Companion*. We have
assembled a small choir for today, who will sing the first verse
for us, so that we can really think about the words written by
Frances Ridley Havergal back in the 1870s. She never thought
of herself as anyone special – just the daughter of a country
clergyman who wished she could do more to encourage others.
But she could never have known how much she really did
achieve through her hymns, which are still urging us to take a
deeper spiritual walk with Christ today."

A solo voice, clear and cultured, rang out around the
church as people strained to see who was singing.

"Take my life, and let it be
Consecrated, Lord, to Thee.
Take my moments and my days;
Let them flow in ceaseless praise."

"Good gracious!" whispered Iris, so that everyone around
her could hear. "It's that awful Carole woman from St Jude's.
She's hardly a good example of someone who puts others
before herself..."

"Shh!" hissed Harry, his eyes twinkling with mischief.

139

"Actually," said Val under her breath, "she's really rather good."

At this point, the whole congregation were invited to join in.

Take my hands, and let them move
At the impulse of Thy love.
Take my feet, and let them be
Swift and beautiful for Thee.

Take my voice, and let me sing
Always, only, for my King.
Take my lips, and let them be
Filled with messages from Thee.

Take my silver and my gold;
Not a mite would I withhold.
Take my intellect, and use
Every power as Thou shalt choose.

Take my will, and make it Thine;
It shall be no longer mine.
Take my heart, it is Thine own;
It shall be Thy royal throne.

Take my love, my Lord, I pour
At Thy feet its treasure store.
Take myself, and I will be
Ever, only, all for Thee.

"Might I suggest," continued Neil, once the last strains of music had died away, "that before you leave Iona today, you each go and find a place down on the shore and pick up two pebbles. Throw one out into the sea, as a symbol of something in your life which you would like to leave behind here. Take the other with you, as a sign of your new commitment to Christ in your heart. Make this your own covenant with God, your promise to do his will.

"And if you doubt your strength to devote your life in this way, then know you aren't alone in your fears. Even the great Martin Luther had his doubts, which he expressed in this heartfelt prayer."

It was the Methodist minister, Maurice Brown, who then stepped forward to read.

"Behold, Lord,
an empty vessel that needs to be filled.
My Lord, fill it.
I am weak in faith; strengthen me.
I am cold in love; warm me and make me fervent,
That my love may go out to my neighbour.
I do not have a strong and firm faith;
At times I doubt and am unable to trust you altogether.
O Lord, help me.
Strengthen my faith and trust in you."

There was complete silence, the powerful silence of prayer. And then from a back corner of the church, hidden from all, a man began to sing, his voice mellow and sweet, rich with emotion, strong with commitment and almost unbearably moving.

"Make me a channel of Your peace.
Where there is hatred let me bring Your love.
Where there is injury, Your pardon, Lord,
And where there's doubt, true faith in You.

Oh, Master, grant that I may never seek
So much to be consoled as to console.
To be understood, as to understand,
To be loved, as to love, with all my soul.

Make me a channel of Your peace.
Where there's despair in life let me bring hope.
Where there is darkness, only light,
And where there's sadness, ever joy.

Make me a channel of Your peace.
It is in pardoning that we are pardoned,
In giving of ourselves that we receive,
And in dying that we're born to eternal life."

There was a stunned hush at the end of the hymn, broken at last by Father Peter, who had come to stand beside Ros and Neil, his Bible open.

"Let us all be encouraged by what St Paul says in the third chapter of his letter to the Ephesians, verses 16 to 19:

> *"I pray that out of his glorious riches he may strengthen you with power through his Spirit in your inner being, so that Christ may dwell in your hearts through faith. And I pray that you, being rooted and established in love, may have power, together with all the Lord's holy people, to grasp how wide and long and high and deep is the love of Christ, and to know this love that surpasses knowledge – that you may be filled to the measure of all the fullness of God."*

"And may God bless you," finished Neil. "May you be an isle in the sea, a shelter in the storm and a beacon in the darkness. And may the power of the Spirit pour on you today and all your days evermore. Amen."

Quietly, prayerfully, the small choir drew the service to a close by singing John Rutter's setting of "Deep Peace", the traditional Celtic blessing, with its words that had become familiar to every worshipper in the chapel.

"Deep peace of the running wave to you,
Deep peace of the flowing air to you,
Deep peace of the quiet earth to you,
Deep peace of the shining stars to you,
Deep peace of the Son of Peace to you."

Lost in the atmosphere of worship, it took a while for the congregation to gather together their thoughts and their belongings, and make their way out of the Michael Chapel.

"Who *was* that?" demanded Betty. "His voice was beautiful."

"How come we haven't come across him before now?" said Sheila. "I haven't heard a voice like that in the congregation at the services on board. Have you?"

"That's because I have only just joined the ship, ladies."

The girls spun on their heels to look into a pale, smiling face with chiselled features that were instantly recognizable, in spite of the navy blue knitted hat that was pulled over his head.

"You're…?"

"Rhydian," he agreed. "Wasn't that service in this place just the most inspirational experience? I'll never forget it, ever." With a nod, he turned to start back towards the abbey.

"We'll be there tonight, cheering you on," Betty yelled after him.

He looked over his shoulder to give them a big smile and a cheery wave, before striding around the corner of the abbey and out of sight.

"That was a stroke of genius," commented Bishop Paul as he followed Brian, Neil, Ros and Clifford out of the chapel.

"Rhydian singing?" asked Brian. "I didn't even need to ask him. He asked me. Coming to Iona and being able to worship here obviously meant a lot to him."

"Well, yes, but that wasn't what I meant. Getting Carole to sing a solo – that was the real triumph! What's more, she sounded very good, which is a great relief all round. Your chat with her obviously worked, Clifford. How on earth did you do it?"

"I've no idea," grinned Clifford. "I hardly said a word."

"Well, I'm certainly looking forward to Rhydian's performance tonight," said Sylvia as she joined the group. "Do you plan to go, Cliff?"

"Oh, I don't know," he mused. "I might…"

As he turned to walk away, Neil could have sworn he saw Clifford wink.

***

It was nearly five o'clock as the weary travellers made their way up the gangplank of *The Pilgrim* after their unforgettable visit to Iona.

"Right!" said Sheila. "You come with me, Jill. You're bang on time for your appointment in the spa."

"What about Rob? I ought to let him know what's happening."

"Don't worry about him," said Marion. "I'll knock on your door and let him know to meet you at seven outside the main restaurant, all ready for a formal night in his very best bib and tucker."

And with that, Jill was dragged unceremoniously away in the direction of the spa.

Coming up behind them, Neil was just about to climb the stairs to their cabin when he became aware of a figure approaching him. It was Brad.

"Neil, can you spare a moment for a quick chat?"

"I bags first in the shower, then," announced Claire. "As it's a formal night, I intend to sparkle with the best of them. And getting ready is going to take me time, *lots* of time…" With a quick peck on Neil's cheek, she headed up the stairs.

The two men found a quiet corner in one of the small bars, where a waiter quickly organized a coffee for them both.

"How are you?" asked Neil.

Brad shrugged. "I don't know. My thoughts fluctuate so wildly. I make a decision one minute, then feel completely different the next. But it seems I'm not the only one in turmoil…"

"Oh?"

"I had an email from Joanne this morning. She wants to come and see me."

"Come up from Dorchester, do you mean? When?"

"She's talking about getting the ferry from Portsmouth over to the Channel Islands."

"So she'll meet you on Tuesday in Guernsey?"

"She says she'll get there the evening before, and can see me any time I'm free that day."

"And what's your reaction to that?"

Brad gave a deep sigh. "Honestly, I don't know. I love Joanne. There's no one else I'd rather see. But so much has happened, so much has been said – words we can't forget or take back."

"Well, she certainly cares enough to make the journey to see you."

"But what will she want to say? I think she may have come to the same conclusion as me – that enough's enough."

"Or she may be hurting and confused, just as you are, and wanting to talk things over with the man she loves."

"Used to love. Before I killed our son."

"But you two shared happy years before this awful tragedy happened. Don't lose sight of that."

"She'd be better off without me."

"Well, there's only one way to find out if she agrees with you. Meet her."

Brad ran his hand through his hair, distracted and thoughtful. "I don't know how to reply to her email. The very last thing she needs is me. That's what I want to say."

"But you don't quite have the courage to write that?"

Brad fell silent.

"Perhaps because you know that's not what she wants – and, in your heart of hearts, not what you want either."

"I'm no good for her."

"Why don't you let her be the judge of what she needs? And perhaps it's better to say very little in your reply, then you can give yourself time to think through exactly what you want to say to her when you meet."

"I should agree to meet her, then?"

"It's what she wants. She's proving that by making the journey. At least be kind enough to meet her. She deserves that."

"And a great deal more."

"You're in my prayers, Brad, both you and Joanne. I pray that you find comfort for your terrible loss, and strength to move on from the despair I see in you now."

Brad's eyes looked suspiciously shiny as he suddenly leaned forward to drain his coffee cup and pick up his diary. "I'll go and write that email, then. Keep it short, you think?"

"Short and sweet."

And Neil watched as Brad visibly pulled himself together before giving him an abrupt nod and walking away.

***

One by one, couple by couple, they met up in the bar beside the grand entrance to the main restaurant. They all agreed that every single one of them looked splendid, the men handsome and distinguished in their dinner suits, and the women in sparkling cocktail dresses and evening gowns.

"A group photo!" suggested Barbara. For once, she did not have her own camera in hand, but she had spotted that the ship's professional photographer had set up ready to take photographs just outside the restaurant.

"That's a wonderful idea," agreed John, as he began herding the assembled members of Neil's two congregations from Dunbridge and Burntacre into some semblance of order in front of the elegant backdrop.

"Has anyone seen my wife?" asked a disgruntled voice. "She's gone missing again. Never where she should be…"

Marion, resplendent in a deep green velvet jacket and flowing evening trousers, stepped up to answer Rob. "Jill will be here in just a minute."

"That woman's late for everything. What's the point of telling me to be here at seven if she can't be bothered to make it on time?"

"By my watch, it's still only five minutes to. In fact, that looks like her now…"

Betty and Sheila were walking together towards them, grinning from ear to ear. Finally, as they reached the assembled group, they stepped apart to reveal someone walking behind them. A gasp went round as people realized that the woman in the shimmering gown before them was Jill, transformed and glorious. Golden highlights glowed in her new chin-length bob, a silky dress clung to her trim frame, and glistening earrings matched the sparkling necklace which perfectly suited the plunging neckline of her robe. But the crowning glory was her face, subtly made up to accentuate her eyes and bring out the softness and colour of her skin.

"Jill! You look absolutely beautiful!" exclaimed Claire, and that sentiment was echoed and endorsed by everyone in the group, who gathered round to comment on her new hairstyle and her lovely dress.

"Really gorgeous," agreed Neil. "You must be very proud of your wife, Rob."

Heads turned towards Rob, curious to see his reaction to Jill's make-over. In fact, there seemed to be no reaction at all. He was simply staring at her, his mouth slightly open.

"Come on now, everyone, the photographer's waiting," ordered John. "Dinner will be served soon, and we want to get this photo done first. Arthur, we'll put a chair for you over on the right here, with Peter and Callum beside you. Julia, can you angle Ida's wheelchair inwards a bit over on the other side? Sheila, Betty and Marion – you need to be in the front there. And Rob, stop gawping and bring Jill over here to join them. You stand behind her, next to Clifford – then you gentlemen can make up a back row with Brian and Peter and your ladies in front of you. Neil, you go in the middle – after all, you're the one who's brought us all together. Claire, stand in front of Neil, next to Iris. Harry, can you tuck in behind the two ladies? And Raymond, you're the tallest, so make sure you don't mask poor Mark. That's right, Deirdre, where you are is fine – and Carole, where are you? Carole?"

Carole and Garry were standing to one side of the group, uncertain whether they wanted to own up to belonging to this giggling, chattering group.

"Oh, don't worry about us. We aren't keen on group photos…"

"Nonsense. You're going to be in this one," commanded Bishop Paul, as he and Margaret squeezed themselves into one side of the crowd. "Look, there's plenty of room for you both over here. And Barbara and John, stop issuing orders and come and join us."

It took a couple of minutes before the photographer was satisfied with the way they all looked. Finally, he asked everyone to smile before he took several shots. Later that evening, when all the photos were put on display in the library, Betty and Sheila were the first to take a peep. Everyone looked wonderful. Even Garry, whose expression suggested he had a bad smell beneath his nose, didn't detract from the obviously friendly atmosphere among the group. Most eye-catching of all, right in the centre, was Jill, looking radiant – unlike Rob, caught in a rather awkward pose by the camera, his expression unreadable as he looked sideways towards his wife rather than forward like everyone else.

Neil had arranged for the whole group to be seated around three circular tables in one corner of the large dining room, and conversation and laughter flowed throughout the four-course meal as wine was sipped and then dainty petits fours were offered by gloved waiters when they finally served the coffee.

"So, are we all going to see Rhydian's performance this evening?" asked Bishop Paul.

"Certainly!" said Iris. "He has a magnificent voice."

"So good looking, too," chirped Betty.

"Well, I hope he's planning to include some opera in his repertoire," commented Carole. "It will be a terrible waste if he only sings popular numbers. He may think the audience here would never appreciate highbrow music."

"Excuse me," said Clifford, rising from his chair. "I have to go."

"You will be coming to Rhydian's concert, won't you?" asked Carole.

"You might see me there," replied Clifford as he smiled a general goodbye and left the table.

"Who fancies a bit of dancing before the show begins?" asked Sylvia. "The band will be playing for an hour before Rhydian comes on stage, and if we go up now, we can all make sure we get good seats near the front."

By the time they reached the lounge, several couples were already on the dance floor and the band was playing a jaunty quickstep. Peter and Val had been taking ballroom dancing lessons since before they married the year before, so they took to the floor immediately with a routine of fancy footwork and swirls which had them laughing breathlessly together. Brian and Sylvia joined them, gliding effortlessly along with the familiarity of a couple who had enjoyed dancing together for more than thirty years. The rest of the group settled themselves around the small tables at the edge of the dance floor, and Jill joined them, swaying in time with the music as she stood watching. Her face lit up when Rob arrived, and she looked expectantly in his direction. Rob hesitated for a moment, staring at her, but then turned away to find another table as Jill stared bleakly after him.

Standing not far away, Mark's heart lurched as he saw the disappointment on her face. Turning to Deirdre, who was at his side, he realized that she too had been watching Rob. With a quiet look of mutual understanding, he squeezed her arm before making his way over to Jill.

"I wonder, lovely lady, if you would care to dance?"

Jill glanced towards Rob, but her husband appeared to ignore her, so she turned back to Mark and took his hand.

"I'd love to," she smiled, and he led her to a corner of the dance floor where they were in Rob's direct line of sight.

"You dance really well," she laughed as Mark expertly twirled her around in time to the music.

"I learned at school, believe it or not. I was a really geeky teenager, so if we had a disco I never had the courage to ask any girl to dance, because I knew she'd say no. But then I discovered the school had a ballroom dancing class, where there were two girls for every boy. They'd literally fight each other to get a partner. I've never been so popular in my life. My wallflower days were over once I'd shown them my cha cha cha!"

Laughing, Jill followed his lead, singing along to the music as they circled the floor together. When that number finished, Mark led Jill back to the edge of the floor, where Brian was waiting to offer her his hand for a foxtrot, with Peter and Raymond forming an orderly queue to take their turn as her partner for subsequent dances.

"Well?" Iris turned to look meaningfully at Harry. "Are you going to ask me to dance?"

Harry grimaced. "My dear Iris, the heart is willing, but my knees won't let me. Sadly, my dancing days are over."

"Well, mine aren't – not when the band are playing a rumba," she sniffed in reply, looking around to see if she could spy a more suitable partner.

"Madam."

Paul, the dance host, appeared at her side holding out his hand in invitation. With a coquettish look that had probably won her many a suitor in her younger days, she slid into his arms as they took to the floor.

"You remember that Joyce Grenfell song about Mrs Fanshaw at the Old Tyme Dance Club?" Carole hissed in Garry's ear as the two of them watched Iris glide into action. "'*Stately as a galleon I sail across the floor…*'"

Garry chuckled as he remembered. "Woe betide anyone who gets in *her* way! I thought the man was supposed to lead…"

"Oh, come on, Neil," urged Claire. "Please!"

"I've got two left feet. You know that. I'll only make a fool of myself."

"Well, let's be fools together. There's no need to bother with proper steps. We can just lean on each other and have a nice cuddle on the dance floor."

Neil's face lit up. "Oh, now you're talking."

Returning to Deirdre's side, Mark squeezed her hand. "You're quiet."

With a small smile, she shrugged her shoulders dismissively.

"Worrying about tomorrow?"

She gave a small nod, saying nothing.

"I love you."

She turned to look at him then.

"And I'll be there, however you need me to be. You're not alone any more, Deirdre. You are loved. I *love* you."

Wordlessly, she leaned forward to rest her head on his shoulder. His arm slipped around her waist as he started to sway to the music, and then gently, as he felt her respond, he drew her onto the dance floor, where they clung together, their feet hardly moving, their bodies entwined.

When the rhythm of the music changed to a waltz, the floor cleared a little as some couples left and others joined.

"Julia!"

Julia turned with surprise at the sound of her name. Paul, the dance host, was standing at her side.

"Look at your mum," he whispered. "She's tapping her foot in time with the music."

In astonishment, Julia stared at Ida's foot, which was barely moving but definitely flexing along with the rhythm of the waltz.

"I didn't realize she could move her legs," he said. "I've only ever seen her in a wheelchair."

"She can walk about at home reasonably well. We've arranged the furniture so she's always got something to grab. When we're out, though, she feels more secure in the chair.

But it really looks as if she's hearing that beat." There was wonder in Julia's voice as she spoke. "I'm not imagining that, am I? Usually she seems to connect with so little of what's going on around her."

"No, you're right. The music's getting through to her. In her own way, I think she's dancing."

Julia cupped her hands over her mouth, her eyes glistening with emotion.

"Let's give her a show. Dance with me!"

"Oh Paul, thank you, but I couldn't. It's years since I danced…"

"Time you started again, then. Come on. Nothing fancy. I promise to be gentle with you."

She looked at the kindness in his face, then slowly rose from her seat to join him as he drew her onto the dance floor. Firmly, but with the lightest touch, subtle movements of his arms and body guided her steps until she found herself forgetting about how awkward and out of practice she felt, and simply relaxed and followed his lead.

Two songs later, the band leader announced that they were coming to the end of their set so that the stage could be prepared for Rhydian's show, which would be starting shortly. "So take your partners, please, for the last dance!"

Finding herself without the offer of a partner for the first time that evening, Jill stood to one side, pink-faced with the exhilaration of so much dancing. She glanced across at Rob, who was looking everywhere except in her direction, although as she'd been dancing, she'd caught him several times watching her with an expression on his face she couldn't read. Finally, taking a deep breath, she made her way over to his side.

"Dance with me, Rob."

As he turned to stare at her, she glimpsed something in him that she hardly recognized. He looked unsure, even vulnerable, in spite of the brusqueness of his reply.

"Why? You've not been short of partners all evening. Why bother with me?"

"Because this is the last dance – and you always save the last dance for the one you love."

There it was again. Hesitation, uncertainty, before he finally got to his feet, taking her outstretched hand. They came together with the familiarity of all their years together pulling them into their own private bubble of intimacy, Jill's cheek brushing his as they swayed to the music.

"You look really nice." His words were so quietly spoken in her ear that she wondered if she had actually heard them. "Your hair, that dress. You look different."

She pulled back, her face almost touching his as she smiled at him. She didn't reply. She had no idea what to say. Instead, she stepped a little closer into his embrace and laid her head on her husband's shoulder.

***

Rhydian's performance was magical from the moment it started with just his solo voice echoing around the huge lounge, which tantalizingly remained in darkness. Suddenly there was a blaze of colour as the stage was bathed in brilliant gold. Rhydian was standing at the mike in the centre, immaculate with his gleaming blond hair, the sharp features of his face dramatically highlighted by the spotlight that encircled him. He was dressed all in black, his tailored tuxedo jacket casually open to reveal the tight black T-shirt clinging like a second skin to his honed body.

And the voice! Years of classical study had brought out the best in its warm, deep richness, so that he could sing with unbearably sweet, hushed tenderness one minute, then ramp up the volume the next so that the lounge chandeliers trembled above them. He sang opera and songs from the shows. He sang in his native Welsh, as well as English and Italian. A delightful sense of humour and modesty came across in his introductions, especially when he came to his final song, which he described as being very close to his heart.

"I grew up in a small town in Wales, where going to chapel was very much a way of life, especially in my family. The first singing I ever did in public was in chapel as part of the choir, and from the start I've loved hymns. I love them because of the depth of meaning in their words, and the insight they give into the experience and faith of whoever penned them. The man who wrote the words to the hymn I'm going to sing now made his living as a captain on a slave ship, profiting from the misery and mistreatment of others. One day, when he was bringing his human cargo back across the Atlantic, the ship hit a terrible storm, and in despair he found himself calling out to the God he didn't believe in, to save his life. When he was dramatically spared, it was a turning point. He left the sea, trained for the ministry and finally became a vicar in the small English country town of Olney. There's something about John Newton's words in this next song which touches the heart and soul of every single one of us.

Amazing grace! How sweet the sound
That saved a wretch like me!
I once was lost, but now am found;
Was blind, but now I see.

'Twas grace that taught my heart to fear,
And grace my fears relieved;
How precious did that grace appear
The hour I first believed.

Through many dangers, toils and snares
I have already come;
'Tis grace that brought me safe thus far,
And grace will lead me home.

The Lord has promised good to me,
His word my hope secures;
He will my shield and portion be
As long as life endures.

When we've been there ten thousand years,
Bright shining as the sun,
We've no less days to sing God's praise
Than when we first begun."

Tumultuous applause rang out, and some of the audience got to their feet to show their appreciation. Rhydian took bow after bow, until at last there was enough hush for him to speak.

"Thank you so much, everyone, and thank you for allowing me to join you, all too briefly, on this wonderful Christian cruise. It has been a pleasure to meet you all – and a special privilege that the ship's band has been led this evening by a keyboard player who is remembered as one of the best musical directors in the business. He says he's retired now, but no one of his talent ever truly retires. Ladies and gentlemen, a huge round of applause, please, for Mr Clifford Davies!"

Stepping out from the shadows at the back of the stage where the musicians had largely been hidden, Clifford took a bow. Gasps of recognition and admiration resounded around the room, especially among the groups from both Dunbridge and Burntacre.

"Well," breathed Neil, "what a dark horse. He never let on that he was so famous."

"Clifford's not one to blow his own trumpet," said Brian, grinning broadly. "He's always been the shy, retiring type, as you well know."

Neil nearly choked with laughter at Brian's words as he stood up along with Sylvia and several others around them to give Clifford a cheer.

"How could you not have realized?" asked Carole, her voice loud and patronizing. "It was obvious to me from the moment I met him that he was a musical genius. When it comes to professionals, it takes one to know one."

CHAPTER 6

⇒ DUBLIN ⇐

Our God is the God of all things.

St Patrick

*N*eil and the family had decided not to book an organized trip that day, because the ship was arranging a regular shuttle bus service to take passengers to and from the centre of Dublin. Harry took a detour along the deck on his way back to the cabin after breakfast, and leaned over the rail to gaze at the Dublin docks laid out before him.

What memories they brought back! He tried to work out what year it was that Rose had organized a trip here so they could celebrate their wedding anniversary in "Dublin's fair city". It must have been right at the end of the eighties, because the statue of Molly Malone had only just been put in place. They'd stood beside it talking about the nicknames they'd heard for the statue: "The Tart with the Cart" and "The Trollop with the Scallop", and he'd said that Dublin's fair city didn't have any girls as pretty as her. She'd looked at him as if he'd said something irrelevant – a typical response from his wife. They'd been married nearly thirty years by then, but they'd never been a particularly demonstrative couple. Oh, they were deeply committed to their home and each other, and had always been the best of companions – but love? That word had never been used between them: not by him, nor by her. It had always seemed unnecessary. Of course they loved each other. They both knew that. It was woven into the fabric of their life together every day for nearly fifty years.

There it was again. That hard knot of grief and loss which caught him by surprise and lodged in his throat until he felt he might choke. He reached into his pocket for a neat, ironed hankie, and dabbed it over his mouth and suddenly hot face. Stupid old man! That's what he was. Stupid, old – and only half the man he used to be when Rose was at his side.

A door banged behind him as a couple of passengers came out to take a stroll around the deck. Hurriedly stuffing the hankie back in his pocket, he walked away from them towards a part of the deck he'd never discovered before. He soon came across an area labelled "Smokers' Corner" and was about to turn back to find another way to his cabin when he saw a familiar figure huddled over the rail. The man was so obviously lost in his own thoughts that Harry started to turn away for fear of disturbing him.

"Hello, Harry."

Harry stopped. "Brig! I haven't seen you for a while. Daisy said you'd not been feeling too well."

"Oh, I bet she did. Told everyone, I expect."

"How are you now? Better, I hope."

"My seasickness is very short lived. It was only those strong currents up north there. I'm fine now."

Harry wasn't sure how to continue, and was wondering whether he should just take his leave, when Brig turned round to look at him steadily.

"Go on, ask! Ask how I could have been a sailor all those years if I suffer from seasickness. Pretty illogical, eh? Ask if I'm making everything up. Just a deluded, idiotic old fella who's living in a past that never really was. I must have been a crap sailor, mustn't I? Go on, ask!"

"You tell me," was Harry's soft reply. "Tell me what you'd like me to know."

Brig took a deep breath, sighing heavily before he spoke. "You're married, aren't you, Harry? To Iris?"

Harry laughed. "No, we're just widowed neighbours who keep an eye on each other now we're both getting on a bit. Iris is Neil's mum, and Claire's my great-niece, so it feels as if we're all one family nowadays."

"What was your wife like? Did you get along?"

"Rose? I lost her to cancer five years ago. Yes, we had a good marriage. No children, and that was a sadness for us both, but we rubbed along OK. How about you? Do you and Daisy have a family?"

"Two daughters, both married and living locally with children of their own. I lived in a household of three women for years."

"Aah," smiled Harry. "A mixed blessing, I imagine."

"Daisy taught the girls well. They know women are superior, in charge of everything and don't expect to be challenged by a man in any way."

"I see. That must be very difficult."

"Impossible is the word I'd use. Daisy's an impossible woman – patronizing, bossy and insensitive. It's partly my own fault; I admit that. After all, she married a sailor, and sailors go to sea. When the girls were young, I was away more than I was home, so Daisy had to cope with everything on her own. She'd got her routine and didn't take kindly to her arrangements being disrupted. Every now and then, I'd arrive back home with my dirty washing, my stories of life at sea – which plainly bored her – and my totally unreasonable wish to be allowed once in a while to take charge of the remote control for the television I bought for us.

"I also had the unreasonable expectation that I might have her company, even her affection, once in a while – but she made it very clear that she no longer fancied me, not in any way. Did she ever? I wonder now. She was never really that keen, even when we were first married. I came to the conclusion that I was no more than a meal ticket for her, the mug who provided the house, the money, the children and the lifestyle she felt was due to her. After that, I was irrelevant, surplus to requirements."

"And now the girls have left home and you're no longer at sea, and there's just the two of you left in the house?"

"We've got a dog, a collie. I chose him, so she hates him. Says he messes up the floor and leaves his fur all over the furniture. I spend a lot of time with him, out walking, doing anything to get me away from the house."

"Have you got friends of your own to spend time with?"

"There's the Naval Association club. I often drop in there for a drink at lunchtime, and they have some nice social nights there at weekends. Daisy won't go, though. She says it's common."

"But at least you meet other seamen there, who understand what it's like to have been in the forces."

"Yes, they're a good crowd. We've got a lot to talk about. Speak the same language because we share similar memories."

"And it's not easy to share all you've seen and been through with people back at home, is it?"

Brig looked at Harry carefully. "You've obviously been a military man, to say that."

"Just four years, straight out of school because it was a job and I couldn't think what else to do. I learned a lot in the army, about myself as much as anything."

"The lads you serve with," said Brig with passion, "they become your family. It's hard to explain to anyone who's not been there. But when the chips are down, when you're faced with real danger, so scared you can hardly speak, you have to work together to save your own life as well as theirs. That makes a special bond."

Harry nodded in agreement. "And it's very difficult for family members back home to understand…"

Brig grunted. "Daisy never could. She never tried. She

wouldn't even listen. She always switches off the news because she doesn't want to know about anything outside her little world. She's not interested, because she thinks everyone should just get on with each other and there shouldn't be wars between one country and another. Because she believes it shouldn't happen, she refuses to see it does happen, and that military men like me and you have to deal with it. Blinkered, disinterested, full of her own righteous opinions. It wears me down."

There was a catch in his voice as he spoke. "I'm tired of it. Tired of her."

"Would you honestly want to live away from her, your girls and the grandchildren, though? Can you imagine being on your own? Wouldn't that be quite lonely?"

"I'm already lonely. I've been lonely since the day I married her."

Harry fell silent, unsure what to say.

"I bet she loved telling everyone I was seasick. Did she make an announcement to a nice big crowd? Because that's what she normally does. Makes sure there are plenty of people listening when she puts me down."

"It was a bit of a shock to hear you were ill, especially when you obviously love the sea so much. We've all been impressed by how knowledgeable you are about everything."

"I've never felt seasick under water. I was in subs, so I was always OK once we'd dived. It's the motion of the waves up top that gets me. I thought in a big ship like this one I'd be OK, and mostly I am. It was just that really rough night that laid me low."

"I see. That makes sense."

"So I'm a laughing stock, am I? I bet everyone thinks I'm a bit of a joke."

Harry considered his words for a moment before he answered. "I don't think we've had much chance to get to know you. You've come across as such an expert, it's made you seem a bit daunting. But the way you're speaking now, just being yourself, you're really good company, Brig."

"Daisy doesn't think so. She never misses a chance to tell everyone how boring and delusional I am."

"Well, maybe you should hold back a bit on the seafaring lectures and just talk more generally about things we can all contribute to – this trip, the places we're seeing, the entertainment, the food. I sometimes think the best conversations I have are the ones where I do most of the listening."

Brig grinned. "That's your tactful way of saying I need to shut up about myself and let other people get a word in edgeways once in a while."

"It's always worked for me."

Brig laughed then, before stepping forward to lay a hand across Harry's shoulders. "Fancy a coffee?"

"When we know the girls are looking for us?" grinned Harry. "That will really infuriate them."

"Quarter of an hour in that little coffee bar upstairs, out of the way?"

"Sounds great," agreed Harry as they headed for the door. "When it comes to the ladies, it's never a bad idea to play a little hard to get. Treat 'em mean, keep 'em keen!"

***

As Deirdre emerged into the sunshine at the top of the disembarkation ramp, her heart lurched to see the unmistakeable figure of Clodagh waiting beyond the wire barrier of the quayside. The nervous stomach cramps and nausea that had kept her awake all night now washed over her again as she thought about what this day might hold. She stood at the top of the ramp, the competent, accomplished forty-two-year-old woman she'd become. Yet just looking at the dockland area, here in the city that had been her childhood home, instantly catapulted her back into the fear and confusion of the teenager she'd been when she had last stood on Irish soil.

She felt Mark's hand slide onto her shoulder, solid and reassuring.

"It's OK," he whispered. "I'm right beside you. Is that Clodagh over there?"

Deirdre nodded dumbly, her throat constricting with dryness.

"Let's go and meet her, then," he said. "You can do this. You want to do this."

At that moment, Clodagh spotted her sister and started waving to catch her attention. There was something about Clodagh's obvious excitement at her arrival that made Deirdre's feet pick up speed as she made her way down the ramp. There followed a frustrating delay while she and Mark had to go through the quayside security check for all passengers, but as Deirdre stepped out of the exit, Clodagh was there, her arms open, warm and welcoming as she drew Deirdre into an emotional embrace.

"I can't believe you're here after all these years. Oh, Deirdre, welcome home!"

In spite of her good intentions not to cry, Deirdre felt hot tears running down her cheeks into Clodagh's hair as the two sisters clung together.

"You've brought someone with you."

Deirdre pulled back so that Mark could move closer to join them.

"This is Mark Stratton."

Clodagh's eyebrows raised with curiosity as she shook hands with Mark.

Deirdre smiled. "Yes, we're together. Mark's very special. He's one in a million. I'm very lucky to have found him."

"Well, Mark, you're most welcome. This is a big day for Deirdre. It won't be easy."

Mark stretched out to take Deirdre's hand in his. "That's why I'm here. I plan to stay in the background, because I know she has to do this alone…"

"… but whatever happens today, Mark's here to pick up the pieces," added Deirdre, looking lovingly at him. "I don't think I could face this without him – and you. I'm so nervous."

"Look, let's go into the café over there and get a cup of coffee," suggested Clodagh. "We can talk things through and decide on a plan of action."

Ten minutes later, Mark noticed that Deirdre's hand was trembling as she picked up her mug of steaming coffee to take a sip.

"Mum and Da still have no idea I'm coming?"

"None at all."

"Do they ever speak of me?"

"Mum does sometimes, but only to me. I don't think your name's ever mentioned in front of Da."

"So he meant it when he said I'm no longer his daughter. He's erased me from his life. I'm nothing to him."

"Da's not an unfeeling man, in spite of how it seems. He's mellowed a lot over the years."

"So how do you think he'll react if I turn up on the doorstep?"

"Honestly, Deirdre, I just don't know."

"Are they both definitely home today?"

"I'm pretty sure Mum will be, because I said I'd pop over to see her this morning. I don't know about Da. I didn't dare ask in case I had to explain why I was bringing it up."

The blood seemed to drain from Deirdre's face. Mark slipped his arm around her rigid shoulders.

"I think," she said at last, "I'll just pop into the ladies' room to powder my nose – and then we should go. The anticipation's worse than just getting on with it. If this turns out to be a disaster, then I'll leave and that'll be it. We've lived without each other for twenty-four years. If I have to live the rest of my life that way, well, so be it. I'd rather spend my time with people who really care about me." She looked into Mark's eyes for a few seconds before leaning down to pick up her handbag as she got up to head for the restroom.

"I worry that this will hurt her," Mark said as he and Clodagh watched her go. "Being estranged from her family has been a huge sadness for her, especially because Brendan's had to grow up not knowing his grandparents."

Clodagh nodded thoughtfully. "We're talking about a very different time then," she said. "In those days there was still a huge stigma associated with getting pregnant outside of marriage."

"It does take two to make it happen," retorted Mark. "She was just a kid, immature and scared. She was abandoned by Brendan's father and then her own mum and dad – in fact, everyone except you. It seems unbelievable to me that they'd turn on their own so heartlessly."

Clodagh shrugged. "We're a Catholic family in a staunchly religious community. Mum and Da are regular churchgoers. A pregnant daughter would have brought disgrace and shame to the whole family."

"Very Christian."

"I agree – and perhaps if the same thing happened now, generally parents wouldn't react like that. But I think Mum and Da were completely shocked by it. It was the last thing they expected and they didn't know how else to respond."

"Do you think they've regretted it over the years since?"

"Yes. Yes, I do. Da's never said anything, but Deirdre was always daddy's girl, and I know he's missed her."

"Right, let's do this," said Deirdre, appearing at their side. "Let's do it before I change my mind and scuttle back home again."

Clodagh ushered Deirdre into the front seat of the car so she could have a clear view of the familiar streets as they travelled back to the house she'd grown up in. Mark felt she was unnaturally quiet as she took in every detail, sometimes turning to stare at something she'd almost missed as they passed, sometimes simply gazing straight ahead.

"It's probably changed a lot from what you remember," said Clodagh, glancing at her sister's pale face.

Deirdre nodded without answering.

They drove past the shops and offices of the city centre,

and on into the suburbs, where the buildings became more residential. Ten minutes later, Clodagh turned off the main road into an estate of large terraced houses built in the elegant style of Edwardian days, though a century of city life had definitely taken its toll.

At last Clodagh pulled into a space halfway up a tree-lined street. Mark heard Deirdre catch her breath as she looked across at the house immediately opposite. It was tall and solid, joined on both sides by identical dwellings. Beyond the gate, a neat lawn was laid out to one side of the path, which led to a small porch framing a black front door.

"They've painted the door. It was dark blue."

"Really?" smiled Clodagh. "I'd forgotten that. It's been black for so long."

"And there's ivy up the wall. That wasn't there."

"Da says it's a weed and he's no idea where it came from. He's always hacking bits off it."

Deirdre's deep breath was almost a sigh as she stared at the house.

"Ready?" Clodagh reached over to still Deirdre's fingers, which were twitching nervously in her lap.

"I don't know…"

"Would you like me to go in first? I can see who's there, then come out and let you know."

Deirdre nodded wordlessly. With one last squeeze of her sister's hand, Clodagh got out of the car, crossed the road and walked up the path. Pulling a key out of her pocket, she unlocked the door and disappeared inside.

The wait seemed endless. Mark leaned forward in the back seat to put his hand on Deirdre's shoulder as she sat with her eyes fixed on the front door. At last it was pulled open, but not by Clodagh. A small, elderly woman was clutching the door, her eyes anxiously scanning the street for Clodagh's car.

Deirdre reacted immediately, throwing open her door, hardly looking as she ran across the road, through the gate and up the path. And then she stopped, but the woman moved for her, her arms outstretched as she cried Deirdre's name, stepping forward to pull her into a tearful embrace of longing and love. And there they stood for long minutes, hugging, crying, loving, as two long decades fell away. Her mother pulled back to cup her daughter's face in her hands, taking in every detail of her, stroking her hair, caressing her skin.

"Come in, come in!" Her mother started to guide Deirdre towards the house, but stopped as she glanced back at the car. "Is that your friend over there?"

"That's Mark. He's happy to stay out here, if that's best. He doesn't want to intrude, but I needed him with me today."

"If he's important to you, then I'd like to meet him. Clodagh, ask him to come in, would you?"

The moment Deirdre stepped inside the door, it hit her, achingly dear and familiar – the smell of home. The colour of the walls in the hall had changed and there was a new stair carpet, but what overwhelmed her was the indescribable, unmistakeable aroma of a house and family, the family she used to belong to. *Her* family.

She knew her mum was watching her reaction closely as she led her past the parlour door and into the back room. Deirdre stopped by the door to take it all in, the things she recognized and the things that were unfamiliar. There was a smart new suite of settee and chairs in a fabric that complemented the swirling beiges and browns of the wallpaper. And they'd had central heating put in! She could picture the coal fire that used to be lit all year round in the cosy, comforting room which was the hub and heart of their family life. This room had been a warm refuge no matter how cold the other rooms in the house might be – especially the bedrooms, where hot water bottles had to be placed between the covers on chilly winter nights before any of them dared to go to bed.

A shiver went through her. This was the room where she'd last spoken to Da. Her final conversation in this house had been right here, when Da turned his back on her and ordered her to leave. She was dimly aware that she was starting to shake, unable to control the trembling that gripped her.

"He's not here, love," said her mum quietly. "He's at the allotment. He'll be back soon."

"Should I leave?"

"Deirdre, you've come home, and I've prayed for this moment every day since you left. You're our daughter…"

"Da threw me out. You packed my bag. He told me I meant nothing to him."

"I know, I know…"

"I'd made a terrible mistake. I knew I was wrong – but the people I loved turned their backs on me. I left the only life I'd ever known that day. I was so alone and scared…"

"I know, love; I do." Her mum's eyes were glassy with tears, and her voice choked on the sob she was trying hard to suppress. "There's so much we have to talk about, but let's put the kettle on first. Do you have a job now…?"

Realizing that her mum was finding this as difficult as she was herself, Deirdre allowed herself to be diverted from the conversation they both knew they needed to have. They talked instead about safer topics, like her post as a teacher and her home in Burntacre. By the time the tea was made and her mum had loaded a tray, Mark and Clodagh were sitting on the settee in the back room.

Mark jumped up immediately to greet Deirdre's mother, but she gestured to him to sit down again.

"You're very welcome here, Mark. You look after our girl. You care for her. You're a welcome guest in this house."

Time ticked by as they chatted about the old days, remembering school friends and neighbours. They talked about how the area had changed, with lots of examples of where it had improved, and just as many tales of how change had brought nothing but problems. They spoke of *The Pilgrim* and their itinerary for the week. Mark described his job as a research scientist, and how they'd met because they both sang in the church choir – and Deirdre watched with a creeping sense of warmth and worth as her mum nodded her head approvingly, pleased that churchgoing was still an important part of her daughter's life. Of course, she had changed her allegiance from Catholic to Anglican, but that was most certainly better than nothing. The thought of a life without God was unthinkable to her mother, and Deirdre knew that she was probably throwing up a heartfelt prayer asking the Virgin Mother to protect her daughter anyway, even if she was temporarily misguided in her choice of church.

Clodagh dug out her phone to show her sister the latest pictures of her two daughters, both now married with children of their own, and they pored over the photos with smiles and chatter. They laughed again at funny stories of when Clodagh and Deirdre were small. They were saddened to think of much-loved neighbours who had died, and others who had moved away through scandal, good fortune or in search of a bright new future.

Mark watched as colour gradually crept into Deirdre's cheeks as she spoke and listened, sympathized and smiled. He saw how, during one heart-warming tale of the old days, her mother clasped Deirdre's hand. Neither mother nor daughter chose to take their hand back. They sat side by side on the settee, and Mark could see the likeness – they shared the same oval-shaped face, auburn highlights in their hair and faint freckles scattered across their cheekbones.

Suddenly, Clodagh looked out of the window towards the garden. Even after all these years, Deirdre recognized the sound straight away. The latch on the back gate had been lifted. Da was back from the allotment. All eyes turned to her, wondering what they should do, but Deirdre was first on her feet.

"I'll go. I have to do this."

The kitchen door was already ajar, so Deirdre was able to step outside but remain in the shadows, so her father didn't immediately notice her. That bought her time to study him as he pottered slowly down the garden, checking this plant and that cutting, reaching for twine and secateurs, totally absorbed in his beloved vegetables. Holding her breath, she stared at him, this man who brought out such mixed emotions in her, from the deep love of a daughter, to pangs of cold hatred for his heartlessness and the years of pain and isolation he had caused her.

And yet, there he was, homely and familiar, wearing the same old gardening trousers and well-worn donkey jacket that she could have sworn were the actual garments he'd been in when she last saw him. His hair had changed. It was silver now and much thinner than before. She watched his hands, weathered and agile as she always remembered them, his arms muscular and wiry.

Slowly, she stepped towards him until suddenly the movement caught his eye and he looked up with a smile, probably thinking it was her mum. That smile disappeared the moment he realized who he was looking at, his jaw dropping, blood draining from his usually ruddy face.

"Hello, Da."

He didn't reply. He didn't move. He hardly seemed to be breathing. He was still, as if every fibre of his body was shocked and rigid. And then, almost as if in pain, he turned away from her, drawing some twine and scissors out of his coat pocket.

"I'm growing broad beans this year," he said. "The runner beans were rubbish last year. Not enough rain. Broad beans'll be better. Mum and I like broad beans."

"Da? It's me: Deirdre."

He nodded a very slight acknowledgment before crossing the path to the vegetables growing on the other side of the garden.

"This is a new strain of onions. I thought I'd give them a try."

"Da, will you talk to me?"

"And potatoes. Mum likes them new. These'll be ready to lift next month."

"Da!"

He looked right at her then, his mouth quivering as if he was trying to speak, but no words were coming out.

"And tomatoes," he managed at last. "Tom Thumb. Great in salads. Your mum likes salad."

"Say something, Da!" Deirdre's body felt like lead, her feet rooted to the ground. "Say anything! Have you nothing to say after all these years? No words for me at all?"

Again, he looked at her, turmoil and confusion etched across his face, the twine hanging uselessly from his hand.

"You wanted me to leave. You told me I had no place here. I've stayed away until today. Do you still feel the same now?"

But he just stood, silent and shocked.

"Do you want me to leave? Da, do you?" She took a step nearer him. "Should I go?"

With a choking sob, she spun on her heel and started back towards the house. It was just as she reached the kitchen door that she heard him.

"Deirdre, no! No…" The scream came from the very depths of him. She turned in time to see him buckle before her, dropping to the ground, his hands spread out on his knees, his distraught face lifted up to her. This was her Da, her strong, dogmatic, dependable, unjust Da, as she'd never seen him: crushed, helpless, crying out in anguish.

She moved back towards him then, falling to her knees, stretching out to pull him to her. His arms gripped her and she heard him saying her name over and over as he clung to her.

"I thought I'd never see you again. I thought I'd lost you forever…"

Deirdre became dimly aware that she was being lifted to her feet, and she leaned back against Mark, watching as her mum and Clodagh put their arms around Da to help him up. He seemed disoriented and unsteady, and as he stumbled towards her, Deirdre reached out to support him. The others were doing the same, and the five of them stood together, arms around each other in a circle of shock, regret and relief. There they stayed for several minutes, no words, nothing to say, while their need and love for each other were blatant and tangible.

It was Mark who eventually broke the circle, tenderly guiding Deirdre and her family back through the kitchen into the back room. Then he stood to one side as Mum sat beside Deirdre, while Clodagh led Da over to his favourite chair by the fire.

Finally, Deirdre broke the silence, her voice subdued and filled with emotion. "The day you threw me out was the worst day of my life. If it hadn't been for Clodagh and Terry, I'd have been completely lost. They took me down to the docks, and this morning I stood there again, when I stepped off the cruise ship that brought me here today. Twenty-four years ago I was terrified and lonely. I got on a ferry to a new country and a new life, knowing that the family I loved had turned their back on me and I could never come home again. Oh, I know I did wrong. I've lived every minute since knowing that, regretting the moment of madness that ended up with me getting pregnant. You called me a slut, Da, and that's how I felt. Worthless, useless, unloved and unlovable. But God is kind – at least my God is. Yours is a God of damnation and fury, but the God I've come to know is loving and forgiving, a God of second chances.

"Clodagh's friend Catherine and her family gave me that second chance, a living example of God's love on earth. They supported me. I've never been afraid of hard work, Da, and I worked hard. I had my son. I studied every spare moment I could, and I qualified as a teacher. I got a job and my own house. And I found my spiritual home too. I went to see my son in the nativity play at the local church, and I felt as if a warm pair of arms were wrapped around me. I've stayed there ever since."

She stopped for a moment to look at Mark. "I found something else too. I found the love of this wonderful man. We've known each other for years, but till now we never allowed ourselves to be anything more than friends. I was too scared. I've been terrified when it comes to relationships, Da. The only time I ever allowed myself to get close to a man it caused all this, so I've kept men, all men, at a distance. How could I burden anyone else with the guilt and shame you laid on my shoulders the day I left? That burden's crippled my ability to find love. All my love's been for Brendan – your grandson, Da. The boy I named after you."

Da's face was unreadable, but from his silence and the tension in his body, it was plain that he was struggling to cope with her words.

"And he's wonderful. Brendan took a law degree. He's a solicitor now, in south London. He has your eyes, Da. And your strong hands – those hands I saw gardening today, those hands that always fixed things and made everything right. You'd like him. And you will meet him, Da, because I want to bring him here to see you and Mum. You'll understand why I'm so proud of him, why I love him so much, why I know you'll love him too…"

She broke down then, unable to hold back the gulping sobs that overwhelmed her – until, through the fog, she thought she heard him call her name. When she opened her eyes, Da was right there on his knees in front of her, his arms wrapping tightly around her. In the strength of that embrace, surrounded by the feel of him, the familiar, reassuring smell of her da who protected her and always made bad things go away, she became a little girl again, *his* little girl, safe and loved beyond words.

"I'm so sorry, so very sorry."

His words were so choked with emotion, she could hardly hear him.

"You're right," he whispered. "If God the Father is love and we're supposed to try and live in his image, then what sort of father was I to turn away my own child when you needed help?"

She pulled back then, smiling at him through her tears. "We have a lot of catching up to do, Da. So much to tell each other…"

"Brendan, eh? You called your boy Brendan? I never knew that."

"She's got photos, Bren," said Mum. "Show him, Deirdre. Oh, he's a looker, her boy. There's something about him that reminds me of the young man you were when you courted me."

Deirdre fumbled in her bag and pulled out her iPad to show her Da the latest pictures of Brendan. Suddenly Da was full of questions about what he was like, what he was interested in, which sports he played and teams he supported. By the time Da had seen all the images, Mum had pulled out the photo albums from the dresser cupboard, and they all pored over old photos, cuttings and mementoes of their family life. They stayed close, hands holding hands, arms around shoulders, as if by touching each other they strengthened the invisible cords which would tie them together, heart and soul, from that day on. Their own dear family, whole and complete again at last, bound in love.

All too soon, it was time for the visitors to leave. Mark found himself smiling with relief to see Deirdre hugging her mum as if she would never let her go, and the emotion-filled embrace she shared with her Da.

"We'll be back," she promised, slipping her hand into Mark's. "We'll be back, and we'll bring Brendan with us."

And then it was over. Deirdre hung out of the car window, waving at her mum and da at the front gate, until Clodagh's car turned the corner. Then she threw her head back against the seat and started to laugh with delight and joy. She laughed and laughed – and Clodagh and Mark couldn't help but laugh along with her.

***

"Pam!"

As Reverend Ros made her way into the buffet restaurant for afternoon tea, she spotted Pam Rhodes and her husband carrying cups and tea plates out to a table on deck.

"Ros," smiled Pam, "I've been hoping to bump into you. Come and join us when you're ready."

They sat in the surprisingly warm May sunshine, looking across at the Dublin docks.

"So how are you getting on with finding people to take part in your 'Songs of Praise'?" asked Ros, tucking into a plate of dainty sandwiches.

"Not bad," answered Pam. "Quite a few people have said they might like to take part, and I've heard some really moving stories. I've definitely found at least two people I'd like to include, and there are a couple of others I've arranged to meet up with tomorrow. What about you? Have you met anyone through your Chaplain's Corner who might be suitable?"

"I've come across a couple who used to do missionary work in India, and I've mentioned the idea. They seemed quite interested. Here's their cabin number, so you can contact them yourself. And there's another lady who told me an incredibly inspirational story, but I'm not sure she'd want to speak about it publicly."

"Well, that's understandable. It's not easy to talk about something that's been painful, especially in front of an audience."

"But we're all human, aren't we?" said Ros. "Life throws up challenges for all of us, and our feelings can be similar even though our circumstances are different."

Pam nodded as she answered. "I'm constantly hearing from people who've been helped by something they've heard during one of our *Songs of Praise* television interviews. I'm sure it'll be the same with our domestic version of the programme here on *The Pilgrim*. No television cameras, but just as encouraging."

"I'm looking forward to it," replied Ros. "By the way, how's the choir coming along?"

"The gospel choir's great. We were really thrilled when so many people came along to that first rehearsal."

"A few good voices, then?"

Pam grinned. "Well, some better than others, but enthusiasm counts for a lot. It's more about having a good time than trying to be a perfect choir – and we certainly had a great fun rehearsing. In fact, we've got another get-together this evening. I'm hoping they might have the words under their belts by then, so we can concentrate on the movements and staging."

"And when will we see the finished performance?"

"On our last evening as we sail out of Honfleur, during our 'Praise Away' service on this deck. Mind you, we *are* heading back to Tilbury and English weather that night, so we might be standing here in our raincoats!"

"Don't they say the sun shines on the righteous?"

"Ah, that's where I'm going wrong, then," chuckled Pam. "I'd better bring my brolly!"

***

"Jill!" yelled Betty. She had spotted her friend walking ahead of her on her way to the gospel choir rehearsal.

Jill turned immediately, smiling a welcome as Betty hurried up with Marion and Sheila not far behind.

"We've not seen you all day. What happened? How's that husband of yours behaving?"

"Well," replied Jill, leaning back against the corridor wall, "it's better. We're better. Not good, but certainly better."

"He liked the way you looked last night, then," said Sheila. "He couldn't take his eyes off you when all those other men were queuing up to dance with you."

"We noticed the two of you dancing, of course," interrupted Marion, "but after that we didn't see you again."

"Well, after that dance we sat down to have a drink, but the lounge started to fill up fast with people coming in for Rhydian's concert. In the end, we found a quiet corner in one of the smaller bars upstairs, and that's where we stayed talking for ages."

"You've been talking, then? What's he saying? Anything you want to hear?" demanded Betty.

"Yes – and no," was Jill's careful reply. "A lot of what you thought might be our problems were spot on. We *have* got ourselves in a rut, and after all these years I probably don't make much of myself. I know I look a bit of a mess when I'm at home. And there he is, working in a big office with lots of smart people, particularly women. And he's a man – he looks and he compares, and then he comes home to mumsy old me!"

"But he saw you in a different light last night," suggested Marion.

"He did. That was quite an eye-opener – not just for him, but for me too. I looked at myself in the mirror after you and the spa had done your stuff on me, and I saw someone I'd forgotten I could be."

"But it sounds as if all you talked about was him, justifying his behaviour. What about you and your feelings? Was he interested in talking about that?"

"Yes, he was, because I made him listen. I'm not sure how much of it went in, but he did listen."

"So that was last night," said Sheila. "What about this morning? How much of all that did he remember?"

"Enough for him to suggest that we take ourselves into Dublin for a day on our own. We didn't even stop for breakfast. We went into the city instead and it was really lovely. We didn't talk about anything deep or difficult. We just had a nice time in each other's company."

"How wonderful," said Marion. "Sounds like a great way for the two of you to spend the day."

Jill smiled. "Yes, it really was."

"Heavens, look at the time," squeaked Betty, staring at her watch. "If we're late for that rehearsal, I'll end up standing next to Raymond again and I won't be able to hear myself think, let alone sing!"

***

"Well, that went well."

Pam came across to Clifford just as he was putting away his music at the end of the gospel choir rehearsal.

"They're certainly getting better," he agreed. "Some nice harmonies this evening, now they're a bit more confident with the words. How do you think the movements are coming along?"

Pam shrugged her shoulders with a smile. "There's definite room for improvement, I think that's how I'd put it. But it's all very new to most of them, so they're doing really well. By the way, did you notice Ida in her wheelchair? I'm sure she was trying to wave her hands in time with the music, and her face was a picture."

"I've heard that before about people with dementia," said Clifford. "It seems music can break through to them in a way nothing else can."

"I wonder whether, instead of just watching, she'd like to be included in the choir," said Pam. "I'll have a chat with Julia about it when I next see her, but we could put Ida's chair at the side, next to where Arthur's sitting. At ninety-one, I'm not surprised he can't stand for long, but he knows all the words better than anyone."

"Raymond's the one I notice most," said Clifford, "but then I'm used to him singing really loudly at St Stephen's. Usually in a completely different key to everyone else."

Pam laughed. "Well, he certainly catches the eye when he does the movements. When it comes to enthusiasm, Raymond takes first place!"

"Do you fancy an early dinner, Clifford?" interrupted Andrew, who'd been playing the electronic keyboard for the rehearsal. "Sharon, Michael and I have to eat soon because of getting ready for the show this evening. My mum and dad are coming too. They'd all love to see you."

"That'll be nice. What about you and Richard, Pam? Are you hungry yet?"

"Honestly, I don't think I'll ever be hungry again after this cruise," she sighed.

"Anyway," said Richard, coming up to join them, "we've been invited to join Bishop Paul's table in the dining room tonight, along with Neil and his family."

"Ahh, you'll have to mind your Ps and Qs with Iris," smiled Clifford.

"We'll try and behave," laughed Richard as he helped Pam scoop up all the words sheets to take back to their cabin.

"We're meeting up in the buffet restaurant in fifteen minutes," said Andrew. "Is that enough time for you, Cliff?"

"Should be. I'll see you there."

***

"So tell me about yourself, Sharon."

Maureen had made sure she was sitting next to the beautiful young dancer who seemed to be her son's constant companion. After so many years of waiting for Andrew to bring home a girlfriend, this vision of loveliness who obviously enjoyed his company was a wonderful surprise. But would this girl, whose skills as a dancer enabled her to travel the world, ever want to settle down? Would she make a good wife? Or mother?

"Well," began Sharon, "this is the second six-month contract I've had on a cruise ship. The last one was much bigger than this, but I like what I'm doing here better. Most of all, I like the choreographer. We've known each other for ages, so when he approached me to ask if I wanted to be lead dancer on *The Pilgrim*, I snapped up the chance. It's a step up for me, being head girl – that means that as far as the dancers are concerned, I represent him on board. He choreographed and produced the shows back in London, before we all started this contract, and now we're left to get on with it. So it's my job to make sure the standard of dancing stays high, and if there are problems, like one of the dancers being ill or injured, for example, I sort things out."

"Michael does the same for the singers, Mum," said Andrew, joining their conversation. "He's got an amazing voice, but then he did operatic training before he came on this cruise."

"A bit of dancing and movement too," added Michael, who was sitting beside him. "And stagecraft – you know, how to make the best use of the performance space so you engage properly with the audience?"

"It sounds like a real science," said Bill. "I didn't know there was so much to putting on a bit of a show."

"More than a *bit* of a show, Dad," retorted Andrew. "So much goes into it. All the musical parts have to be written and the musicians engaged. And the costumes are spectacular. Just wait till you see the fantastic masks they use in tomorrow night's performance. And the sets – they're different for each production. The stage crew are putting up and taking down sets every day, so you can watch a completely new show every night. And then there's the lighting and the sound. It's a real team effort, putting on highly professional shows like these."

"And it all looks wonderful, dear," said Maureen, patting Andrew's hand. "Especially the dancing. You're very talented, Sharon. Your mother must be proud of you. Where do your family live?"

"Brighton, and my mum runs the biggest dancing school in the town," said Sharon with pride in her voice. "I teach there too, when I'm home. I expect I'll take the school over some time in the future when Mum wants to hang up her tap shoes."

"Oh," said Maureen, apparently concentrating on spearing a bit of roast beef with her fork as she spoke. "No plans to settle down and have a family of your own, then?"

Sharon laughed. "Not yet. Some time, maybe, but definitely not for ages. Besides, no one would have me."

Maureen had to bite her tongue to stop herself saying that Andrew would.

"She's too much of a workaholic," grinned Michael. "But that's as it should be, because she's very talented. But then so is your son, Mrs Bragnall. I love to listen to him play."

"Oh, me too," Maureen gushed, happy to talk about her wonderful son for as long as anyone was prepared to listen. Frustratingly, she wasn't allowed to, as her husband quickly changed the subject to talk about the cruise itinerary and the places they'd visited in their travels. Maureen chose not to join in that conversation. She was too busy watching Andrew and Sharon together, thinking what a handsome couple they made.

***

"Now, will you be all right, Harry?" asked Iris. "I do hope so, because Bishop Paul's asked me to sit beside him at dinner this evening."

Harry chuckled. "How lovely for you – and the bishop too, of course!"

"It will be nice to have such sophisticated company," agreed Iris, oblivious to the irony in Harry's reply. She drew closer and lowered her voice before continuing. "And he could be very helpful to Neil in furthering his career…"

"How kind you are, Iris, but don't worry about me for a moment. Arthur and I have already decided to sit together and reminisce a bit. We've not had the chance for a proper chat yet. I must say, Neil seems to have taken on a lovely congregation up at St Jude's."

"Well, don't go overdoing it," snapped Iris. "You've been looking a bit peaky for the last couple of days. That coach trip round Dublin today sounded relaxing, but it really wasn't, when we were getting off, then back on the coach every ten minutes. You need to rest."

"Well, a pleasant meander down memory lane with a veteran like Arthur will set me up for a peaceful night. Memories are good, Iris. I'm very fond of mine."

"Of course you are," agreed Iris with a delicate sniff. "But don't forget – no butter or cream, and stay off the red wine. It never agrees with you."

Arriving at the table with Neil, Claire overheard the end of their conversation and came over to lay her hand on Harry's arm as Iris left him to greet the bishop.

"You *are* all right, aren't you, Uncle Harry? We're all finding the cruise timetable a bit relentless. That heart operation of yours wasn't that long ago, and you're definitely not allowed to put us through all that worry again."

"Thanks for your concern, Claire dear, but I do know my limits. And I'm enjoying every moment of this trip, even if today was a bit tiring. An early night is definitely my plan, because tomorrow's the day I'm looking forward to most of all."

"Tresco Gardens," smiled Claire. "It'll be heaven for a pair of gardeners like us. We can wander round together and quote Latin names to each other."

"That's exactly what I have in mind," agreed Harry.

"With plenty of stops along the way to sit and watch the flowers grow and let the world go by," finished Claire, just as Neil called her over to take her place beside him.

Harry stood beside his seat while Pete manoeuvred his dad's wheelchair into position so Arthur could climb out to take his place at the table. Pete sat down on the other side of Arthur, with Callum sitting next to Harry.

"Two old boys together," quipped Harry.

"You're a young whippersnapper compared to me," grinned Arthur. "I clocked up my ninety-first birthday last month."

"So I'm ten years younger than you. Actually, I shall call it a decade. That sounds a lot longer."

"Do you feel your age?" asked Arthur, suddenly serious.

"Yes," answered Harry, "but I try not to act it. I suppose being eighty means I'm finally a grown-up."

"Do you keep well?"

"Had a bit of a drama with my heart a couple of years back, but not bad since then. You?"

"My legs seem to have gone. I reckon it was all that

dancing Beryl and I used to do, right up till we were both pensioners. We were senior dance champions in Derbyshire thirty years ago. It was the samba that got me. That was my dance. Everyone said I was a lovely mover. The ladies were queuing up to dance with me. Beryl used to get quite ratty about it. Mind you, I'm paying for it now. It's not natural for a man to wiggle his hips like that."

"Gardening, that's my thing, but it gets harder. All the bending and digging takes its toll on your back. Sometimes, when I bend over, it takes me ages to straighten myself out again."

"No fun getting old, is it?"

"Not much. I wouldn't have missed a moment, though."

"A married man, are you?"

Harry nodded with a smile. "My Rose was the very best. We nearly made our fiftieth anniversary. She died five years ago. Cancer. She was in a lot of pain. It was dreadful to see."

"Beryl got knocked over when she was just seventy. It was the strangest thing. She'd crossed that road every day for years, but that morning she stepped out in front of a car and that was it. Whatever was she thinking? I'll never know, will I?"

"You still miss her?"

"Every moment," replied Arthur. "Beryl was a girl in a million."

"Do you find yourself thinking about things you wish you'd known or done or said when she was still with you?"

"Oh, all the time. Everything she did for me, all the things I didn't get round to doing for her – I remember them all. I took her for granted. That's what marriage is, I suppose. But I wish I could say thank you and sorry and 'You were right, love'! All those little words I should have realized were important at the time."

"I love you." There was deep, painful regret in Harry's eyes as he said those words. "I never told Rose I loved her. I thought she knew and it went without saying, but she told someone just before she died how much it would have meant to her. I never knew, so I never said it. I can't get that out of my mind now."

"Oh, well," sighed Arthur, "we'll be seeing them again soon. I expect Beryl will have a lot to say to me when we meet at the pearly gates."

"So what made you decide to come on this cruise?"

"Just one day on the itinerary. Wednesday, the last port on our trip. We dock at Honfleur, and I've been near there before, but not for over seventy years. It's just up the coast from where I landed on D-Day. That day changed my life, and yet I've never been back there. I couldn't face it. Now, though, I find myself wondering how much more time I'm likely to have, and I know I've got to go back. I need to stand on that beach again as it is today. If I can see that our sacrifice brought peace and prosperity to the land my comrades gave their lives for, perhaps at last I'll find some peace right here, in me." He thumped his chest as he spoke, his eyes focused on some far-away memory.

"And your son and grandson have come along to make sure you're OK?"

"That's what they probably think, but I've got my own reasons for wanting both of them with me. There are things I should tell them. It's time."

Harry waited quietly for Arthur to speak again. Eventually, the old man seemed to shrug himself back to the present.

"And you?" he asked. "What made you come?"

"Tomorrow. We're at the Scilly Isles, and we're taking the trip to the gardens on Tresco. Rose and I went there together once, years ago. I loved it then and I'll enjoy it again now, probably talking to her all the way round, batty old man that I am."

"You're surely not going on your own?"

"No. My great-niece Claire's going with me. She loves gardening as much as I do. The rest of the family are coming too, but tomorrow will be our day. We've worked out a long list of plants we want to see."

"We're both men with a mission, then," said Arthur, his eyes twinkling.

"We are," agreed Harry. "And here come our starters."

CHAPTER 7

⇒ THE ISLES OF SCILLY ⇐

And on the eighth day, God made Tresco.

O n the morning they arrived at Scilly, *The Pilgrim* moored offshore. That meant passengers heading for either the main island of St Mary's or the second largest island, Tresco, had to make the trip to the jetties by local tender boats. Several boats were on hand to ferry them to and from the shore throughout the day.

It soon became clear that Iris was going to have a problem getting onto the tender boat. She simply couldn't get to grips with the idea of stepping off a large and comfortable ship onto a relatively small craft that was bobbing up and down with the movement of the waves. As the rest of the group heading for Tresco queued up behind her on the ramped stairs down the side of the ship to the level of the tender, Iris panicked. No amount of reassurance or cajoling from Neil made any difference, and eventually he was politely moved to one side as the professionals took over.

The ship's crew were well used to this. With a supporting arm on each side, and a helpful nudge from behind, she almost leapt into the arms of the good-looking crewman who was waiting to catch her. If she was embarrassed by the fuss she was causing, there was no evidence of it – instead she complained loudly to anyone who'd listen that it was ridiculous for passengers to be subjected to such danger when they'd paid a small fortune to come on the cruise. All the other passengers boarded the tender boat with enthusiasm and ease, except for Sister Maureen. She looked terrified, until the waiting crewman smiled into her eyes as he caught her, and she stayed mesmerised in his arms for several seconds before she allowed him to release her.

And then they were off, skimming across the waves towards the tiny island of Tresco, all seven hundred and fifty acres of it. For two hundred years, it had been the home of one family, who had deliberately held back the march of time – no cars, no crowds, no neon lights, crime or noise. Some would say true heaven on earth.

From the small jetty where they spilled out of the tender, a long pathway led off through banks of gorse dotted with late spring flowers towards the centre of the island, where a thousand years earlier a Benedictine monastery had once stood.

First up the path were Barbara and John Curtis, looking the business in their walking boots, sensible anoraks and backpacks. They set off from the boat at a marching pace, having announced that Barbara intended to photograph examples of every individual family of flowers they came across, as well as the exotic birds and butterflies that John had read up on in advance.

"We are most certainly not going to walk all that way," wailed Iris as she saw the long path winding off into the distance.

"Don't worry, ma'am," smiled a friendly-faced man who was waiting on the shore to greet the party. "If you feel you can't manage the walk, we do have a horse and cart service to transport you up to the Abbey Gardens."

"Well, it's not for me, you understand," huffed Iris. "My friend Harry here has a bad heart. A walk like that could kill him."

"Thank you, Iris," commented Harry. "Actually, I think a stroll would do me good."

"But don't forget," said Claire, "there's a lot of walking to do within the gardens. Why don't we all take the cart up, so we can save our energy for wandering around inside?"

"How sensible," agreed Iris, striding off towards the waiting cart, followed by several Catholic mothers and Sister Maureen, who was reading out snippets from the guidebook as she took her seat.

"Just twenty-eight miles from Land's End, the toe of the county of Cornwall at the most south-westerly tip of England, lie the Scillies, a group of one hundred and fifty small islands, which are both buffeted by the Atlantic and warmed by the Gulf Stream. Only five of the Isles of Scilly are inhabited by a population which doesn't total many more than two thousand people. That means that the peace and tranquillity of the islands, along with their sub-tropical climate, make them magical places of wild and exotic flowers, sparkling white sands and crumbling castles."

The others were gazing around at the passing scenery as they listened.

"Back in the 1800s the Abbey Gardens here on Tresco were laid out in their present form to nurture and display the exotic seedlings brought back from all corners of the world by Scillonian mariners. From the start, the Abbey Gardens collection has been regarded by botanists as one of the most interesting and varied horticultural experiments in the world."

Claire and Harry smiled at each other. They were both looking forward to seeing those plants.

A few minutes later they climbed down from the cart to make their way through the Abbey Gardens entrance.

"I need the loo!" declared Iris. "And Neil, I want a cup of milky coffee and a cake before I go a step further. Wait for me in the café."

"Harry?" Claire linked her arm through his. "Would you like a coffee now?"

There was real excitement in Harry's eyes as he turned to answer her. "Do you know, Claire, I've longed to be here for ages. It was our fortieth anniversary treat when Rose and I came all those years ago. I can have a coffee any old time, and now I'm here I'm raring to go."

"Well, we'll take it easy, with lots of stops along the way."

"You're plotting to escape with Harry, aren't you, and leave me with Mum!" said Neil, coming up to join them.

Claire giggled. "Harry and I know how much you value quality time with Iris."

"You're heartless."

"I love you," returned Claire, as she and Harry moved off. "Enjoy!"

"Oh, I remember this," exclaimed Harry as they walked across the Blue Bridge towards a vista that ran onwards and upwards through a profusion of trees and shrubs towards the Mediterranean Garden. In the centre stood the Agave fountain, surrounded by exotic and glorious plants.

"Those are *proteas*, aren't they, those cacti with the bright red flowers?" pointed out Claire.

"I think so," said Harry. "And all these trees with the huge round balls that look a bit like palms are *dasylirion*. It says so on this label. This one's a native of Mexico. I'm sure I saw these in Kew Gardens."

Poring over the information on each plant label, they wandered through a bank of clipped olive trees and up a series of steps towards the Olive Terrace, peppered with the dark red and purple heads of succulent *aeoniums*. Here they turned to look out over the treetops towards the sea, where they could just glimpse the outline of the island of Samson.

"I would like to sit inside the Shell House," said Harry, nodding towards the delightfully decorated little building ahead of them, with its sparkling, patterned floor and pointed roof covered in old terracotta pantiles. "Rose and I sat in there and held hands while we watched the world go by."

Claire reached out to take his hand. "Let's go and do the same now, shall we?"

And so they did. They climbed inside the little shelter and sat hand in hand for several peaceful minutes, each with their own thoughts as they gazed out at the gardens spread before them. Their peace was eventually disturbed by the arrival of Sister Maureen and the Catholic mothers at the bottom of the steps leading up to the Shell House. Claire and Harry watched the group gather around the nun as she read aloud to them from the guidebook. Suddenly there was a commotion, with several of the mothers squealing in fright as they looked down at the ground.

"Spider! It's a spider, a *massive* one. It's probably poisonous. Stamp on it, quick."

"You know, you shouldn't kill something just because it's ugly." These words from one particularly upright lady rang out across the garden just at the moment when Sister Maureen brought down her heel to crush the spider to a pulp.

"Time to leave, I think," said Harry. "Sister Maureen may need this seat for a while."

They meandered along the interlinking pathways, each offering a different display of exotic blooms in all colours of the rainbow. The next bench they found was in the Middle Terrace, the very heart of the gardens, where rockeries tumbled with flame-red spikes, cascading waves of green, purple and yellow flowers, and sheets of pink *oscularia* hanging down like carpets.

"I'm ready to join her, you know." Harry spoke so quietly that Claire could hardly hear him.

"Rose?"

"I feel as if I'm living in black and white without her; as if all the colour's faded away."

Claire nodded.

"Five years, that's a long time. Long enough. I want to be with her now."

"But Harry, you're still so busy. Lots of friends and neighbours, everyone at church, and here you are on a luxury cruise. There's a lot of life in you yet. Aunt Rose wouldn't want you to waste a minute of it, would she?"

Harry smiled. "Rose hated waste. She never threw anything away that might be useful some time. Especially food – she'd use leftovers for days in different guises rather than throw away a single mouthful."

"So she'd want you to make the most of everything you are now, wouldn't she? She wouldn't like this talk about wanting to be with her, knowing what you really mean."

"But I'm tired." Harry's eyes were deep pools of sadness as he turned to Claire. "I'm tired and I'm lonely and I've done everything and more than I ever wanted to do."

"Don't wish your life away, Harry."

"I'm not worried about what's ahead, you see. I welcome it. I'll be with my Lord and my Rose. That will be so much more wonderful than the half-life I'm in now."

"Don't, Harry, please," said Claire. "Don't talk like this."

"I need you to understand, Claire, for when the time comes. I'll be moving on with joy. Whatever else you feel, remember that. Share my joy. Keep it in your heart always."

She stared at him, her eyes filling with tears.

"Come on," he said suddenly. "We've still got a lot to see before we get anywhere near a cup of coffee, and I could murder a cup right now. Couldn't you?"

Helping Harry to his feet, Claire pulled him to her, and for several long moments they stood with their arms around each other, moved beyond words by the conversation they'd just shared. Then they linked hands as they walked over to the Neptune Steps, down past the statue of Gaia, the Earth Mother, before peeling off to the left towards the gardens surrounding the old abbey ruins. It was just as they drew near the Pebble Garden that Harry stopped abruptly.

"My goodness, there it is, after all these years!" He was staring at a glorious old climbing rose which wound its way up the wall, covered in a profusion of small golden-yellow roses.

"We stopped here," he exclaimed. "Rose always loved her name because she loved the flower, and yellow roses were most definitely her favourite. She thought this was the most beautiful rose bush she'd ever seen."

He moved across to stand close to the wall, his nose buried in the blooms. "She dragged me over to do this. She said this was the very sweetest perfume, nature at its best. We stood here for ages before she'd let us get going again."

Claire came up beside him, cupping a branch of flowers in her hand as she breathed in their fragrance. "I can see what she meant. These are superb."

"And when we got home after our visit here, I bought her yellow roses whenever I saw them, so we'd never forget the special time we spent here."

"What a lovely memory," agreed Claire, warmed by the sheer delight in her great-uncle's face as he soaked up the moment – this place, the rose bush; its colour and aroma weaving together to carry his thoughts back to one of the happiest times in his life with Rose. Claire had never seen him look as contented as he did then, lost in an experience so deeply personal and intimate that she feared she was intruding simply by being there.

When he was ready, he crossed to join her where she waited a few steps away, by the old gate. Without a word, she took his hand and they walked on in silence, warmed by what they'd just shared: a moment in time both knew they would never forget.

***

After several hours of walking around the gardens, the group returned to the tender and sank gratefully into their seats, exhilarated but exhausted.

"We'll be just in time for afternoon tea," announced Iris. "I will have one scone with cream and jam and a cup of Earl

Grey, then go and put my feet up for an hour. You must do the same, Harry. You're no spring chicken, you know."

"Oh, Iris, I wouldn't have missed today for anything," sighed Harry. "It was wonderful."

"Well, you need to pace yourself," retorted Iris. "Lots of tea, nourishing food – preferably cooked by someone else – plenty of sleep and a clear conscience. That's the secret of good health."

"Well, I'm due at the final gospel choir rehearsal at five," replied Harry, "so I'll settle for a cup of tea in my cabin and a lie down for a while."

Having walked with Harry back to their cabins, where they dropped off their bags and coats, Neil and his family joined their friends up in the lounge for afternoon tea.

"It's a *chocolate fest*," squealed Betty, practically running up to the long tables on which was spread the most mouth-watering and colourful buffet. "Look, Sheila! I've never seen so much chocolate all in one place."

Sure enough, it was everywhere – on cakes, pastries, sandwiches and biscuits, in dainty little pots of mousse and puddings, and from a fountain flowing with hot creamy chocolate for profiteroles, strawberries, marshmallows, or just by the spoonful!

"Chocolate can't be all bad," mused Betty, her eyes greedily scanning the table. "After all, it's made from cocoa beans, and everyone says we should eat more vegetables."

"It's so unfair," wailed Sheila, shovelling a large piece of gooey fudge cake onto her plate. "I only want two things: to lose weight and eat chocolate."

"Well, I reckon chocolate brownies are definitely good for my health," decided Marion. "My mental health, that is…"

And the three friends split up to head for different sections of the spread, so they could pile their plates with as many chocolate treats as possible.

***

"Neil, can we have a word?"

Neil looked up to see Deirdre and Mark standing beside him. "Of course. Pull up a couple of chairs. There's plenty of room."

"We don't want to disturb you, so we won't stop long. We just wanted to share a bit of news with you." Mark smiled down into Deirdre's face as he spoke. "This wonderful woman has agreed to become my wife."

"That's terrific news," beamed Neil, "and not totally unexpected, I must say."

"I'm glad you think so," smiled Deirdre.

"You two have been making eyes at each other for ages. *We* all knew what a great couple you'd be before either of you did, I think!"

"Oh, I think we knew too," agreed Deirdre, "but it felt too important to get it wrong, so neither of us got round to saying anything – until this cruise."

"Well, I couldn't be more delighted, and I know the whole congregation will feel the same."

"Good," said Mark, "because as soon as we get back home and you've got the church diary to hand, we'd like to book a date for our wedding."

"Even better," beamed Neil. "I think you can safely say the whole choir will be there that day to see two stalwart members celebrate such a special occasion."

"And," said Deirdre, looking lovingly up at Mark, "I'm hoping that my Mum and Da will be able to come. In fact, the whole family. We saw them while we were in Dublin yesterday."

"That worked out well, then," said Neil.

"Oh," said Mark, "you have no idea how well."

***

Realizing he'd left his music case by the piano after the service that morning, Clifford glanced at his watch anxiously. He only had a few minutes before he was due at the last gospel choir rehearsal. The piano stood on the stage in the small lounge where the service had been held, but there was no sign of the case.

Thinking it must have been discovered and put away somewhere safe, he was taking a look behind the dark curtains at the back of the stage when he heard voices. Two men were emerging from the small room beside the stage where artistes could wait out of sight before they enter the spotlight to start their performance. It only took a moment for him to recognize whose voices he was hearing.

"I'll see you later, then." Andrew came out first, looking round to smile at the person who followed him through the door.

"You will come and see the show tonight?" asked Michael, standing so close that the two of them were almost touching. "I've been rehearsing that new number. I need to know what you think of it."

"I like everything you do…"

Michael laughed. "I know that, but I want your professional musical opinion. Tell me straight. If I can do it better, let me know."

Andrew put his hand on Michael's arm. "I will. You'll get the brutal truth from me."

"I'll see you after the show, then, up in the cocktail bar before you start your set."

"I'll look forward to it."

"Me too…"

Their heads inclined to one another for just a second before Andrew pulled back.

"I'll be late for the gospel choir rehearsal if I don't go."

"It's good of you to do that. You don't have to."

"I know," grinned Andrew. "I'm a very nice person."

"You certainly are…"

"See you then – and break a leg tonight! Don't worry, that new song will be great."

Clifford waited until the two of them had left the lounge before he emerged from the shadows.

So that was how things were. It didn't look as if Maureen Bragnall was going to be welcoming Sharon as a daughter-in-law any time soon.

***

"Don't go!"

"Rob, I must," replied Jill as she was about to leave the cabin, her gospel choir sheet in her hand. "It's the last rehearsal."

"*Dirty Dancing*'s showing on the ship's television system today. That's one of your favourites, isn't it?"

"Yes, but I've got a rehearsal."

"I thought we could cuddle up and watch it together."

"You hate musicals. You've always been really rude about me liking that film."

"Well, I fancy watching it now – with my wife."

Jill turned, her hand on the door handle. "That's a lovely thought, Rob. Unexpected, but lovely – and I still have to go to the choir rehearsal. Why don't you come?"

"Why don't you stay?"

"Look, I'll be back soon, and I'd love to take up your offer of cuddling up in front of that film later tonight, perhaps after dinner?"

"I might have changed my mind by then," he said, narrowing his eyes in a way he hoped looked seductive.

"That's a risk I'll have to take."

"If we leave it until later, will you wear that dress again?"

"What? To cuddle up on the bed?"

"You're right, that's a *bad* idea. Just slip it on for a while to remind me how nice you looked in it, then you can take it off again before you come to bed…"

"I'll think about it," replied Jill, her lips twitching with the effort of trying to control the smile that was creeping across her face.

"Please do," suggested Rob as she shut the door behind her.

***

"Well, that was really brilliant. Well done, everybody!"

A round of delighted applause and cheers rippled around the choir at Pam's encouraging words.

"Keep an eye on the people either side of you," Pam continued, grinning as she raised her voice to be heard. "If everyone else is swaying to the right and you're swaying to the left, it's probably you who's doing it wrong. And gentlemen, don't forget *not* to sing when it's supposed to be women only – but do remember to sing when it's your turn. OK?

"Right, well, the actual performance is the day after tomorrow, as we leave Honfleur heading for Tilbury. I'm told that sail-away time is scheduled for five forty-five, so our service will start a quarter of an hour before that, at five thirty. Could I ask you all to assemble here at five, so we can have one last run-through before we go upstairs? We need to be up on deck in good time to make sure everyone knows where to stand."

There was general agreement all round as the choir members began to disperse.

"Carole, Sylvia, Peter and Val, Betty, Sheila and Marion, Julia, Mark, Deirdre, Father Peter and John – can you spare a minute to come up and have a word, please?"

Once they were all gathered around her, Pam carried on. "Thank you for all agreeing to be part of my Good Heavens! choir for our 'Songs of Praise' tomorrow afternoon. I know you've already had a rehearsal with Brian of the hymns we'll be singing. Viewers are used to hearing musical pieces sung beautifully on the television programme, so we need to make sure our hymns are as moving and musical as we can make them tomorrow. Knowing you're all experienced church choir members, used to reading music and holding harmony lines, I'd like you to stand round the microphones at the side of the stage, so you can give a strong and melodic lead. We'll probably have at least three hundred people in the audience tomorrow, so with your help the sound should be wonderful."

"We'll need a proper sound check," declared Carole, "so we get the voices balanced correctly. Obviously the strongest and most perfectly pitched voices should be nearest the microphones."

"You're right, we do need a sound check, and for just that reason I'd like you all to be in the lounge by half past four, thirty minutes before we start. Is that all right with everyone?"

"What should we wear?" asked Marion.

"You're on holiday," smiled Pam. "Whatever you might wear to go to church while you're on holiday."

"What? No uniform?" asked Carole. "We'll look like a very ragamuffin choir if we're all in different colours and styles."

"That's why I call it the Good Heavens! choir. We're not pretending to be a group who've sung and practised together for years. This choir's made up of new friends who've come together specially for this occasion. Good heavens, we might look a bit unusual, but our hearts and voices will most definitely be in the right place."

Carole said nothing, although her expression said rather a lot.

"You all know Richard now," continued Pam, smiling at her husband beside her. "He's well used to leading the singing during our 'Songs of Praise'. He'll be with you all the time, to make sure everyone knows when to stand up for each hymn and when to sit down again so you can listen to the interviews. Just keep your eye on him. I really hope you find it a lovely experience. Thank you again. We'll see you tomorrow."

Once the crowd had dispersed and the room was almost empty, Clifford moved over to where Andrew was sorting through his music.

"A word in your ear, dear boy."

Andrew looked up in surprise.

"Completely by accident, I happened to see you taking your leave of Michael this afternoon, just before this rehearsal."

Andrew's jaw dropped.

"Don't worry! I've no problem with the two of you being that close, and I see you haven't either."

Andrew raised his chin as he replied. "Michael's an extremely talented performer and a good friend."

"Much more than just a good friend, I venture to suggest."

The younger man fell silent.

"Look, Andrew, you can't help who you love, and none of us has the right to impose our opinions on others. But in saying that, your mother does come to mind…"

"You're not going to tell her, are you?"

"Of course not, but I hope that one day, before too long, you might feel ready to tell her and your dad yourself."

"They'll never understand."

"I'm sure it'll be a new thought to them, and at first they may struggle to accept it. But you're their only son, and your happiness is important to them. It's easy to see how much they love you."

"I just don't want to disappoint them."

"Well, whether you do or you don't will be as much about them as it is about you."

Andrew nodded as he thought this over.

"In the meantime, if you need a good listener – one who's faced a similar dilemma in the past – I'm here, OK?"

"OK," agreed Andrew, his face pale.

And with what he hoped was a reassuring smile, Clifford picked up his music case and turned to leave. Andrew sat down heavily, his fingers going instinctively to the keyboard, where they started to play.

CHAPTER 8

❧ ST PETER PORT, ❧ GUERNSEY

God is near to all those who call on Him.
The kingdom of heaven can be reached
from any land.

St Samthann

The passengers breakfasting on deck the next morning were treated to a panoramic view of the waterfront of St Peter Port, with its grey and white stone buildings interrupted by rows of colourfully painted houses. The spires of churches and monuments reaching up from its winding streets and leafy alleys were dwarfed on the southern side of the town by Castle Cornet, the magnificent granite fortress which had stood guard on that spot since the eleventh century. Etched into the castle were the war wounds it had gathered over the years, especially during the English Civil War – Guernsey had supported Cromwell, which meant that the island's Royalists had to hold out in the castle for eight long years.

"The Channel Islanders were so brave during the Second World War, you know," Arthur explained to his grandson Callum. The seventeen-year-old was tucking into a hearty breakfast of bacon, sausage, black pudding, eggs, mushrooms, beans and tomatoes, along with buttered toast to mop up the juices.

"These islands were the only British territory to be occupied by the enemy, for five years from 1940 to 1945. We'd left them undefended, so they were almost handed to the Germans on a plate. When they sent a squadron of bombers over to pummel St Peter Port and the main harbour on Jersey too, the Germans soon realized there was no real resistance. You can imagine what a triumph it was to take over this jewel of British territory. They thought it was a strategic stronghold, the gateway to an invasion of Great Britain."

"Well, that never happened," said Callum between mouthfuls, "so the islanders must have been OK."

"They had to become self-sufficient, because they were cut off from the mainland. And that was easier said than done, with the Germans helping themselves to any rations and produce they were able to grow themselves. Some people practically starved before the end of the war."

"That wouldn't happen now," said Callum confidently. "Military planning's much more sophisticated these days. That's why I want to join up. With all the terrorist groups in the world who need sorting out, the British Army's always at the front when it comes to getting the bad guys. They either stop what they're doing, or we'll stop 'em – dead!"

Arthur sighed. "Callum, you've got no idea about war. I hope you don't find out the hard way how naïve you are. Soldiers die on all sides. Bombs and missiles don't discriminate. If you're in the way, you're the one who dies, probably without you ever seeing the whites of your enemy's eyes."

"Well, I'm joining up as soon as I'm eighteen, Grandpa," retorted Callum. "It's a proper job. I've been on training exercises with the school cadet force, so I'm not that naïve. You fought for your country. Why shouldn't I?"

Arthur eyed his grandson thoughtfully before his gaze focused further away. "Just over there, about twenty-five miles away, is the Normandy coast. We'll be there tomorrow. It'll be the first time I've set foot on that shore for more than seventy years."

"Yeah, I'm looking forward to that. Can't wait to hear the story of your war, Grandpa. I've never heard you talk about it much."

Even when Arthur eventually spoke again, Callum failed to notice the pain in his grandfather's eyes.

"Well, I'll tell you tomorrow. Then we'll see if you're still as keen to march off to war."

But Callum was too interested in ploughing through his breakfast to listen – and the thought of the reality of war, which his grandson simply couldn't grasp, upset Arthur enough to put him off the thought of any breakfast at all.

Back at the buffet restaurant, Neil was just heading for the door when he bumped into Brad coming out.

"I was hoping to see you," said Neil. "Are you still meeting Joanne today?"

Brad glanced at his watch. "She'll be here in about ten minutes. We're having to meet early, because I'm on duty here this afternoon."

"How are you feeling?"

"Terrified, resigned, sad beyond thinking…"

"Well, perhaps it's best not to over-think what'll happen today. You and Joanne have got a lot to talk about."

Brad nodded forlornly.

"Just remember how much you've always loved each other, and how you both loved Chris. Joanne may need your love very badly right now."

"I think she needs me like a hole in the head."

"You're thinking again," smiled Neil. "Go with an open mind. Listen as much as you talk."

Brad took a deep calming breath. "I might need a chat with a mate later today. What time are you back?"

"We're on the *Guernsey Highlights* trip around the island," replied Neil. "Back about four, I think. We're all going to the 'Songs of Praise' at five."

"OK."

"And Brad, I'm praying for you."

"Thanks." Brad's expression was grim as he replied. "I definitely need that."

Several minutes later Neil had been joined by Claire and Iris. They'd all selected their breakfast and chosen a table overlooking the quayside. Glancing down, Neil saw Brad walking away from the ship towards a woman who stood just inside the gate. She looked very small and alone as she watched the man who was striding over to meet her. When he reached her, they didn't touch, but exchanged a few words then turned to go out of the gate, as distantly as two strangers who had just met for the first time.

"Where's Harry?" Brig came over to ask the question.

"He's a bit tired this morning," sniffed Iris. "He's been doing too much. I did warn him."

"And he had such a wonderful day yesterday on Tresco," added Claire. "We did a lot of walking there, so I think his legs are giving him a bit of trouble this morning."

"He'll miss out on Guernsey, then," said Brig. "One of the most famous seafaring islands around the British Isles. Their sailors and fishermen are legendary."

"Brig!" snapped Daisy, stepping up behind him. "Let those poor people eat their breakfast in peace."

A momentary look of embarrassment shot across Brig's face before he pinned on his usual resolute smile. "Well, I'll take my leave of you, then."

"Thanks for asking after Harry, Brig," said Claire. "I'll tell him before we head out on our trip today. Have a good time yourself."

Brig shot a doubtful look towards Daisy, who was busy spooning melon pieces onto her plate at the buffet. "I'll try." And with a click of his heels and a smart salute, he marched off in the direction of his wife.

Before Claire left the restaurant, she gathered together a simple continental breakfast and a strong cup of tea, and carried the tray down to Harry's cabin. Using the extra key she'd been given, she knocked before stepping into the darkened room.

"Uncle Harry?" she whispered. "Are you asleep?"

"No," came the muffled reply from under the covers. "I'm just resting my eyes."

Claire smiled, putting the tray down on the bedside table. "Well, your eyes might like to feast themselves on the breakfast goodies I've brought for you. There's a mug of tea too, just the way you like it."

He stirred then, his eyes peering over the bedclothes. "Thank you, Claire. I'll have some later."

"You need something to eat now, so you can take your pills, and that tea will wash them down nicely. Come on. Let me help you to sit up a bit."

Reluctantly, Harry allowed himself to be propped up on his pillows so he could see her clearly, sitting on the bed opposite his.

"How are you this morning?" she asked.

"There were a lot of steps up and down in Tresco, weren't there?" groaned Harry. "And all that walking too. I loved it, but my knees weren't so keen."

"Are you going to take things easy today, then?"

"I think I should."

"It's a pity you'll miss Guernsey. They say the island is really pretty."

"With pedigree cows that produce the most marvellous cream, so Iris tells me," said Harry. "I gather you'll be having a strawberry cream tea on your tour today."

"Iris has mentioned that three times already this morning."

"She certainly has a sweet tooth – although she always protests when I say that."

Claire leaned forward to lace her fingers through his. "I'll miss you. Wish you were coming with us."

"Well, I promise to behave. I'm thinking of taking my book out on deck in the sunshine somewhere. That sounds like the perfect day to me."

She smiled, but there was concern in her voice as she stood to leave. "You are all right, though, aren't you? You don't need anything? You know you can always ring the steward from the phone right here."

"I do know that, and I'll be fine. Have a wonderful time. Enjoy the cows – and Iris."

With a quiet chuckle, Claire planted a loving kiss on his cheek and gave him a quick wave before closing the door behind her.

Half an hour later, Harry stood up to draw back the curtains in the cabin. The small window gave a view of the quayside, where a row of coaches were waiting to ferry passengers around the island on various trips. Suddenly, he saw the group who interested him most: Neil, hand in hand with Claire; Iris following on with Peter and Val Fellowes at her side. He banged on the window, wondering if there was any chance they could hear him. He soon realized they couldn't, but he carried on watching as they gave in their tickets and climbed into the coach. Minutes later, as the bus pulled away from the ship, he glimpsed Claire's face looking back at him, almost as if she sensed him watching her.

And then they were gone.

***

"Well, Neil, is this church small enough for you?" grinned Peter as they all walked up the lane towards the Little Chapel at Les Vauxbelets.

"I wouldn't fit much of a congregation in there," laughed Neil, looking up at the two sets of curved steps leading to the chapel. Behind them, Sister Maureen arrived with her guidebook, Catholic mothers in tow.

"This Little Chapel is a labour of love," she read loudly. "In December 1913, a de la Salle monk called Brother Deodat arrived in Les Vauxbelets, and when he saw this woody slope of land facing the valley, he had the idea to build a grotto here like the one at Lourdes. By March of 1914, he had built a tiny chapel nine feet long and four feet wide, but when his efforts were criticized, he spent the following night tearing the building down.

"But he couldn't forget the idea, so he set to work on another chapel, which ended up being the same width but a little longer than his original attempt. This chapel survived until September 1923, when Brother Deodat tore it down again after the Bishop of Portsmouth had got stuck in the doorway."

"Well, no wonder," frowned Iris, eyeing the tiny entrance. "Any normal-sized person who likes cream teas would get stuck in that door."

Sister Maureen chuckled before continuing to read.

"So Brother Deodat set about building a third chapel, which is the one we see now. It was hard work, as day after day he had to collect pebbles and tiny pieces of broken china to decorate the shrine. Then, following an article in the *Daily Mirror* newspaper showing a picture of the chapel, the shrine became famous, and gifts arrived from around the world, bringing everything from pieces of exotic mother-of-pearl to brightly coloured chips of china donated by the locals.

"Over the years since, decoration has been completed on the walls and ceiling in the crypt, and a Way of the Cross has been built around the chapel mirroring the Way at Lourdes, with fourteen traditional Stations of the Cross. The fifteenth, symbolizing the Resurrection of Our Lord, is deemed to be the Little Chapel itself."

All those listening were plainly moved by the story, none more so than Sister Maureen herself, who seemed close to tears as she closed the guidebook.

"Come, mothers!" she cried as she set off up the sparkling, colourful stairs. "Prayers and penance. Follow me!"

***

At exactly that moment back on *The Pilgrim*, Harry was opening the door onto the side deck, looking up and down the long rows of loungers for somewhere to stretch out and read. The ship was unnaturally quiet with all the passengers ashore on Guernsey, and he smiled at the thought of the peace and quiet he would be able to enjoy for an hour or so. Glancing up at the sky, he decided the sun probably wouldn't hit this part of the ship for some time, so he climbed a nearby staircase to the next deck level. Here, he found a line of lifeboats suspended above his head as he made his way along to find a small area of deck right at the very front of the ship. Just a handful of loungers were on offer there, so he rolled up his towel as a cushion for his head, and with a sigh lay down with his book open on his chest.

Small bundles of cloud scudded across the blue sky, and he shaded his eyes from the warm sun, rising to its height as the clock ticked towards noon. Perhaps he nodded off, because when he opened his eyes again he wasn't sure where he was or why he was there. His head felt muggy, there was a dull ache in his chest and his limbs felt too heavy to lift – but he was so warm and comfortable, he had no wish to move.

Slowly he became aware that he was not alone. There was a woman standing a few yards away to one side of him, and he sensed that he knew her, although it was hard to see her clearly. He closed his eyes for a moment to help him focus, and when he opened them she was right at his side.

"You're tired, Harry; so tired…"

Was he hearing those words, or was her voice just echoing around inside his head? Squinting to see her image more clearly, he breathed in sharply. "Rose?"

"You found our roses, Harry. You remembered…"

Struggling to find his breath, he would have stretched out to touch her if only he could lift his arm. It was then that he realized she was carrying a bunch of small yellow roses, and that fragrant golden petals were tumbling around him.

"I never told you…" he began.

"… that you love me? I know, Harry. I've always known."

"Is it time?"

"Yes."

He felt her hand touch him then, and suddenly his arm was weightless as he reached out to her. He was standing beside her now, looking down at her dear face as he remembered her on the day she'd become his bride, her eyes full of love, yellow roses in her arms. Breathing in the sweet aroma, he was dimly aware of their golden petals swirling around them as he bent to kiss her.

***

The lounge was filling up quickly as several hundred passengers took their seats for 'Songs of Praise'. Richard and the ship's technical team had already run sound checks on the Good Heavens! choir. There had been a somewhat heated discussion with Carole, who felt her professionally trained voice should be right in front of the sopranos' microphone, but the engineer pointed out that once she started singing, no one else could be heard at all, and he moved her to the back line, where she glowered with indignation. As musical director for the event, Brian was checking the order of the hymns he would be conducting. Clifford was at the grand piano, while Andrew made final adjustments to the sheet music spread out on the electronic keyboard. The drummer and guitarist from the ship's band had joined them too, so the music would have rhythm and harmony. Pam was sitting in the front row alongside the interviewees, looking over final details before the event began.

"Has Claire still not found him?" asked Iris as she walked in with Neil. "He can't have gone far."

"No, you're right," agreed Neil. "He's probably disappeared into someone else's cabin for a chat – or he did mention there was a film showing downstairs in the cinema which he fancied seeing. Either that, or Claire's wandering round the ship one way, just missing him as he wanders in the other direction."

"Harry's been talking about coming to this 'Songs of Praise', though," Iris pointed out. "Perhaps he's lost track of time. That happens as you get older."

"Well, Claire will keep looking for him and bring him down to join us. Let's save a couple of seats for them."

"Good afternoon, everyone," greeted Pam as she moved to the middle of the stage, microphone in hand.

There was a general hush as people settled down.

"Well, I'm not sure if you can raise the roof on a ship, but we'll have a good try as we sing together some of our most popular hymns, old and new. So let's start by getting to our feet to sing 'To God Be the Glory'."

***

Claire wasn't having much luck. She remembered that, faced with all the decks and different locations on this large ship, Harry had become quite confused about which end was which, what deck he was on and where he was heading. He always preferred to be in the company of someone he knew, so being alone today might well have left him disorientated. She'd knocked on Arthur's cabin door, as well as Val and Peter's and Brian and Sylvia's, but there was no reply from any of them. They were obviously all at "Songs of Praise".

Next she tried the library, thinking he might have settled down to his favourite pastime of completing the *Pilgrim* crossword, as he did most days. She looked into each corner and around every shelf of books, opening doors which led to rooms containing computers, jigsaw puzzles, handicrafts and a selection of CDs and videos. There was no sign of Harry.

The cinema! She remembered him saying earlier in the week that he liked the look of some of the films that were being shown there. Perhaps today he'd realized that a favourite of his was playing, and he'd gone down to watch in comfort? After a few minutes of being totally lost as she tried to locate the cinema, she eventually opened the door to find it completely empty.

Where on earth was he?

***

The first person Pam welcomed onto the stage to chat to her was Brian, who had retired from being a builder about ten years earlier. Soon after, he had received a call from his daughter, who was doing voluntary work in a particularly needy area of India. They had a problem and she wondered if her dad might help. There was no school building in the village, and one was badly needed. Would Brian give them some guidance from England – and then, please, please, please, would he come out to India to supervise the building? She was sure that under his direction it wouldn't take long. Much against his better judgment, Brian found himself agreeing to go, and set to work designing a very simple building, then sending over a list of supplies she'd have to requisition before he arrived.

Two weeks before he was due to leave home, she rang with bad news. She'd managed to find everything except bricks, of which twelve thousand were needed. Bricks could easily be made and baked by men in the village, but what they required was a certain type of clay and a plentiful supply of water. The clay was only found on one particular plot of land, which was owned by a lady who was very sceptical about their plans. She said they were welcome to the clay, but what would be the point? It hadn't rained for months, and the water hole near the village had completely dried up. No one could argue with that. Their task was impossible.

"Well, there's no point in me coming if you haven't got any bricks for me to build with," Brian had said, quite reasonably. "If you've not managed to sort something out within the week, I'll have to postpone my visit."

But Brian hadn't reckoned on the absolute faith of the local teacher who, like many in the village, was a devout

Catholic. He called a village meeting and told them all that they had to pray as never before. Hopes faded, as for days nothing happened – and then one night, without warning, it started to rain for twelve hours non-stop. The curious thing was that the rain was very local. It fell heavily around their water hole, but a mile up the road on the land where the clay was, there was no rain at all.

"Quick!" ordered the teacher, calling on every available pair of hands in the village. By the time they had worked non-stop for the first day, they had crafted nearly two thousand bricks by hand. The next morning, though, they arrived to find that the land was drying out quickly in the hot sun. All around the water hole the ground was cracked and dusty.

"But look, it's a miracle!" said the teacher. They realized that the water level in their hole had not gone down at all, in spite of all they'd used the previous day.

"The sun will have dried it up by the end of the day, though," the elders warned, so villagers of all ages worked tirelessly, mixing, shaping and baking brick after brick until, by the end of the second day, they had one third of the bricks they needed.

For five more days they worked, and for five days the water level in the hole stayed high. The morning after they finished, the hole was empty again.

Obviously deeply emotional, Brian halted his story at this point, aware of the gasp of wonder that echoed around the audience.

"And did you go and help them build their school?" asked Pam.

"I did. The villagers worked alongside me for two weeks before we hung the last door and put the paint pots away. That school teacher was taking lessons in there a few days later."

"And looking back, what do you think about the way those bricks were made?"

"I think prayer has power. I think that the teacher and

those villagers had the kind of faith that moves mountains. I think God was in that project."

"Did that experience change you?"

He nodded his head thoughtfully. "We live very comfortably in Britain, don't we?" he answered. "Our faith isn't challenged every day in the way it is in communities like that. That's the kind of faith that keeps them alive, working and praying together. I find that so humbling. Never again will I doubt that prayers are heard and answered. It's amazing."

Turning to the audience, Pam thanked Brian, then introduced the hymn he had chosen to express the wonder he felt at God's goodness and grace.

"Let's all stand to sing 'Great Is Thy Faithfulness'."

***

Claire was beginning to wonder if Harry had decided to take a stroll off the ship after all, and got confused about the time. Panic gripped her as she realized the ship was due to set sail in about ten minutes' time. Surely they wouldn't leave unless all passengers were accounted for. Reception – that's where she could find out – and her purposeful stride had turned into a frantic run by the time the reception desk came into sight.

"I've lost my Uncle Harry," she panted to the receptionist. "Harry Holloway, Cabin 126. I'm worried that he might have gone ashore and not come back. Is there a way you can check?"

"Certainly," smiled the smartly suited, rather glamorous receptionist. After long seconds of tapping into her computer, she looked up at Claire. "Mr Holloway hasn't left the ship today."

"And he hasn't booked himself in for anything I might not be aware of? With the doctor, perhaps? Would you have a list of the surgery's bookings?"

More tapping. "He's not booked for an appointment anywhere that I can see."

Claire ran her fingers through her hair with frustration and worry.

"Look," said the receptionist kindly, "this is a large ship. There are so many places where people can get away from it all for a bit of peace and quiet, or even for a chat with someone they've only just met. He's definitely on board somewhere. I'm sure he'll turn up soon."

"Maybe." Claire still looked doubtful. "Well, I'll do the rounds again, but can you bear in mind that an eighty-year-old man, who isn't brilliant when it comes to his sense of direction, has gone missing? Could you pass the message on to the crew, just in case they spot him somewhere?"

"Of course. Perhaps you could let me know when he returns to his cabin, as I'm sure he will."

Feeling she was being patronized and dismissed, as if she were an over-protective mother, Claire walked away, wondering where to try next. Slowly she climbed a set of stairs winding rather grandly up the decks in the centre of the ship. She was about to carry on climbing when she realized that on either side of the stairs on that level were doors leading out to the sun decks. She had walked right around those decks several minutes before, but perhaps Harry had made his way out there since she'd left.

Encouraged by the thought, she set off again.

***

There was complete hush in the packed lounge as Pam's next guest told her story. Many of them had got to know Bishop Paul's delightful wife, Margaret, but what she shared with them that afternoon stunned them into silence.

She explained how, four years earlier, she had been diagnosed with an incurable form of blood cancer which was attacking the cells of her bone marrow. It was hard enough simply coming to terms emotionally with the word "incurable", but the treatment she needed to fight the condition would also demand every ounce of physical resilience she could muster. There had followed a challenging period of five months of chemotherapy, then later a very difficult and painful session of injections to harvest her own stem cells. That left her traumatized and exhausted, dreading what else lay ahead of her. She knew the next step to be faced was when she'd be put under general anaesthetic so that the stem cells could be transplanted back into her. The procedure was known to be risky and the outcome very uncertain. She remembered feeling at rock bottom as she was waiting to be wheeled into the operating theatre.

"But I knew I wasn't alone, that God was in it with me. I just had to trust him. And some of the old words I'd known all my life from Psalm 121 kept coming to me:

> I will lift up mine eyes unto the hills, from whence cometh my help.
> My help cometh from the LORD, which made heaven and earth.
> The LORD shall preserve thy going out and thy coming in from this time forth, and even for evermore."

"Did that prayer help?" asked Pam.

"It wasn't just my own prayer which became so important to me," Margaret explained. "It was all the other people who I knew were praying for me too. I could feel its power in a way that gave me reassurance and comfort. And every day that followed, through three long months when I had to stay in a sterile environment, not seeing people or going out so that it felt as if my life had been put on hold, I never stopped being strengthened and reassured by prayer."

"But now, four years later, you look wonderful, and we've all seen how full of energy you are. How are you?"

"Honestly, not as well as I look. The condition is taking hold again, and in two weeks' time, after this cruise, I'll be starting that whole procedure again. But I've been through it once, and I know that the strength I need to face this lies in my faith. This is the situation I've been given by God, and he's in it with me. Through him I've learned the need for trust and patience. And I find myself looking at everything differently, valuing what's really important, thankful for every morning, every person I love, every moment I cherish. As my health diminishes, so my faith grows all the more. That's why I've chosen this hymn – because it speaks of Christ's triumph over death."

"Thank you, Margaret," said Pam, as moved as every other person in the room by the impact of her words, especially knowing that she was shortly to face another round of painful treatment.

"Let's all stand to sing with Margaret the great hymn of praise she's chosen: 'Thine Be the Glory'."

***

Claire walked right around the decks on both sides of the ship, but Harry was nowhere to be seen. Finding herself back where she started, she was just about to open the door to step inside so she could check whether he'd returned to his cabin, when she spotted a small staircase she hadn't noticed before. The stairs led up to a narrow gangway lined overhead by a row of huge suspended lifeboats. Surely, with his sore knees, Harry wouldn't have come all the way up here!

Eventually the path opened out onto a small, almost hidden, deck area right at the front of the ship. There were just a handful of loungers there, and at first when she glanced around she didn't see anyone.

"Harry!" she called.

Suddenly, she spotted him, stretched out in the pale, late afternoon sunshine, his book on his chest, fast asleep.

"Thank goodness I've found you. You certainly tucked yourself away up here. Come on, you're missing 'Songs of Praise', and I know you were looking forward to…"

She stopped mid-sentence. He was so quiet, his face relaxed, with a secret smile as if he were having a dream he was enjoying.

"Harry!" she called again, kneeling down close to him so that she could stroke his face to wake him.

He was cold.

Snatching her hand back, the shock punched the breath out of her.

"Harry?" she whispered softly. "Wake up, Harry. It's me."

Slowly, so slowly, she stretched out her fingers to touch his arm. He didn't move. She knew he couldn't. He would never move again. And as she leaned her head forward to rest on his shoulder, she felt something flutter down and brush past her face.

It was a single golden petal.

***

The next person to share their story on "Songs of Praise" reminded everyone of the fateful events of 7th July 2005, which shocked the whole country.

Nigel was the chaplain at a private school in Reading, and he had gone to London that morning to take part in a conference. He'd taken the tube from Paddington to Kings Cross shortly after half past eight, then headed down to the Piccadilly southbound line. When the first train came in, it was packed, and he became aware that a lady near him was desperate to get on. As he was in no hurry, he let her take his place and remained on the platform to wait for the next train – a gesture that was to seal his fate. When the train came, he got into the third carriage from the front, standing shoulder to shoulder with several others near the door. Minutes later, in the middle of the tunnel, there was a deafening explosion and they were plunged into darkness. With panic all around him, he was surprised to hear himself saying very clearly above the noise, "Lord, if it's possible, please get us out of this mess."

That seemed to calm everyone down. There followed thirty endless, harrowing minutes while they waited for help, thinking that any minute they might be engulfed in flames, and in that time he found himself considering the possibility that he might die. At last they saw lights through the gloom as rescue workers prised open the door and told the passengers to follow them back down the tunnel to the platform at Kings Cross which they'd just left.

Making his way upstairs, lending an arm on the way to other people with various degrees of injury, Nigel emerged at ground level into a scene of chaos. He realized for the first time that this was not a simple accident or a fire. It was a bomb – and as news came in that other bombs were going off in strategic places around London, the order came to evacuate the station.

Dazed and covered in grime, with all tubes and buses halted, Nigel set off to walk the two or three miles back to Paddington station. There he got a train for Reading, then a bus to his church, where he knew his wife would be helping out with the senior citizens' lunch club. When he walked into the building, exhausted and covered in dust, cheers rang around him as his wife fell into his arms, sobbing with relief that he was safe.

"How do you feel now," asked Pam, "about the people who planted those bombs?"

Nigel's eyes clouded with the memory of the carnage caused by the explosions that went off in central London.

"Fifty-three people were killed that day, twenty-six of them in the front two carriages of the train I was on." He stopped for a moment to gather his thoughts before continuing. "But I believe in a loving God, a God of forgiveness. God's love is revealed in Jesus Christ and, more than ever, I know we must stay true to his commandment to love one another. So, for me, there is nothing to forgive. It has made me realize, though, that you just don't know what's round the corner, and because of that, we should never let the sun go down on anger, or leave important words unsaid. Seize the day and every opportunity to put things right."

"It's interesting to hear you say that when a lot of people would find it very hard to forgive such violent acts against innocent people," said Pam. "How much has the support of others helped you through this?"

"I simply couldn't have managed without their love and prayers, not just from people I know, but from so many others I don't know from around the world – people who were moved to hear what happened.

"One thing I ask, though. If someone you know has gone through a traumatic experience, make sure you're a good listener. One thing I noticed was that after some people had asked me how I was, I barely got a word out before they announced that they knew exactly how I felt, because of something *they'd* been through. They couldn't possibly know how I felt, because every experience is different. I needed to talk and for them to listen, but it often ended up the other way round. So my advice would be this: if someone opens up enough to want to talk about pain they're going through, remember that your compassion and love are what they need most of all."

Just as Nigel went on to answer Pam's question about which hymn he'd chosen, Neil became aware of someone making their way across the room. Looking around in surprise, he saw the assistant cruise director, Jane, come up to kneel beside him.

"Neil, you're needed urgently. Dr Osbourn sent me."

"Oh, I know what that's about," Neil said. "Tell him I'll come down for a chat as soon as this finishes."

"No, Neil."

He frowned at the urgent tone of her voice.

"You have to come now."

Neil leaned across to whisper to Iris that he'd been called away very urgently, but she was engrossed in what Nigel was saying, and just shrugged with irritation.

A sense of foreboding swept over him as he followed Jane through the audience towards the door. Something terrible must have happened to Brad – but what?

***

As Nigel's hymn, "In Christ Alone", came to an end, Pam introduced the last person to share their story that afternoon. Fiona, a middle-aged lady, talked about her early career as a nurse.

One night she was working in a special care baby unit in a London hospital, looking after twelve newborns who needed the help of incubators to give them the best chance of survival during the first vital hours and days of their lives. One little boy was so desperately ill that the hospital chaplain was called to be with him and his parents. The child was expected to lose his fight for life at any time. Fiona helped to detach the baby from all the tubes and lines in the incubator, gently handing him to his mum so that she and his dad could hold and talk to him for a few minutes as his life ebbed away. They sat in a circle of light as the chaplain prayed for the baby, asking God for his blessing and protection for the tiny child.

"I'd never been much of a believer," explained Fiona. "I honestly had no faith at all at that point in my life, but what happened that night has stayed with me always. I can only say it felt as if suddenly there was a huge presence in the room, like the most loving embrace, so real that I felt gripped by it. We all watched as the baby very gradually stopped breathing, but there was no feeling of panic or distress; just an overwhelming sense of calm and peace, and the absolute knowledge that he was safe with God, just as we too were safe and supported in our loss and grief."

That was a turning point for Fiona. She now knew that God was real and present, and her hunger to learn more about him led eventually to her being ordained a minister in the Church of England. Years later, she was offered the opportunity to become a hospital chaplain herself, and she said what a privilege it was to be with patients and their families at poignant and painful times in their lives.

"Very often I've been with people at just the moment when their lives come to an end, and I'm aware of the same presence and calm which touched me so deeply all those years ago. Sometimes when the body takes its final breath or the heart beats for the last time, it's hard to know for certain when death comes – but there's a definite moment when you can almost *see* that person's soul leaving their frail body. They've gone to God in what is often the most intensely calm and loving atmosphere."

"It's only human, though, to fear death, isn't it?" Pam's voice was gentle as she asked. "How do you feel about death now?"

"I worry about how I'll die. The thought of being very ill, in pain or disabled *is* frightening. But I don't fear what waits for us beyond death. I've seen God's real and loving presence in life, so I know that same loving God is there for us in death. We can take comfort in that because it's true."

***

When Jane set off upstairs instead of downstairs towards the doctor's surgery, Neil was filled with curiosity. He tried to get more information out of her, but she was obviously reluctant to say any more than that he was urgently needed. She led him onto the outer deck and up a small set of stairs. Following her, Neil found himself ducking to avoid hitting his head on the lifeboats hanging above the gangway.

They emerged onto a small deck at the front of the ship where he'd never been before, and in the gathering gloom of early evening, he struggled at first to make out what he was seeing. Then he saw the huddled shape of Claire sitting next to Brad beside one of the sunbeds. A chill ran through him as he followed her gaze. Harry was stretched out on the bed. Deathly still. Neil didn't need a doctor to know that Harry was gone.

Claire's tear-streaked face was gaunt and pale as she looked up at him. Neil sank to her side, putting his arm around her stiff shoulders, drawing her to him.

"What happened?"

"I just found him here." Claire's voice was hesitant and husky, choked from too many tears. "But look at him. Look at his face. Can you see he's smiling?"

Neil leaned forward to peer more closely at Harry.

"I've been staring at him for ages and all I can see there is contentment," said Claire. "Joy. That's what it is. He warned me. He told me he wanted this, and he said he felt nothing but joy at the prospect of dying. Can you see that in his face? I can."

"Do we know what caused his death?" Neil asked Brad.

"Now you've come, we'll move him downstairs so I can examine him properly, but the first indications are that his heart failed."

"He had a major heart operation a couple of years ago."

"Really? Well, from what I can tell at this stage, it looks as if everything simply stopped. He closed his eyes in the sun and fell asleep. There's no sign that he suffered at all."

"I'm glad," said Claire. "He deserved that."

After a few moments of silence, Brad quietly suggested that arrangements should be made to move Harry inside.

"We need to tell Iris," whispered Claire.

"Yes," agreed Neil. "Let's do that together."

"Come down to the surgery when you're ready, Neil. I can tell you more about what needs to be done then. See to your family first. And Claire, you've had a tremendous shock. If you need anything to help you sleep or calm your thoughts, let me know. I'm here to help."

Neil eased Claire onto her feet, wrapping her jacket tighter around her shoulders. "Come on, love. Let's go now. We need to break the news to the others."

They knew that "Songs of Praise" would be over by that time, so Iris was probably in her own cabin. Knocking on her door, Neil almost hoped there would be no reply, but within seconds his mother swung open the door.

"Well, you're a fine one, rushing off like that," she snapped at Neil. "And you didn't even bother to come to the 'Songs of Praise', Claire! I know you're not a card-carrying Christian, but you might have found it very enlightening. And where's Harry? He'll need to know what time to be ready for dinner."

Something in Neil's expression finally got through to her, because she abruptly stopped talking.

"Can we come in, Mum? We've got something to tell you."

But Iris was ahead of them. She stepped back to sit down heavily on the bed. "He's gone, hasn't he?"

Neil nodded wordlessly.

"I found him lying on a sunbed right up at the front of the ship," explained Claire. "Heaven knows why he ended up there – I don't think any of us have been up there before. He just looked as if he was asleep, really peaceful, almost a smile on his face."

"But he was dead," concluded Iris.

"The doctor said it looked as if he just dropped off to sleep and never woke up again."

"Silly man!" chided Iris. "I told him he was doing too much. Would he listen? Of course not."

"I think he'd had enough," said Claire. "He was tired. He ached. He wanted to go home."

"I never imagined Harry as a quitter."

"He didn't quit. He just felt that he'd done everything he wanted here, and he was ready to move on."

"What about me?" Iris wasn't crying. She wouldn't let herself cry, but there was such forlornness in her voice that Neil sat down on the bed beside her. "I needed him. We looked after each other. Whatever will I do without him?"

She started to tremble then, her knuckles white as she linked her fingers around her knees.

"I think the doctor should come up and see you," said Claire. "It's such a shock; too much for you to cope with."

"I'll go," volunteered Neil. "Will you stay with her?"

Claire didn't answer, gathering Iris to her as hot, tumbling tears at last began to slide down her mother-in-law's ashen cheeks.

***

When Neil knocked on the surgery door, it wasn't Brad who greeted him. From his glimpse of her on the quayside earlier that morning, he recognized Joanne immediately. Close up, he was struck by the warmth and compassion in her eyes, and the prettiness of her face, which was framed by chin-length dark brown hair.

"You must be Neil," she said, beckoning for him to come in. "Brad's still with Harry."

"I thought they were bringing him here."

"There's a mortuary on board. That's where they are."

A *mortuary*. The finality of that word felt like a punch in the chest.

"Sit down," ordered Joanne, pulling up a chair. "You've had a tremendous shock."

This is stupid, thought Neil, embarrassment washing over him as he realized he was in danger of crying. He was supposed to be strong, the man of God, the minister called to provide answers and comfort to people when they lost a loved one. *A loved one!* What a trite description of someone who has been a cherished, valued, adored presence in the family for years!

"Nothing prepares you for it," said Joanne quietly. "You're a minister. I'm a trained nurse. But when it's your son or father…"

And there they sat, no more words needed – two strangers, each with their own memories, united in grief.

A couple of minutes later, Brad and the nurse walked into the surgery. Joanne stood up immediately.

"I'll go." She gave a small smile, her eyes meeting Neil's. "Take care."

She left, closing the door quietly behind her.

Brad was in business-like, doctor mode as he explained to Neil what procedures had to be followed after a death on board a cruise ship.

"I'll have to check with the relevant authorities in the morning, but my guess is that Harry will stay with us until we dock in Tilbury on Thursday morning. That's where the paperwork and official procedures really kick into action. He'll be taken to a holding facility at the docks while all that's organized."

"How long is that likely to take?"

"Possibly as long as a couple of weeks. It depends what's needed. They'll have to contact his own doctor and get a complete picture of his medical state before they'll release him. They may even need a post-mortem."

"And have you any more thoughts on why he died?"

"I think he just stopped living. His heart and breathing ceased, and he passed away. Officially I'll put on the death certificate that he died from heart failure, but he was an old man and he just died in the most peaceful way."

"Well, I thank God for that."

"You OK, Neil?"

"It's been quite a shock. I must get back to Claire, and my mother is very upset. Do you think you could come down later and see her? She might need a sedative to help her sleep tonight."

"Of course."

"I'll have to tell the others too."

"Do you want me to come with you now?"

"No, I have to do that on my own."

Neil's expression changed as he looked across at Brad. "And you? How are you doing?"

Brad nodded, considering the question before answering. "All right, I think. Better. Joanne coming has been good."

"I like her," said Neil. "She seems very intuitive, warm…"

"She is. It's easy to forget that when we're apart. When I'm on my own, I lose her somehow."

"So you've done a lot of talking today?"

"Yes. She's grieving as much as I am, but I sense she's moved on from her initial grief. I still feel so guilty. If I'd acted differently, could I have saved him?"

"This time, maybe…"

"Yes. There would have been another…"

"So what happens now?"

"Joanne's staying on board until we dock in Tilbury, so we have more time to talk."

"I'm glad," said Neil, getting to his feet. "It seems you and I both have difficult conversations ahead of us. God bless you, Brad."

"You too. I'll speak to you in the morning."

On the way back to his mother, Neil realized he was passing Peter and Val's cabin, so gave the door a knock. Val answered, laughing that she must look a mess because she hadn't yet changed for dinner. Surely they weren't *that* late, were they?

Five minutes later, after Neil had told them the news, their mood was sombre as the couple struggled to come to terms with the loss of their dear friend.

"Could you tell the others?" Neil asked as he stood up to leave.

"Of course," agreed Peter. "And we're here. Anything you need, you or the family, just yell. We're so sorry, Neil."

***

"Have you heard?" Betty hurried back across the lounge to the table where Marion and Sheila were waiting. "Carole was telling us over at the bar. Claire's Uncle Harry – you remember him? Such a lovely person. Well, he dropped dead this afternoon, right here on the ship. They'd gone ashore and left him, so he was all alone, poor man."

"Poor Neil. He and Claire must be beside themselves," said Sheila. "Do you think they need any help? Should we offer?"

"Better not disturb them tonight," replied Marion.

"Perhaps we could get a card from the shop and drop them a note from us all."

"That's a lovely idea!" cried Betty. "Shall I nip up and grab one before the show starts?"

"Too late," said Sheila as the sparkling chandeliers around the huge lounge started to dim.

The band struck up a rhythmic introduction as Cruise Director Ramon Moreno strolled onto the stage wearing a sparkling red jacket that made him look like a diminutive circus ringmaster. Clicking his fingers and smiling suggestively at the audience, he launched into his version of an old Demis Roussos favourite.

"Oh, he can definitely love me forever and ever," sighed Betty, closing her eyes dreamily.

"That voice…" agreed Marion.

"Pity he's so vertically challenged," commented Sheila.

"I'm not that tall," said Betty. "I think he'd be perfect for me."

"Getting involved with a man at sea?" quipped Marion. "You know what they say about sailors – a girl in every port!"

"You may be right," agreed Betty. "I can't exactly see him settling down in Burntacre, although Carole might welcome his voice in the choir."

"We'd all welcome him in the choir, whether he sang or not," grinned Sheila.

"Do you know him?" asked Betty, turning to Andrew, who happened to be sitting beside her as they all watched the show.

"Ramon? Yes, he's my boss. He's all right."

"Married?"

"I think so. He talks about his children."

"Oh!" huffed Betty. "The best ones are always taken."

"Actually," continued Andrew, his eyes glued to the stage, "I think the one to watch is Michael, the singer about to take centre stage now."

They all followed his gaze to watch as the tall, good-looking young man, surrounded by a whole company of other performers, launched into an upbeat song.

"Hmm," mused Betty. "Married?"

"No, Michael's not married."

Andrew sat back in his seat and smiled to himself in the darkened room.

CHAPTER 9

⮞ HONFLEUR ⮜

*Do not be afraid, for we have God as our guide and
helper. God will guide as God pleases.*

St Brendan

"*I*'m going to say this now in case I forget to say it
later," said Jill, grasping the handle of the cabin
door as she and Rob were about to leave. "I'm
really glad you're coming to Honfleur today."

"I remember being here on a school trip years ago," replied
Rob. "It's a nice old town."

"I'm sure it is," replied Jill, turning to look at her husband.
"Honestly, though, I don't really care where we're going. I'm
just glad you've decided to be with me today."

"Last day. Better make the most of it."

"And when we get back home again?" she asked softly.
"We've done a lot of talking this week. We've moved on,
haven't we? Learned a lot about each other."

He moved towards her, touching his forehead to hers. "I
think so."

"Will it last, do you think, when we get back home?"

"That's up to us, isn't it?"

"It's certainly what I'd like. Being close to you again has
meant so much to me."

"We'll have to work at it. Stop taking each other for granted."

His lips touched hers for a few lingering seconds before he stood back with a chuckle. "And that old dressing gown of yours has got to go! Agreed?"

"Definitely!" she laughed, and the two of them picked up their bags and headed off to where the coaches were waiting.

***

Hearing the quiet knock, Claire opened the cabin door to beckon Val inside.

"Come in. Neil's downstairs talking to the doctor now. They're sorting out the paperwork for Harry so that everything's ready for when we dock tomorrow."

"And you?" asked Val gently. "How are you holding up?"

"It's been a shock. Harry's been so much more than just an uncle to me. He felt like my grandad really – always there, always sharing adventures, ready with a plaster, a hug or a silly story to make me feel better. I wonder if I'd ever have become a gardener if it weren't for Harry sharing with me his own passion for growing things."

Putting an arm around Claire's shoulders, Val led the distraught young woman over so they could both sit on the bed.

"I'm going to miss him so much."

Val nodded, saying nothing.

"You're a nurse. You're used to this. But I've never seen a dead body before."

Claire was very still for a while before suddenly turning to look at Val. "Can I show you something?"

"Of course."

Claire leaned over to pull open her bedside drawer. With great care, she drew out a folded piece of paper tissue.

"When we were in Tresco, Harry was really excited because he'd been there with his wife Rose years ago, and he remembered quite a lot of places and views he'd shared with her. Then, towards the end of our walk round the gardens, we came across a huge old rose bush, and it almost moved him to tears. It was covered in beautiful golden flowers, and yellow roses had always been her favourite. He remembered that when they'd been there together, she'd said it was the loveliest thing she'd ever seen."

With trembling fingers, Claire opened up the tissue to reveal a single golden petal.

Val smiled. "Did you bring a petal back with you?"

"No, neither of us did."

Curiosity registered on Val's face.

"This petal fluttered down on me just as I discovered Harry yesterday. We were on a ship in the middle of a harbour, no bushes of any kind nearby – and this came out of nowhere."

"And you think…?"

"I think Harry's with his love, his Rose. And I think this is their way of letting us know."

***

A row of coaches waited on the quayside at Honfleur to take passengers on a variety of tours, including *Monet's House and Gardens*, *The Norman City of Bayeux* and *The Spirit of Normandy*. Alongside them stood a smart black people-carrier that had been adapted with ramps so that a wheelchair could be pushed up into it. Pete was supervising Arthur's safe placing in the back of the vehicle, while Callum sat in the front passenger seat playing a game on his mobile phone.

"So, where exactly are you taking us?" Pete asked as Bertrand, the driver, secured the back door. Pete had booked Bertrand through a local company specializing in private trips to the Normandy beaches. There were always plenty of people who wanted to visit the landing area for thousands of Allied troops on D-Day, 6th June 1944.

"We'll head for Ouistreham. It's about an hour's drive

away from Honfleur," Bertrand replied in what was thankfully excellent English. "On D-Day, the eight-kilometre stretch of coastline from Ouistreham to Saint-Aubin-sur-Mer was given the code name of Sword Beach. You said your father was with the 3rd Infantry Division? About twenty-eight thousand men from the 3rd landed on the most eastern point of Sword Beach, between Ouistreham and La Brèche d'Hermanville. We'll start there, and see if we can find exactly what he's looking for."

Arthur was surprisingly quiet on the journey.

"You all right, Dad?" asked Pete.

"Seventy years," said the old man, gazing out of the window. "It's a different world now, a peaceful world. I remember this land at war."

"It's not easy to imagine the past when we're travelling on main roads like this," said Bertrand. "But these modern roads will help us to get you there as quickly as possible so that you have plenty of time to look around. Do you see the sign up ahead?"

Arthur squinted to read the lettering, then exclaimed, "Caen!"

"You remember that name," smiled Bertrand.

"That was our mission," recalled Arthur. "To take control of the beach and the town of Ouistreham and move inland to capture Caen and Carpiquet airfield."

"And, of course, you know the famous landmark at Caen?"

"Pegasus Bridge. It was over the canal between Caen and Ouistreham. The airborne boys had done their stuff before our division got there."

"I've seen that film," interrupted Callum, suddenly lifting his head from his mobile phone game to join the conversation.

"That was *The Longest Day*," said Pete. "John Wayne, Robert Mitchum and Henry Fonda: all-American heroes winning the war single-handedly!"

"It was a real-life triumph though," said Bertrand. "In the dead of night, it took six gliders, less than two hundred men and about twenty minutes to take the enemy by surprise. They claimed the bridge in preparation for thousands of troops who were already making their way across the Channel, heading for the beaches on this coastline. Did you know the original bridge is no longer there, Arthur?"

"They've put it in a museum."

"They have. It's only a short detour. Would you like to see it?"

"No. I never got there. I didn't see it then. I've no need to see it now."

Bertrand nodded. Although Pete was full of questions, which Bertrand endeavoured to answer, Arthur was lost in his own memories as they travelled on. Eventually Bertrand pointed out a sign indicating that they were entering the town of Ouistreham. Arthur stared earnestly out of the window as the car wove its way through the streets, until at last they emerged onto a wide, grassy area with a huge expanse of white sand and the sea spread out ahead of them.

"Is this it, Dad?" asked Pete with excitement in his voice. He noticed that Arthur's hands were trembling.

"It's OK," said Bertrand. "We'll take this slowly. If you like, Arthur, we can take a stroll along the path here?"

Arthur nodded, plainly too emotional to reply.

Within minutes, Bertrand had expertly manoeuvred the wheelchair out of the car, and the group stood for a moment taking in the scene.

"What's that?" asked Arthur, his eyes fixed on a huge flame-shaped structure.

"That's the Kieffer Flame Monument, a memorial in honour of the one hundred and seventy-seven Free French Commandos who fought here that day."

Arthur's gaze misted over, picturing past rather than present scenes. "They wore green berets. We all respected them. Philippe Kieffer: wasn't that his name?"

"You're right," agreed Bertrand. "He was a sailor fighting for the French Free Forces because, like so many other brave French people, he would never surrender to German occupation. He joined the British Navy and then was so impressed with the Commandos, he asked to be allowed to set up a similar unit of Free French fighters. The training he and his unit went through was brutal, but they excelled to the point that British officers would salute anyone wearing the green beret because that meant they were tough enough to be a member of Kieffer's Commandos."

"They were the first ones to set foot on the beach here," recalled Arthur. "They led the way. Took a lot of casualties."

"Kieffer himself was wounded twice that day, but they fought on to meet up with the British paratroopers at Pegasus Bridge."

Arthur looked intently at the peaceful beach ahead of him. "This takes me back – but I don't think it was here."

"Neither do I," agreed Bertrand. "From what you've described, I think we need to go a little further west."

It was a short drive down the coast road to where Bertrand drew the car to a halt. Arthur's body tensed as his chair was pulled out and he was able to look around.

"Recognize anything?"

The old man nodded slowly.

"Come!"

They pushed the chair down the path for a while before Bertrand indicated that they needed to take Arthur down onto the beach. With the three men lifting the wheels off the ground, it took very little effort to carry him across the sand until, not far from the sea line, they turned his chair around to look back towards the land.

Arthur gasped. "That's it!"

"The monastery has not been used for many years now," said Bertrand quietly. "The monks left long ago and the building has fallen into disrepair."

"I was there…" breathed Arthur. "They saved my life."

"How?" demanded Callum. "Were you wounded, Grandad?"

"They called it the Longest Day," began Arthur, "but honestly it had been the longest week. We'd been waiting near

Shoreham, on the south coast, for days, expecting the order to come any time. At first they told us D-Day would be the 5th June, but they hadn't reckoned on the British weather – it was as foul as it could be. They loaded us all on the landing crafts anyway, and we waited there all day, packed like sardines, in pouring rain and high winds. We didn't have much in the way of rations, but we hardly wanted it. I was sick as a dog. Everyone was – and we hadn't even left the shore! The worst thing was having time to think. We didn't really know what we were going to meet over here. I thought I might die. I was twenty years old, and I really thought I was going to die.

"The waiting was agony. When the order finally came, we were too exhausted to care what happened at the other end, just as long as we were doing something. So we set sail in this huge armada of landing craft and warships, thousands and thousands of us, sailing through the night. The sea was really rough, high enough to knock us off our feet when it crashed over the sides of the craft, as if we weren't already soaked enough from the belting rain. I remember someone praying out loud. The Lord's Prayer – *Our Father who art in heaven, hallowed be thy name.* We all joined in, even the ones I knew would never call themselves Christians. It was as if that prayer was our souls calling out for help, whoever we were, whatever we did or didn't believe.

"And then, about seven in the morning, we saw this bit of coastline looming up ahead. The noise was deafening. There were other landing craft on the beach ahead of us, and the Germans were shelling them without mercy. Those lads were falling where they stood, with their comrades running on without them. They told us not to stop. Whatever happened to people around us, we had to keep going and not look back."

Arthur rubbed his face with his hand, as if to clear his vision of those long-ago days.

"As the front of our boat was lowered, one landing craft ahead of us took a direct hit and bodies tumbled out into the sea. And then the German guns took aim at us, and about half a dozen men at the front of our boat fell where they were standing. They were my mates. I'd trained with them, and they were dead before they'd even jumped in the water.

"And then we were all running to the front, stepping over their bodies, jumping down and wading towards the shore. Shells were exploding all round us and I remember just focusing on my feet and splashing on, not daring to look up at whatever was ahead. And then I reached the sand and just ran. I ran and ran until my lungs ached. I ran up the beach and was almost there when it happened. I didn't realize it was machine-gun fire till my legs collapsed under me. I dropped like a stone, with a searing pain in my thigh, the carnage of hell all around me.

"I don't know how long I lay there. Hundreds of men ran past me. Some fell. Some seemed to be getting through. I knew no one would stop for me, though. I was on my own.

"It took a while for me to realize it was just my leg that had taken a hit. There was a huge hole below my hip and I was lying in a pool of blood. So I dragged myself inch by inch up this beach, leaving a trail of blood behind me. Slowly, so slowly, I was almost fainting with the pain as I used my elbows to drag myself along. I didn't know where I was heading, because all I could see was smoke and feet and bodies and confusion. Then I looked up and I saw that."

Arthur's eyes narrowed as he gazed towards the old monastery building.

"Would you believe it! That little iron gate is still there. That's what I made for. There's a pebble path through it and I remember the agony as I dragged myself over the stones to get to the building. I thought it might give me some sort of cover. I had no idea, though. It could have been full of Germans. I was beyond caring.

"I'm not quite sure what happened then. I might have blacked out. I've got a hazy memory of being lifted up, faces and voices and hands on me – and then silence. When I came to, I was in a long room, lying on one of about ten bunks lined up along the wall. All the bunks had soldiers in them, looking as bad as I felt."

"So was it a hospital?" asked Pete.

"No, but when the monks found themselves in the middle of a battlefield, they just did what they could to comfort the wounded, whoever they were."

"What do you mean? Whose side were they on?"

"The side of God and mankind. Apparently as the Allies were falling through the doors of their monastery on the beach side, the Germans they'd been helping were climbing out of the windows on the other. Some were too ill to leave, though, like the man in the bunk next to me. I could see he was badly wounded."

"He was German?"

"Yes. Most of them in that room were."

"But they could have killed you!" exclaimed Callum.

"By then the killing was over for all of us. We were beyond that. We were just young boys caught up in our countries' war, doing our duty – and almost dying for it. The man two bunks along from me did die that afternoon. He was German, and I felt nothing but compassion. He was calling for his mother…" Arthur's voice faltered then, his eyes glassy, his breathing heavy and laboured.

"Steady, Dad," soothed Pete. "Rest a bit."

Visibly pulling himself together, Arthur touched Pete's hand, which was resting on his shoulder, and continued.

"I was there for ten days before the regiment realized where I was. They were organizing transport for hundreds of wounded soldiers, and I was less important because at least I was being cared for. I didn't realize how much blood I'd lost, but that very nearly cost me my life. If the monks hadn't picked me up and stemmed the bleeding, none of us would be here today."

"How bad was your wound?" asked Callum.

"There was a bullet lodged in an awkward position right up near my hip. It was too delicate an operation for the monks to try, even with the help of the local doctor from Hermanville, who was a wonderful man. So I stayed there while I got my strength back and waited for transport to take me home."

"What about the Germans there with you? Didn't they arrest them as prisoners of war?" the young man demanded.

Arthur smiled. "There were no enemies in that room. We shared too much in common to feel anything but fellowship. Those monks treated us all as equals, because that's what we were."

"They should have shot them," retorted Callum. "It was a war. Look at how many Allied lives they'd taken that day – *your* comrades, Grandad. They showed no mercy – and neither should you have."

Arthur sighed as he looked at Callum. "If you can say that, it's clear you've got a very limited view of war. Unfortunately that's not something you'll learn just because I've told you. It's a lesson you only learn through experience. But to get that, I fear you may not live long enough to value it."

"So what about that man in the bed next to you?" asked Pete. "Did he get better too?"

"When I first came round, I heard them saying they thought he could die any time. I kept staring across at him, thinking that it could have been me. He was wearing a crucifix, I remember, very similar to mine. I found myself just *willing* him to live. Whenever the monks came to tend to his wounds and help him take a sip of water, they would pray for him and I prayed with them too. We'd been through hell, all of us, and I wanted that connection with God from the very depths of me. All those years of going to church meant nothing until I called out to God on this beach and in that monastery, and my prayers were heard. I was alive – and more than anything, I wanted that young man, who looked so like me, to live too.

"And he did. On the third day, his fever had gone and he opened his eyes properly for the first time. He looked over towards me and sort of smiled – and do you know, I could have hugged him."

Arthur stopped for a moment to compose himself.

"We spent another week together before I left, and in the whole of my life before and since, that was the deepest, most meaningful friendship I have ever known."

"How did you talk to each other," asked Pete, "if he was German and you were English?"

"He'd got some English relatives and had been over to stay with them a couple of times. He spoke well enough for us to understand each other. His family had their own farm in Lower Saxony, and as he was the only son, he would have taken it over if the war hadn't got in the way."

"So what did you talk about?"

"Our families, our homes, how much we hated the war that had pitted us against each other, when in fact we felt like kindred spirits divided by nationality rather than nature. We had hour after hour to do nothing but talk. By the time I left, I didn't just like him, I loved him – and I hated my part in the injuries he'd sustained from a bullet I might have shot. The bond between us was so strong that it shaped my life ever – a beacon of inspiration that's never left me."

"Is he still alive?"

Arthur smiled. "I had a letter from one of the monks here a few weeks after I'd arrived at the sanatorium in Nottingham to recover from my operation. He never made it home. His internal injuries were too severe. He died a few days after I left.

"His memory lives on, though," Arthur went on, looking up at his son. "After the war, when I got back home to Derby, I took over Dad's hardware shop. Over the years I built up the business, so eventually I had to take on a secretary. That was your mum, of course. Beryl had lost her fiancé in the war, and it took us a while to work out we'd be good together. We had a little daughter, but she died after three days. We'd been married for five years by then, and as time went on we thought we could never have any more children. And then, miracle of miracles, you came along. You were perfect and we loved you so much, the most unexpected blessing from God. I knew life would never be the same after that. I found myself thinking again about that other man who'd made such an impact on my life. His name was Pieter – and Pete, you were named after him."

* * *

"Come in a bit closer, everyone," called Pam as the gospel choir members tried to arrange themselves into a shape that worked in the space available. The open-air deck outside the buffet restaurant had been specially cleared for the "Praise Away" service. "Try not to leave any gaps between you – don't be shy!"

"Where would you like Mum?" asked Julia, wheeling the chair up to the performance area.

"How about over there at the side, Ida?" smiled Pam. "Would that be OK for you?"

"I think that's a yes," grinned Julia, as Ida's normally vacant expression brightened just a little.

At that moment Pete arrived, pushing Arthur in his chair.

"I hope you're not too tired for this, Dad. You've had a long day."

"I've never felt better. It's been the most wonderful day and I'm really looking forward to singing tonight. This is an act of worship, and I've got a lot to thank God for."

"Right!" shouted Pam over the happy chaos as the choir shuffled into place. "Take a look at the rows of seats down either side of the deck. Those are for you, so when the choir's invited up to sing right at the end, you can all walk smartly into the places where you're standing now. Shall we just rehearse that? Follow each other off to the seats in the order you stand when you sing, and then when you come back to perform, you should be able to lead straight to your places again. That's the theory, anyway."

Pam caught Richard's eye as he was handing out worship sheets to the passengers who were already coming up to find a good place to sit for the service. They chuckled at each other over the heads of the choir members as they tussled over who should sit where. Minutes later, though, with seats selected and after a successful run-through of getting to their right positions on stage, the choir members settled down and waited for the service to begin.

"*There* you are," exclaimed Betty, sliding into a spare seat next to Jill. "I haven't seen you for a proper natter for ages. How are you getting on with that husband of yours?"

Jill laughed. "I think you, Sheila and Marion ought to set up business as relationship counsellors. Your make-over on me that night certainly had his eyes out on stalks."

"And now he won't let you out of his sight?"

"Yes, that has been a bit of a surprise," Jill grinned. "But better than that, we've done a lot of talking, which is probably what we needed most of all. Being on this cruise has been perfect, away from all the things at home which have been getting both of us down. We've not bothered with any organized trips since that evening. We've just wandered out from the ship and found a nice view or a cosy café where we could sit and talk. We got out of the habit of doing things like that years ago. We'd forgotten how much we enjoy it."

"And has it helped? What have you talked about?"

"Well, there was me thinking he loved his work and wanted to spend as much time there as possible just to get away from me. But when he eventually opened up about his job, it became clear how much it's worrying him. He's had a new boss for quite a while now, and they don't see eye to eye at all. Rob knows he's being passed over for younger, more ambitious people who've only been there five minutes, and that makes him feel as if his years of experience aren't valued at all. He was looking at the prospect of having to work there until he retired, and was getting really depressed about it. He saw himself as the main breadwinner, responsible for all our family bills, and couldn't see a way out.

"So he's been burying his sorrows down the pub each night

after work, along with a bunch of other disgruntled employees, and that's made him feel even worse. Then he would come home to find me looking very comfortable and homely. He ended up feeling that I was living very nicely, thank you, while he was burdened with having to pay for it all."

"But he's the one who stopped you having a career of your own."

"That's male pride for you. He's quite old-fashioned about not wanting his wife to work, because it would suggest he's not a good provider, whereas I'd love to use my brain and skills, not just for my own sense of fulfilment, but also because I'd like to earn a bit of extra money for *us*!"

"So now you both know this, where does that leave you?"

"Well, Rob's going to leave – not me, but that job he hates. We've decided to work together and set up our own business."

"Wow! What have you got in mind?"

"We're still thinking it through and we'll have to do a lot of research when we get back home. We thought we'd look for a business franchise we can work on together. We've got a bit of a nest egg put by for when we retire, but it'll do more good for us if we invest rather than just save it. We're both hard workers. I can be very creative when I put my mind to it, and he's always been great with accounts and paperwork. Between us, we reckon, we've got the combination of skills we'd need in business. Maybe we'll take on a shop, or we'll find a product to market and sell. It's early days, but we're both so excited about it."

"That sounds really enterprising," beamed Betty. "And what's more, you've got your husband back. It's easy to see you still love him as much as ever."

"I do. We'd got into a rut where our lives were running on parallel lines, not touching, each of us doing our own thing. We intend to put that right from now on. When we think about what we nearly threw away…"

"Good evening, everyone!" greeted Bishop Paul, bringing their conversation to an abrupt halt as he stood at the mike to introduce the service. "Well, what a wonderful backdrop we have for our 'Praise Away' this evening: the charming old town of Honfleur, the last of the many places we've visited together in recent days. Have you enjoyed the cruise?"

A cheer went up around the crowd.

"And have you felt inspired by it?"

That brought even louder agreement from the crowd.

"Well, I'm glad to hear that. We've travelled as pilgrims together, and I wonder if you, like me, feel you've made some very special friendships here that you will cherish long after *The Pilgrim* has docked at Tilbury tomorrow."

Again, there was enthusiasm from the crowd.

"Talking of friends, one very dear friend was lost to us yesterday. Many of you will have met Harry Holloway, a much-loved family member of Reverend Neil and his wife Claire. Sadly, Harry died yesterday afternoon – peacefully in his sleep. Our prayers and thoughts are with all those who love and miss him, and we ask for God's blessing on them. Harry was a man of great faith, and although he will be missed here by so many, there is comfort in knowing he is with the God he's always trusted, worshipped and loved. Let's bow our heads in prayer for a minute to remember Harry."

Standing with his arm around Iris, who looked pale and drawn, Neil drew her closer just as Claire slipped her hand into his. Together they stood in silence, knowing that Harry had planned to be standing beside them for this farewell service.

"I know you're here, Uncle Harry," breathed Claire to herself. "I hope you know we miss you and how much love there is for you here. I'm trying to remember what you said about joy. I'm not quite there yet, but I will be…"

It was during the singing of the first hymn that everyone on deck realized that the big ship was starting to move. Smoothly, with regal dignity, *The Pilgrim* pulled away from her berth, turning from the picturesque harbour of Honfleur and out to sea.

As the hymn ended, Sister Maureen stood up to take her place at the microphone.

"This is a reading from Mark's Gospel, chapter 4, verses 35 to 41," she said, finding her place in the Bible. "As we sail out to sea this evening, it seems appropriate to remember how when Jesus was in a boat, he calmed the waters in the face of a storm.

"That day when evening came, he said to his disciples, 'Let us go over to the other side.' Leaving the crowd behind, they took him along, just as he was, in the boat. There were also other boats with him. A furious squall came up, and the waves broke over the boat, so that it was nearly swamped. Jesus was in the stern, sleeping on a cushion. The disciples woke him and said to him, 'Teacher, don't you care if we drown?'

"He got up, rebuked the wind and said to the waves, 'Quiet! Be still!' Then the wind died down and it was completely calm.

"He said to his disciples, 'Why are you so afraid? Do you still have no faith?'

"They were terrified and asked each other, 'Who is this? Even the wind and the waves obey him!'"

"Thank you," said the bishop, taking the mike again. "There's good advice and reassurance in the story Sister Maureen has just read to us. Here we all are, sailing on a very luxurious boat for the shores of home. I wonder how you're feeling now as you think about going back to take up the reins of your usual life. Does that fill you with anticipation and pleasure? Or is there part of you that wishes you could stay in this cosseted, comfortable bubble for longer, where everything is organized and done for us, and all we have to do is enjoy it all?

"The fact is that normal, daily life is hard. I don't believe anyone is immune to troubles and worries. That's the human experience – that God-given mixture of blessings and gifts on the one hand, and the limitations and concerns we all recognize on the other, like illness, relationship problems, money, work, disability, loneliness, exhaustion. The list is long and I bet, from your own experience, you could add other examples to make it even longer.

"That's how life is for us today, and it was probably a very similar story for the disciples two thousand years ago. They'd given up their usual way of life to follow Jesus when he asked them. They'd each come to Christ with a glad heart. But can you imagine how many practical problems that decision probably caused them? And then, to top it all, they'd set out across the Sea of Galilee when everything seemed settled and calm, only to run into a sudden violent storm that had them fearing for their lives. Can you think how you'd have felt if you'd been one of them, panicking and terrified, when the man who'd organized the trip appeared completely uninterested, sleeping peacefully through it all?

"But when they woke Jesus, afraid they were about to drown, he couldn't understand why they were so worried. He simply got to his feet, ordered the storm to subside, then wondered aloud why they had so little faith in him, and in God's loving protection of them.

"But aren't we all a bit like those disciples? Don't we get ourselves in a mess of worry and doubt as we try to sort out our problems by ourselves? Yet through the promise of Christ living here with us on earth, we know that God is with us always, especially in the most harrowing of times. He has promised that if we call out to him in prayer, he will listen. Over my years as a bishop, I have so often been moved beyond words at the times I've seen prayers being answered in the most wonderful way – not always as we expect it, but according to God's will.

"So that's the thought I would like you to take home with you when we part company in the morning. Whatever you are going back to, whatever challenges or concerns await you in your everyday life, don't forget God's promise to be with us. Our great God who made the heavens and the earth, the sea and the skies, also created each and every one of us, unique and perfect. He *knows* us. He's made an eternal commitment to us. Let's never cease thanking him and praising his holy name."

At that point, Brian started playing the introduction to one of the most loved and familiar of all hymns, the poignancy of its words touching chords in the souls of the worshippers as they sailed together towards the sun-streaked horizon.

Dear Lord and Father of mankind,
forgive our foolish ways;
reclothe us in our rightful mind,
in purer lives thy service find,
in deeper reverence, praise,
in deeper reverence, praise.

In simple trust like theirs who heard,
beside the Syrian sea,
the gracious calling of the Lord,
let us, like them, without a word,
rise up and follow thee,
rise up and follow thee.

O sabbath rest by Galilee!
O calm of hills above,
where Jesus knelt to share with thee
the silence of eternity,
interpreted by love,
interpreted by love!

Drop thy still dews of quietness,
till all our strivings cease;
take from our souls the strain and stress,
and let our ordered lives confess
the beauty of thy peace,
the beauty of thy peace.

Breathe through the heats of our desire
thy coolness and thy balm;
let sense be dumb, let flesh retire;
speak through the earthquake, wind and fire,
O still, small voice of calm,
O still, small voice of calm!

By the time the last verse had finished, the gospel choir members had quietly risen to take their places across the back of the performance area, poised to start the moment the bishop's introduction had finished. Together, Clifford and Andrew struck up the opening bars of their performance.

If any of them were nervous, it certainly didn't show as they sang their hearts out, swaying, clapping and marching their way through the selection of old gospel favourites. The audience loved every moment, even when Raymond very loudly sang not just the wrong words, but the wrong song without noticing at all what the others were doing around him! And at the end, they finished to rapturous applause and even a standing ovation from some members of the audience who enthusiastically showed how much they'd enjoyed every minute.

Several people mentioned later that they'd found their eyes drawn to one particular lady at the front, whose performance took their breath away. Ida, sitting comfortably in her wheelchair, had come to life with the music. She might have been mouthing words that didn't fit and weren't right, but that hardly mattered when her usually expressionless face was a picture of sublime concentration, as her hands swayed in her lap and her feet attempted to tap to the rhythm.

As the gathering was starting to disperse, Julia was hugging her mother warmly just as Paul came over, plainly delighted at the reaction to Ida's performance in the choir.

"You will come dancing this evening, won't you?" he asked Julia, touching her arm.

"Well, I have got two suitcases to pack…"

"Yes, you have, but this is your last night. It may not be professional for me to say so, but I really want to dance with you – and not just on this trip."

Julia looked at him quizzically. "But aren't you at sea for months at a time?"

"I'm booked on the next cruise for this coming fortnight, starting tomorrow afternoon, but after that they'll send me dates, and I can choose whether I want to do them or not."

"This might be a delicate question, but isn't this your job? Surely you don't want to turn work down?"

"The cruise itself is the payment. They just offer me the opportunity to travel the world with all expenses paid, and in return I spend my evenings dancing with any lady who'd like a partner for a spot of ballroom dancing."

"And you're offering to dance with me…?"

"Not as a dance host. I hope you feel our friendship is already beyond that. I'd like to dance with you as my friend, as someone I'd like the opportunity to get to know better as time goes on."

"Oh!" The surprise that registered on Julia's face was mixed with obvious interest. "But – where do you live?"

"Just outside St Albans, about ten miles away from where you work in Welwyn Garden City."

"Really?" she smiled.

"Really," he stated with a smile to match hers.

"Well," she said, taking hold of the handles on Ida's wheelchair, "I'd better go and pack if I'm going dancing this evening…"

***

As it was the last night on board, there was no big production by the ship's entertainers. It was assumed that people would mostly be packing their bags ready for collection later that evening. The passengers would be reunited with their luggage on the dockside as they left *The Pilgrim* next morning at the end of their holiday.

"We're all going up for a last dance," announced Betty, pushing back her chair. "Are you two coming?"

The smile Carole and Garry shared in reply to her question could only be described as smug.

"Actually, we're meeting the captain for a nightcap. Such an interesting man! We've become rather good friends."

"We're joining you, Betty," said Mark, as he helped Deirdre up from her seat.

"I'm bringing my camera," cried Barbara, "and John will take some video too. Before we part company in the morning, we must all put our diaries together to sort out a time for our holiday photos evening."

"Can I come?" beamed Raymond. "Except I'd need a lift all the way to Derbyshire. Perhaps Peter and Val will go? They've been up to stay with Neil and Claire before. Oh…"

His face fell as he mentioned their names. "Poor Neil and Claire. I always liked Harry. I liked him a lot."

"We all did." Sylvia put a comforting hand on Raymond's arm. "Come on, let's go up to the lounge and get as much dancing in as possible before we all collapse in a heap."

The dance floor was already filling up by the time they got there. The Pilgrim Band was in full swing, belting out a well-known pop song that worked for ballroom buffs as a quickstep, while others did their own thing, as if they were back in their disco days.

"Look!" Brian nudged Sylvia later, directing her attention to Sister Maureen, who was waving her arms in the air as she danced and sang along to "Show Me the Way to Amarillo."

"I love her," laughed Sylvia. "She's my type of woman."

"And you're mine," grinned Brian. "Come on, let's show Sister Maureen how it's done."

Paul was already on the dance floor, partnering one of the Catholic mothers, when Julia wheeled Ida into a space at the corner of the floor. From there they could watch together, joining in with the applause when each number came to an end.

As the floor cleared, the band changed the tempo to a slow rumba, and several couples took to their feet again, their steps smooth and flowing. Paul looked thoughtful for a moment before making his way over to kneel directly in front of Ida's wheelchair.

"Ida," he said very clearly, making sure his face was level

with hers so that he could look straight into her eyes. "Would you care to dance?"

Julia took a sharp breath, wondering what on earth he could be thinking – until she looked down at her mother's face. There was a definite spark there, as if she was trying to make sense of what he'd asked. Then, slowly and deliberately, Ida started to slide her hands along the arms of the wheelchair. Shocked at her mother's reaction, Julia caught Paul's eye as they both moved to help Ida up, watching as she concentrated on making sure her feet were steady before she finally lifted herself up from the seat inch by inch.

And her partner was waiting! Paul slipped his arm around Ida's waist to steady her before lifting her right hand into a traditional ballroom dance hold. Hesitantly at first, but gaining in confidence and momentum, the two of them swayed from side to side to the rumba rhythm. Julia looked on, gulping for breath as tears clouded her eyes. Her mother was dancing! She'd always loved to dance. Somewhere in the depths of that frail body in which her muddled mind and memory were trapped and buried, her beloved mother was still there.

The music lasted for several magical minutes before it drew to a graceful end. The silence that followed was suddenly filled by warm applause from the small crowd around them, astonished and touched by what they'd just seen. Ida stiffened in Paul's arms, and he watched as the light of recognition seemed to dim from her face.

Helped by Julia, he guided Ida back into her seat, kissing her cheek gently as he whispered in her ear, "Thank you, Ida. I enjoyed that very much."

He looked up to find Julia staring at him, her lips trembling, tears brimming in her eyes. He stretched out his hand towards her, and without a word she stepped into his arms, resting her head on his shoulder as the two of them clung together.

"Do you see that?" asked Betty, drawing Marion's attention to Paul and Julia's embrace. "Looks like all the nice girls love a sailor!"

"Aah," smiled Marion, following Betty's gaze. "Paul's not a sailor. He's a money man in the City of London – or at least he was. He took early retirement some years back when his wife became ill. I had a long chat with him the other evening. He admits he's become very isolated and lonely since she died, especially now his son and daughter have families of their own. He took up dancing as a hobby, then ended up meeting someone who suggested he might like to be a dance host. He says it's got him out of the house and back into the world again. Apparently his working life involved long hours and constant pressure, and that meant he and his wife didn't travel as much as they'd have liked."

"Well, it looks like he's come home," said Betty softly. "Julia's a lovely person, and quite lonely herself, I think. If he's Fred, I've a feeling he might just have found his Ginger…"

CHAPTER 10

⇒ TILBURY ⇐

*The extent of your prayers should be
until tears come.*

St Columba

"Right, I'm ready!" Claire zipped up her handbag as she spoke, watching Neil open and shut every drawer and cupboard to check they'd left nothing behind.

"That's it then. The end of our cruise."

Claire stepped across to put her arms around his waist. "Not finishing the way we hoped. I still can't believe Harry isn't with us."

"I know," he soothed, kissing her hair. "We've just got to get through today. It isn't going to be easy."

"Iris will be OK with Peter and Val, won't she?" asked Claire. "It's going to hit her hard, travelling back to Dunbridge without Harry."

"I don't think she could be in better hands."

"Will the undertakers organize everything? Sort out transport and paperwork and stuff? I hope it won't take too long."

"I've known Mr Whalley ever since I first went to Dunbridge as a curate. He couldn't be more understanding, because he knew and liked Harry too. He's assured me Harry'll be travelling home to Dunbridge the very moment he's told the legalities are complete and they're allowed to collect him."

Claire shuddered and Neil held her tighter.

"I wish we didn't have to face that long coach journey back to Derbyshire this morning," Claire sighed, her face nuzzled up against his chest. "Everyone else on the coach will be buzzing about what a wonderful holiday they've had, and that's great, but…"

"… it's not quite the same for us now," finished Neil. "Mind you, this cruise *has* been wonderful; better than I expected, really. So much more than just a nice nine-day holiday on a ship. I've felt a real sense of pilgrimage – not just with everyone else on board, but on a personal level too."

"I know what you mean. There have been some very special moments."

"A few of them in this cabin," said Neil softly. "I've grown very fond of our little room."

"Even the single beds?"

"Definitely. Perhaps we should take up that idea at home."

Claire pulled back in astonishment. "You mean, have single beds?"

"No, just one single bed. I rather liked all the cuddling up we had to do to fit both of us into a bed that narrow."

There was a wicked gleam in Claire's eye as she lifted her head to kiss him. "I like your thinking, Vicar – and can I just say how much I always enjoy your excellent bedside manner?"

***

"Clifford!" called Maureen Bragnall, waving frantically from the table at which she, Bill and Andrew were having breakfast. Standing at the coffee station, Clifford acknowledged her call, then brought his cup over to where they were sitting, and pulled up a chair.

"I'm so glad we saw you," enthused Maureen. "Before

we parted company, we just wanted to thank you for all the encouragement you've given Andrew."

"That's no trouble," replied Clifford, stirring sugar into his coffee. "He's a very able musician. His talent could take him far."

"Well, they've already asked him to extend his contract on *The Pilgrim*, haven't they, son?" beamed Bill.

"Yes," said Andrew, apparently concentrating on the bowl of cereal and fruit he was eating. Cliff understood the young man's reticence. The last time they had spoken with any privacy was the afternoon he had realized the depth of Andrew's friendship with Michael.

"Well, it seems you have some interesting choices ahead of you, Andrew," replied Cliff smoothly. "I certainly wish you well, whatever you decide. And I hope we can keep in touch. I've enjoyed getting to know you."

Andrew looked up then. "Actually, that would be good. Maybe we could swap contact details?"

Clifford pulled out his wallet from his back pocket, extracting a card, which he placed on the table in front of Andrew.

"Any time, feel free to call. I'm a good listener, if you ever want to chat over your options."

A small, relieved smile crossed Andrew's face. "Thank you. I *will* do that."

"My advice would always be to follow your heart," continued Clifford, his eyes locked with Andrew's. "This is your life, your time. The decisions you make must feel right for you."

"Thank you, Cliff, for everything." Andrew's reply was barely above a whisper as he studied the card. "I'll definitely be in touch. I've found our conversations during this trip extremely useful. Challenging, in some ways…"

"Always liked a challenge, haven't you, Andrew?" enthused Maureen.

"And are you two leaving the ship this morning?" asked Clifford.

"Sadly, yes. It's gone all too fast," she sighed. "We're going to miss Andrew so much when we get home."

"It's been good to see where he's working, though," added Bill. "At least we know he's being well looked after, and he has nice friends."

"Sharon is *so* nice." Maureen looked proudly at Andrew as she spoke. "We've told her she's always welcome at our house any time. As *you* are, Clifford. It was such an honour to see you accompanying Rhydian the other evening. Carole was telling us about all the stars you've worked with."

"Was she?" smiled Clifford.

"And then to see you and Andrew working together during the 'Songs of Praise' and with the gospel choir yesterday. It was such a privilege for Andrew; such a privilege!"

"Well," said Clifford, downing the last mouthful of coffee, "our coach awaits. My regards to you all."

"May I?" asked Maureen coquettishly, holding her arms out to him as she leapt to her feet. Catching Andrew's eye over her shoulder, Clifford succumbed to her smothering embrace.

"Thank you so much, dear lady," he managed when he was finally released. "Bon voyage to you all!"

And stepping smartly out of arm's length in case Bill wanted a hug too, Clifford walked quickly away.

* * *

Brad was sitting at his desk when Neil popped his head around the surgery door.

"Come in, Neil. I was hoping I'd see you before you left. How are you?"

"Well," sighed Neil, taking a seat, "it's been tough. Long before we became family, Harry was the first friend I met in Dunbridge, and my neighbour too. He was incredibly kind and patient with me when I was an extremely green curate, and over the years he's become very dear to me. Then, of course, I married his great-niece, and he officially became the relative I'd always felt he was anyway."

"I imagine this has hit Claire particularly hard."

"Oh, yes. She never remembered her real father, so although Harry was a generation older, he's always been a father figure to her. They had a lot in common. Their reactions were so similar sometimes, they were like peas in a pod. She's struggling to come to terms with losing him."

"And Iris? Were Harry and your mother an item?"

Neil smiled. "Not in the sense you mean, but they were the most wonderful companions. Their gardens back onto one another, and it's always been difficult to be sure where one home ends and the other starts. They ate together, went to church together, and enjoyed the same circle of friends and the social life that went with it."

"Will she move to be nearer you and Claire in Derbyshire now, do you think?"

"I hope not, because we have no idea how long we'll stay there. And she's settled in Dunbridge. It's a very friendly little town."

Brad smiled. "From the church members I've met on board, I can tell how fond they all are of you and your family. I'm sure they'll take good care of her."

A small silence followed before Neil spoke.

"And you? How are you getting on?"

"I think we're going to try again. I can see now that me being away travelling all the time has been very hard on her. She was dealing with her concerns about Chris on her own for so long. And I know I wasn't very receptive to listening to her worries, because thinking about him always felt too painful. Besides, I knew I couldn't do much to influence him when I was miles away from home, and that suited me fine. I opted out. I ran away, if I'm honest, and that was unfair to Joanne."

"What about all the guilt you've felt? That's plainly been a burden for you to bear."

"Yes, but the burden Joanne was carrying while she was trying to sort out Chris all on her own was much worse. I can see that now. I was here wallowing in self-pity, while she was having to cope with all the practical stuff with no support from me at all. I'm ashamed of the way I've treated her. I wouldn't blame her for walking out on me completely, because that's what I deserve."

"You did say before that you thought she'd be better off without you. How do you feel about that now?"

"That's probably still true. I've let her down so badly, what can I say? What could I ever do to make things right between us again? But Joanne's quite simply a remarkable woman. I'd forgotten how wonderful she is: how strong, how loyal to the family she loves. And she loves *me*, Neil! After all I've done, my complete failure as a father and a husband, she still loves me – and I intend to spend the rest of my life letting her know how much I love her."

"That's good to hear."

"It's not going to be easy; we both know that. There's been such emotional carnage in our family, we've got a lot of bridges to mend. But we love each other. We'll get through this. We will."

"I couldn't be more delighted for you."

"It's not just us. There's our daughter Livvy to consider as well. I know she could have done with more support from her dad, so I've a lot of making up to do there too."

Neil smiled. "I do wish you all well."

"I'll be leaving the ship, of course."

"Can you leave when you want to? What sort of contract do you have?"

"I've been with this cruise company quite a few years now. I had to tell them about Chris and what I was going through, and they were really understanding. I had a chat with my immediate boss yesterday, and we've agreed I can leave in a month, by which time they'll have organized a replacement doctor."

"So it's back to Dorchester for you?"

"I rather fancy general practice. They're always desperate for locums, so I can fill in with that until I find a surgery I'd like to join on a permanent basis."

Neil nodded thoughtfully. "We've shared our crossroads, you and I, haven't we? We've lost Harry. You've lost Chris. But this cruise has been challenging, changing, decisive and healing in so many ways."

"It has," agreed Brad. "We were well met in those sand dunes on Lindisfarne."

"It always was a special place." Neil pushed back his chair, holding out his hand to grip Brad's. "I wish you every blessing, Brad. God go with you always."

"And also with you, Neil. Also with you."

***

Iris was all packed and ready to go when Claire knocked on her door to collect her.

"Right. I'm ready to leave now."

Noting the brittle determination in Iris's voice, Claire peered at the dark circles under her mother-in-law's eyes, then stepped forward to put her arms around her. At first, Iris resisted, but almost immediately her body slumped, and Claire could feel the quiet sobs that shuddered through her.

They stood there for some minutes in shared grief and sorrow before Iris abruptly pulled back, roughly rubbing the tears from her cheeks. "I'm fine. Let's go. We should have breakfast before we leave."

"No one expects anything of you after this, Mum," said Claire softly. "You don't have to pretend you feel better than you do. Be gentle with yourself. Harry would want that."

"Harry's not here." Iris opened her bag, applying a quick coat of pale pink lipstick before a final check in the mirror.

Claire stayed rooted to the ground, uncertain what to say.

"Well, are you coming?" snapped Iris, stepping out into the corridor.

Full of concern, Claire sighed, picking up Iris's bag before hurrying to catch up with her as she disappeared around the corner.

***

Several familiar members of the ship's crew were lined up for a final farewell as, one by one, the passengers had their passes scanned for the last time. They emerged onto the dockside at Tilbury to an overcast day that threatened rain any moment.

"Good job I brought my pac-a-mac," commented Betty. "I can tell we're home. It's just about to start raining."

"It's been lovely, though," sighed Marion. "After all those gorgeous meals, our beds made, being cosseted and looked after, it's going to be hard getting back to four teenagers and a husband who has no idea how to use the washing machine and wouldn't know a vacuum cleaner if he tripped over one."

"John's gone to an away match with the football lads today," said Sheila. "He won't be back till after nine. He asked if I could have a casserole waiting for him."

"Back to the old routine for us all, then," moaned Betty.

"Not for me," interrupted Jill, who'd overheard their conversation. "The old routine is definitely out for me. I'm never going back there again. Never."

The girls squealed with delight and there were hugs all round.

"You're not allowed to give up the church choir though, Jill. Promise?"

"Of course not," agreed Jill. "My three best friends are in that choir. I wouldn't miss it for the world."

"Look!" cried Sheila. "Poor Neil and Claire. The hearse is leaving…"

All eyes turned towards the sleek dark car that was just pulling away from the dock. Neil drew both Iris and Claire to him, as Brig stood stiffly to attention nearby, his hand raised in salute to the old soldier. Silence fell among the members of Neil's two congregations. Just a week before, they'd met as strangers. Now they stood together as friends to watch as Harry was carried away to the mortuary, where he would rest until he was allowed to make his final journey home to Dunbridge.

"Clifford!" called Carole, as she and Garry supervised the storing of their two expensive cream leather cases in the hold of the coach, apparently oblivious to the sombre mood of everyone around her. Clifford pinned what he hoped was a sincere smile on his face before turning to acknowledge her.

"I just want to say," she continued, not waiting for him to reply, "that it has been a real pleasure to work with a professional like yourself. It's a rare treat nowadays to come across someone who shares the same high musical standards I adhere to myself."

Clifford nodded his head, saying nothing, because he couldn't for the life of him think of anything to say.

"I will be talking to Neil in due course. I think that with you and me at the helm, we should bring our two choirs together for a concert in Burntacre, followed by another in Dunbridge. I've already made a list of the musical items I think we should feature. I'll be in touch within the week to discuss my suggestion further."

"I shall look forward to it, dear lady. Goodbye now. I wish you a pleasant trip."

"I believe you're in charge, madam?" Steve, the driver who had brought the group down from Burntacre, appeared at Carole's elbow, his face as bored and irritated as ever. "We need to round everyone up. Can you *please* get on board? The M25's a nightmare at this time of day."

"That's us too," said Neil, looking down at Iris. "I love you, Mum. I wish we were able to come back with you for a few days, just to make sure you're OK."

"What nonsense!" snapped Iris. "I'll be perfectly all right. I'm used to living alone. Now, get on that coach and give me a ring the minute you're home. Understood?"

Claire stepped forward to hug her. "Understood," she whispered in Iris's ear. "Remember, be gentle with yourself. We love you."

"That coach'll go without you if you don't get a move on," warned Iris, stepping back from Claire's embrace. Allowing

Neil no more than a kiss on the cheek, Iris turned on her heel towards Peter and Val's car.

"Before you go, Neil..." Bishop Paul and Margaret appeared beside him. "I just wanted to say thank you for all you've contributed on this cruise. We're both sorry it has ended so sadly for you."

"Thank you, Bishop – you too, Margaret. It's been lovely to share this time together."

"Vicar, if you don't get on the coach this minute," Steve announced from his driver's seat, "you'll be walking back to Derbyshire."

With a flurry of goodbyes and waves, Neil almost made it up the steps before a cry stopped him in his tracks.

"Hold it there!"

Bustling towards him with the whole group of Catholic mothers not far behind, Sister Maureen arrived, panting and red-faced, throwing her arms around him until he was almost as breathless as she was.

"You need this," she announced, thrusting a small printed card into his hand. "You can't face grief and bereavement without remembering the strength and reassurance you'll find in the words of Julian of Norwich: 'All shall be well, and all manner of thing shall be well.' And all *shall* be well, my dear Neil, even if it doesn't feel that way right now. I pray that you and Claire will be blessed by these words."

"These words and *your* company," agreed Neil, hugging Sister Maureen tightly to him.

"I mean it, Vicar!" shouted Steve. "You're late and I'm leaving. I'm driving away now. Look! Put that nun down, say goodbye to the fan club and *get on board*!"

And with kisses blown into the air from Sister Maureen and the Catholic mothers, and more subdued loving waves and nods from their Dunbridge friends, Neil and Claire kept their noses to the window until *The Pilgrim* was out of sight.

***

It was gone seven when the phone rang in Iris's front room.

"Dunbridge 813293."

"We're home, Mum," said Neil. "We had to fight our way through a pile of post behind the front door, and it's taken me more than quarter of an hour to listen to all the messages on the answerphone – but we're home."

"I'm glad," replied Iris. "You two must be exhausted, and you always did need your sleep, Neil, even when you were a little boy. Leave all the letters and phone calls until tomorrow. Have a nice warm bath, make yourselves a hot cocoa and go to bed."

"We will, Mum," grinned Neil. "You too. You've been through a lot. Have you got any food in to make yourself some supper?"

"Cyn's been over and put a few bits in my fridge. She takes her churchwarden duties to an extreme, I must say."

"She cares a lot about you. Harry was a great friend of hers too. They'd known each other for years."

"Right, well, I must go," snapped Iris. "I want to catch up with *EastEnders*. Good night, Neil."

"Night, Mum. I'll ring in the morning. We love you."

But the line had already clicked dead.

Staring at the phone, Iris sat down heavily on the settee, hugging her knees tightly as she began to rock slowly backwards and forwards. The wail that came from her throat was the cry of an animal exhausted by pain and inconsolable grief. At last, spent and empty, she leaned back against the cushions, bleak desolation etched across her face.

CHAPTER 11

❧ DUNBRIDGE ❧

*Be joyful, brothers and sisters. Keep your faith
and do the little things.*

St David

*H*arry would have loved the weather that day. He would have been out in his wellies tying up his beans, hoeing around his potatoes and spraying any brave greenfly ill-advised enough to land on his prize roses. Year after year, those roses never failed to win top prize in the Dunbridge Horticultural Flower and Garden Produce Show which was held in August. Standing by the French doors, gazing out across Harry's beloved garden, Claire's thoughts came to an abrupt halt. Someone else would win the First in Show rosette for their roses this year.

"Ready?" Coming up to stand behind her, Neil slid his arms around her waist as Claire sighed, allowing herself to lean back against him.

"Perhaps I'll feel better once today is over."

Neil nodded, burying his face in her neck, breathing in the familiar smell of her, loving the feel of her soft skin, loving her.

"The cars are here." David, Claire's stepfather, was standing at the front window as he spoke.

"OK," said Claire turning to her mum, Felicity, who was

sitting alongside Iris on the comfy old settee. Harry had loved to stretch out there when he watched television in the evenings.

Iris was first on her feet, picking up her handbag at once and walking towards the front door. Neil and Claire exchanged a concerned glance. Iris's behaviour had been a worry to them all since they'd lost Harry. To the casual observer, it might seem that she was calm to the point of being unaffected by her companion's death, but those who knew her well recognized that deep emotion and grief lay beneath her apparent indifference.

Along the length of Vicarage Gardens, people stood at their front gates or in small groups on the pavement, waiting to pay their last respects to a much-loved neighbour who had been there for more years than anyone could really remember. They'd grown used to his friendly wave and the chats they'd enjoyed with him over his garden gate – which often ended with the offer of a bag of fresh vegetables or a bunch of flowers. They stood in silence now as Iris appeared at the front door, her step faltering as she saw for the first time the long, black hearse carrying Harry's coffin, surrounded by a mass of wreaths and flowers. Neil tightened his grip on her arm, holding her close as he led the way to the car in which the family would travel behind the hearse. Once the others had settled in beside them, the smartly suited attendant closed the door, and within minutes the procession set off at a slow, dignified pace, led on foot by a sombre gentleman in full morning dress, down the street which had been Harry's home for so much of his life.

As one, the family had agreed on the route of Harry's last journey. He had loved Dunbridge, so it felt right not only that he should have the chance to say goodbye to his home town, but that Dunbridge should have a chance to bid farewell to him. So instead of turning immediately right at the end of Vicarage Gardens to travel the few yards to St Stephen's Church, the hearse turned left, then left again, to make its stately way around the market square in which Harry had always been a familiar face.

Neil wound down the window of the car so they could hear the doleful sound of a single bell tolling from the church tower as it resounded around the square. It was market day, Harry's favourite time of the week. He'd known all the traders, often sharing sweet hot tea with them from his thermos flask when the weather was icy, or chatting about the latest pot plants or vegetables on offer on the stalls. Amid the bustle of a normal shopping morning, a stillness descended as many of the traders and customers turned to watch the hearse pass by. Old men stood to attention at the edge of the pavement. Mums brought their buggies to a halt as their small children pointed out the two gleaming cars.

Outside the Wheatsheaf, right in the centre of the square, where Harry had spent many a happy hour playing bridge well and darts badly, the landlord stood with several of his customers, raising glasses and coffee cups as the hearse went past. The chemist with whom Harry had always chatted when he'd collected his heart pills stood quietly at the kerbside. As they passed the flower shop opened by church members Pauline and Audrey the previous year, they spotted a huge floral display in the window saying WE LOVE YOU HARRY. At the sight of that, Iris took a sharp intake of breath, but her face had resumed its impassive mask by the time Neil turned to look at her.

Once the procession had completed a circuit of the marketplace, the tower of St Stephen's loomed into view. At this point, the smartly suited man got out from the car and donned his top hat to walk in front of the hearse until it reached the porch gate. Through the window, Neil looked up at this church which had become so dear to him during his three years as a curate. Faces, friends and incidents flashed into his mind for just a second or two before the door was opened by a pallbearer, who offered a gloved hand to help Iris from the car.

Bishop Paul greeted Neil in the porch. When it had become clear that Neil would find it too emotional to take the service himself, Paul had offered immediately, for which Neil was immensely grateful.

The family formed a line to follow the hearse up the aisle, and Bishop Paul took his place at the front, ready to move off as soon as the congregation had stood to mark the arrival of the funeral party. As he walked, the bishop recited words of comfort and reassurance.

> *"'I am the resurrection and the life,' says the Lord. 'Those who believe in me, even though they die, will live, and everyone who lives and believes in me will never die.'*
>
> *"I am convinced that neither death, nor life, nor angels, nor rulers, nor things present, nor things to come, nor powers, nor height, nor depth, nor anything else in all creation, will be able to separate us from the love of God in Christ Jesus our Lord."*

A wave of emotion washed over Neil as he began to walk down that familiar aisle, taking him by surprise. He looked around to see so many faces he knew: stalwart congregation members, youngsters only just recognizable as the babies and toddlers he'd baptized, family groups, choir members, musicians, old friends and neighbours who had not only loved Harry, but who had also shown Neil a huge depth of love and understanding during his eventful time at St Stephen's. Their eyes were turned towards him now, full of compassion and sympathy.

It was then that he noticed one face beaming a smile at him from the choir stalls. It was Betty, standing alongside other members of the choir from St Jude's in Burntacre who had got to know Harry on the cruise. Neil knew they were there not just for their new friend. They'd come to support their vicar and his wife at a time of sadness, and Neil caught Claire's suddenly tearful eye as she spotted them too.

The pallbearers gently laid the coffin on its stand in front of the altar rail, leaving just one floral decoration on the top: a magnificent display of fragrant yellow roses.

Once all the family members had taken their seats, Bishop Paul stood to face the congregation.

"It is no surprise that the church is packed this morning for this final farewell to our dear friend Harry Holloway. He has worshipped at St Stephen's for decades. His wife Rose is buried here – and in a short while, we will be laying Harry beside her in the grave he has tended so lovingly throughout the five years since he lost her.

"Harry would have been touched beyond words to see how many of you are here for him today, and most of you know how much he always loved the old hymns he'd sung since he was a boy. So please stand now to sing one of his favourites, 'Abide with Me'."

As Brian played two lines of introduction, the congregation got to their feet to sing words most of them knew by heart, without need of hymn books. In spite of the sadness of the occasion, the sound resounded sweetly around the church, bolstered by the extra choir members from Burntacre, who provided harmonies alongside the regular choir of St Stephen's.

When the hymn ended, churchwarden Peter Fellowes stood to read the psalm that Harry had always said he found most comforting of all: Psalm 23, using the wording from the King James Bible:

> *"The LORD is my shepherd; I shall not want.*

> *"He maketh me to lie down in green pastures: he leadeth me beside the still waters.*

> *"He restoreth my soul: he leadeth me in the paths of righteousness for his name's sake.*

> *"Yea, though I walk through the valley of the shadow of death, I will fear no evil: for thou art with me; thy rod and thy staff they comfort me.*

"Thou preparest a table before me in the presence of mine enemies: thou anointest my head with oil; my cup runneth over.

"Surely goodness and mercy shall follow me all the days of my life: and I will dwell in the house of the LORD for ever."

Once Peter had sat down, Bishop Paul went into the pulpit to read out the eulogy that Neil and the family had put together. It covered Harry's early life, growing up on the family farm. Being older by two years, his brother had taken over the farm, so Harry had looked for work elsewhere. He was taken on to help with a local milk herd, and after delivering milk to a nearby dairy every day for several years, the dairy finally offered him the job that filled his working life for the next four decades. Come rain or shine, he would be up and out at four every morning to do his milk round, making him a very well-known face in Dunbridge and the surrounding villages.

Towards the end of the fifties, he'd met the love of his life, Rose. Their wedding in St Stephen's in 1960 was the beginning of a very happy marriage which lasted just a few weeks off half a century, when his dearly loved wife died after a long illness. One great sadness for the couple had been the fact that their son Archie was stillborn, and they were never able to have any other children. Rose's death was, therefore, a sad blow for Harry, who channelled his energy instead into his church life and his garden, which some said he loved in equal measure.

Bishop Paul then introduced Claire to continue the story. Clutching a page of notes, she stepped nervously onto the podium. It didn't take long, though, for her voice to gather volume and her notes to be forgotten as she spoke from the heart about the man who had practically been a father to her.

"Officially, Harry was my great-uncle. My grandfather was Harry's only brother, but he had died long before I came along.

His daughter Felicity is my mother, and because my own father didn't stay around long enough to know me, Uncle Harry stepped into the role of grandad and dad all rolled into one. I have so many wonderful memories of Harry spending time with me throughout my childhood, telling me stories, playing chase and hide and seek, catching tiddlers from the local stream, patching me up with plasters on my knee and kisses to make everything better. He taught me to look at the world with wonder and gratitude. He found beauty in the ugliest of garden bugs, and ugliness in people who didn't appreciate the glory of the world around us. From Harry, I learned my love of nature and growing things. I became a professional gardener thanks to Harry and his encouragement. He taught me so much – from homespun gardener's tips to the proper Latin names for each and every plant we saw – and what a wonderful gift that was.

"And then Sam came along, my own son, who's now nearly seven years old. Harry became as devoted a grandad to him as he'd always been to me.

"There are few people in the world who are simply good. Harry was one of those unique and remarkable souls, with kindness and care for others coming as naturally to him as breathing.

"And now he's gone. I spent the day before he died visiting Tresco Gardens on the Isles of Scilly with him. It was a heart-warming occasion, because he'd visited those gardens with Rose some years before. Around every corner, he saw something to remind him of her – a bench they'd sat on, a tree they'd admired, a glorious yellow rose bush we saw in bloom that day, just as Harry and Rose had when they were there. It was a day of happy memories and love – his for Rose, and ours for each other. The word he used to describe how he felt was *joy*.

"And I believe that happiness, that *joy*, was with him until the moment he died peacefully in his sleep the next afternoon. He felt very close to Rose, and I know in my heart that they are together now, as devoted in death as they were in life."

She turned then to look towards the coffin. "So goodbye, Harry. We love you. We'll always remember you and miss you being with us, but you're in God's care now, you and Rose."

Putting her hand to her lips, she blew a slow, soft kiss towards the coffin, then made her way back to the pew where Neil waited to put his arms around her.

Prayers followed, led by individual members of the St Stephen's congregation who had worshipped alongside Harry. Then the announcement was made that the coffin would be taken out for burial. The pallbearers led the way, followed by probably a hundred or more people who had been in the church, filling the churchyard.

As the pallbearers lowered the coffin into the grave, Bishop Paul read the Committal Prayer, and one by one, members of the family and close friends came up to throw a handful of soil onto the top of the coffin.

"We have entrusted our brother Harry to God's mercy,
and we now commit his body to the ground:
earth to earth, ashes to ashes, dust to dust:
in sure and certain hope of the resurrection to eternal life
through our Lord Jesus Christ,
who will transform our frail bodies
that they may be conformed to his glorious body,
who died, was buried, and rose again for us.
To him be glory for ever.

Amen."

Raising his hand in blessing, the bishop continued:

"Eternal God,
whose Son Jesus Christ said,
'Do not let your hearts be troubled or afraid,'
take away our fear of death;
bring us to the place he has gone to prepare for us;
and give us his peace for ever.

Glory to the Father and to the Son
and to the Holy Spirit;
as it was in the beginning, is now
and shall be for ever.

Amen."

And then it was over. The sombre mood of the burial was replaced by discussions about the tea that Beryl and her team had prepared for everyone back in the church hall, and in small groups people drifted away towards the church. Claire waved Neil on as he took Iris's arm to leave the churchyard, then waited in the shadows by the grave until all was quiet again. Moving forward, she knelt down, gazing at the coffin for several minutes as if she were unable to let him go. In her hands she clasped a copy of the Order of Service with her favourite picture of Harry on the front cover. He looked tanned and happy, leaning on a spade in his vegetable garden.

"I love you," she whispered at last, turning the booklet over to see the picture on the back cover of Harry and Rose smiling at the camera during their Silver Wedding Anniversary party.

She had to go. The others would be wondering where she was.

It was just as she started to get up that she felt something touch her cheek. Claire smiled, looking around for what she knew it was, but there was no yellow petal to be seen.

It didn't matter, though, because that touch, as soft as a kiss, told Claire all she needed to know. Harry was fine – and she would be too.

***

They were all there. Neil was welcomed back by so many friends and congregation members from St Stephen's who had grown to love the charmingly inept young curate as he had stumbled his way through his early training to emerge, butterfly-like, as a pretty decent minister at the end of his three years with them.

"Have you heard about our new minister?" asked the other churchwarden, Cyn Clarkson, who joined Neil as he was chatting to Peter Fellowes and Bishop Paul.

"There has indeed been a new minister appointed to this church," confirmed the bishop. "He and his family are moving into the rectory in about two weeks' time, so their children can be settled in ready to start the new academic year in September."

"Have you met him?" asked Neil, feeling rather odd at the thought of someone new taking over *his* parish.

"His name's Paul Nicholls, and his wife Anne's a doctor. She's just agreed to join the local surgery as a GP."

"Well, that's great news," enthused Neil. "What sort of church has he been working in until now?"

"He's a very interesting and unusual man, and I am sure he'll have a lot to offer here. He's not actually been ordained all that long. In fact, he's at a similar stage in his ministry to you, Neil. I felt that, as a first church for a new minister, St Stephen's would be the perfect place to start."

"But he has children, so has he been in another career until now?"

"You could say that…" agreed the bishop, leaving Neil with more questions than answers.

"Neil." It was his mother-in-law, Felicity. "Iris is looking a little tired, so we're going to run her back to the house. Shall we see you there in a while?"

"Of course. I'm not sure where Claire is, but when I've found her we'll follow you down."

"Well, keep in touch," said Val, giving Neil a hug, followed by just about every other member of the St Stephen's congregation, including Raymond, who almost squeezed the breath out of him.

"We'll look after Neil," said Betty, appearing at his side along with Marion, Sheila, Mark and Deirdre.

"Yes, and he will be back," announced Carole Swinton, who predictably had been chatting to the musical team at St Stephen's. "Clifford, Brian, Sylvia and I are planning a programme of music to feature our combined choirs, with performances both here in Dunbridge and in Burntacre. I am sure you'll see Neil then."

After a further flurry of hugs and goodbyes, Neil and Claire finally escaped to cross the road, then walk hand in hand down Vicarage Gardens to take one last look at Harry's house.

Standing by the garden gate, Claire put her arms around Neil's waist and looked up at him. "I wonder…"

"What?"

"Well, you know I said that Harry was a wonderful dad to me?"

"Yes."

"Will you be as good a dad as he was?"

Neil pulled back, staring at her. "Is that a hypothetical question, or are you trying to say…?"

"That I'm pregnant? Well yes, I am. You're going to be a daddy."

With a whoop of joy, Neil swept her up in his arms and kissed her soundly.

"But when? How…?"

"When? It's early days yet, but I think we'll be needing a nursery some time in February. And how? Well, I blame those single beds…"

CHRISTIAN-CRUISES.CO.UK

Enjoyed the book? Now experience the cruise!

Pam Rhodes' Saints and Sailors *was inspired whilst aboard one of our Christian Themed Cruises…*

Christian-Cruises.co.uk specialises in the creation of quality cruises with a Christian theme, whether in the UK or around the world. This unique travel experience enables you to unwind in the sumptuous surroundings of some of the friendliest cruise ships afloat, whilst enjoying celebrity hosts, the fellowship of other Christians, and the inspiration of the on-board worship, study groups, and historical site visits.

We are not a travel company, and therefore enjoy the freedom of being able to work alongside different travel providers. Alongside the fun, laughter, and on board facilities, the spiritual side of the cruise is provided by a team of high calibre lecturers, entertainers, leaders, and tour guides.

Our web site offers a further glimpse of why we have become a popular provider of an excellent cruise experience, aboard the best ships afloat for the best value available.

Why don't you join us?